Veng s
in H

By Cassius Cox

For my brother Robert Cox
I miss you every day.

William Shakespeare – Titas Andronicus

Vengeance is in my heart.

Death in my hand.

Blood and revenge are hammering in my head.

"Evil people always support each other; that is their chief strength."

Aleksandr Solzhenitsyn

PROLOGUE

'If you move that again, I'll snap it like a twig,' he said as he used his knee to pin her left arm down. The redness grew on her lilywhite arms as she lost all feeling below her wrist.

A second man used both hands to squeeze her right arm.

'Just give in, enough of this shit.' The third was using all thirteen stones of his bodyweight to crush her legs. He smiled like they were play-fighting, like this was all a joke...only, she wasn't in on it. No matter how hard she tried, she couldn't free herself. Thrashing her head side to side, her muffled screams were silenced as he pushed his sweaty hand down firmly into her face. The stink of cigarettes curled in her nostrils. Her vision blurry and the pain in her head escalated as she tried to gain focus.

As he moved his hand away, she took her chance to beg. 'Please don't, you don't have to do this. I won't tell anyone.'

Her desperate plea cost her a slap across her already bloodied face. 'Stop fighting. This is what you came for, little birdy,' a man snarled from the distance. The others laughed.

'I'm on my period, don't do—'

'We've heard that one before…enough. This is happening. You're not stopping it.'

Hayley Flashman had simply gone out for a couple of drinks that turned into many, easily done when you work up town. It was Friday and her colleague, Denise, had asked her to join her in London's Soho. Most Fridays by 4 p.m. were the same, computers were turned off, office phones were switched direct to voicemail, and e-mails to out of office. Targets had been met. Now it was time to drink, really drink. Hayley worked at a busy recruitment firm. It could be stressful and involved long hours. Heavy drinking was a reward for another working week survived, another reward was the large commission.

With an air of excitement, they took on the busy, cold streets of London. Winter darkness had arrived early, earlier than last week. The bright lights of the city reflected in every puddle. Annie Jacks was the name of the first bar, two large glasses of wine were easily consumed within the hour before meeting up with the director of the company, Slack-bladder Steve, affectionally known for his constant visits to the bathroom throughout the day.

Steve only employed female staff. He'd been advised more than once by Jo in Human Resources that this could and would be frowned upon. His latest non-PC reply to Jo, 'I pay the fucking wages around here. When the government, or whoever the fuck, pays them for me, they can decide who works here. In the meantime, please tell them to kiss my balls.'

Steve had the next round ready, sitting pretty on a corner table in Bar Termini.

They finished their drinks as Dawne, Hayley's friend and boss, arrived. 'Fuck that. It's freezing out there. A polar bear walked past and said he could see my nipples.' She gave an exaggerated shiver and removed her coat. Dawne was driven, could be hard to work for, but great bloody fun socially.

'Hayley, go on then, be a sweetie and get them in. I want a sea of colour on this bar.' Dawne prodded the bar's shiny oak surface before pointing up at the cocktail menu that was neatly written out on a giant chalk board.

Hayley gave a theatrical closing of her eyes before smiling. 'Dawne, sweetie, number one, we are out of the work environment, so we are now equals, no bosses. And two, it's early, and I can't drink anything above 10% proof until after eight.'

Dawne nudged Hayley playfully with her shoulder. 'That's all well and good, however I have a top trump to play, so don't be a twat, put your big girl pants on, and order everyone a drink.'

Dawne waved the company credit card under Hayley's nose. 'It'll just go through on my expenses. Steve doesn't care a toss. Entertainment costs are what they call it in accounts.'

'Dawne, I heard that,' Steve said.

'Shut it, Steve. I've made you a fortune this week. Go and have another piss or something useful.'

'Fair enough.' Steve shrugged. 'Get em in, Hayley.'

Hayley's lips curved into a smile as she swiped the card from Dawne's grasp. 'When you put it like that, you have indeed trumped me.' Hayley waved to get the attention of the bar staff.

Expensive cocktails were consumed far too easily, and the hours passed by lightning quick. Hayley ordered a sneaky water with the next round, hoping it would prevent her getting too drunk, too early. Dawne appeared over her shoulder. 'Lightweight, pussy.'

By the time they hit the next bar, The Billabong, they had met three more work friends who'd been drinking elsewhere. Natalie, Nicky, and Lorna. Two more drinks and a round of shots later, a wobbly Steve announced, 'Ladies, it's that time of the evening when only a club will suffice. Any later and we won't get in. Let's get the fuck out of here…but not before I have a piss.' He turned and headed to the bathroom as Hayley and Denise laughed.

'Gallbladder, I reckon. Has to be. He's getting on a bit,' Dawne announced with authority to the group.

'Infection down there, I reckon,' Nicky said as she pointed to her groin.

Lorna's eyes were half closed and her words slurred. 'Wouldn't be surprised, dirty boy. He puts that thing about a bit. Has a different fella every week.'

'Good on him, top shagging Steve. A toast,' Dawne said as she raised her glass.

Hayley held her arms in the air. 'Okay, that's enough. Leave Steve alone. No more toasting to Steve's sex life. Let the man have his much-needed eighty-seventh pee, and let's just go.'

They hugged each other for warmth as they teetered across Leicester Square in the bitter cold. Hayley's teeth were still chattering as they entered Ciros Bar, a popular club on Shaftsbury Avenue. The music there was a mix of hip-hop, commercial, and pop. As they came down the brightly carpeted staircase, they could feel the heavy bass and raucous atmosphere from the packed club. Hayley shouted loud enough for Dawne to hear, 'No spirits, I'm gonna spew up if I keep drinking that shit. Just a bottle of Peroni. Back in a mo. I need the bathroom.'

Hayley was relieved at the lack of queue and took care of business. After washing her hands, she was about to leave the bathroom when a fellow clubber with short pink hair tapped her pierced nose with her index finger and said, 'Well?'

After a hesitant delay, Hayley politely replied, 'Tempted, but not for me. Not anymore, but thanks.'

The girl with the pink hair smiled and whispered into Hayley's ear, 'Good girl, but if you change your mind,' and then made her way into a cubicle alone.

Hayley returned to find Dawne was only just being served. The bar was four people deep from every angle.

Hayley had removed her coat, sweat beading on her brow, arms in the air, she danced with an award-winning smile across her face.

But then, he changed that.

A man of average height revealed a smile full of teeth that were so white he'd never need a torch in the dark. His open-necked floral shirt took away some of the attention from his mouth full of overly polished tombstones. The offensive shirt was four buttons undone from the top, the kind of look only a skinny male pop star could pull off. He had paddling pool sized sweat marks making their way from his armpits to his chest.

He playfully nudged Hayley. The smile she gave him didn't reach her eyes as he continued dancing uncomfortably close to her. If she gave him the brush off straight away, he'd probably turn nasty. It had happened one too many times before. She had learned over the years how to play this game. There was an art to it with men like this. Never wanting to appear rude through fear of a backlash, she never told a man outright that she wasn't interested. First approach was to gradually put her back to him through dance, message still not received as he thrust his hip into her from behind. She pulled away. Second approach was a playful point at him, like he was a naughty school-boy. He smiled, those Dulux high-gloss white teeth back on full display. He was taking it as an invitation and came in closer. The third approach was to find safety in numbers. She needed Dawne. Her eyes lit up as Dawne waved her over. He backed off, for now.

Hayley tried to tell Dawne what had just happened. 'Perv with giant white teeth. He won't stop dancing into me.'

Pointing to her ear, Dawne mouthed, 'Can't hear, perv, who's Keith.' Hayley laughed it off and continued dancing. She gave a subtle look behind. He was looking directly at her, his horse smile gone, replaced with a snarl.

She grabbed Dawne's arm. 'C'mon, we're going to a different part of the club.' The girls found a good spot where the music wasn't as loud.

Satisfied Seabiscuit had disappeared and relieved that the game was over, her night of fun continued. Ten minutes later, she was back to her happy self, drinking and dancing. Twenty minutes more and she returned to the bar where she drank half a bottle of her Peroni and then re-set it safely on the corner of the bar. Thirty minutes more, she could feel her eyelids getting heavy after she'd finished her drink. A cheeky yawn had crept in. Scanning the club, there wasn't anywhere to relax. 'Bollocks,' she mouthed. This wasn't a club with seats for free. The booths were taken by groups spending up to four figures on a bottle of Grey Goose. She rolled her eyes. 'Fucking bankers. Rich twats.'

Leaning forward, she put her mouth to Dawne's ear and slurred her words. 'Shall we go? Need sleeps. Bankerzz. Seats. Twatzz. Done.'

'Done? No. You're twenty-five, not fifty. Too early, get a Red Bull, Grandma.'

Gesturing to the door, she said, 'Outside, fresshh air. Back in a bit. I just need to wake ups.' Making her way up the stairs her eyelids turned to paving slabs and slammed shut. Her shin crashed into the metal strip at the front of a step. Eyelids back open. 'Fuck.' She momentarily sat and rubbed at the blood appearing on her shin. 'Bollocks.' Holding the railing on the wall, she pulled herself up and looked at the mirrored wall. She could see her face swaying near, then far. Once at the front door, the security staff asked if she was okay. She said she was as she stumbled onto the road.

'Taxis are over there, love. Want me to sort one for ya?'

Hayley waved the doorman away and crossed Leicester Square, heading for a fast-food restaurant. A man held the door open as she walked in.

'No need to thank me, rude cow,' the man said.

Hayley didn't hear him. In a dream-like state, she crashed against the counter and pointed to a meal deal. 'That one plzzzz.' Angered by the staff's weird reaction to her, she shouted, 'Rude!'

And repeated her order. To Hayley, she had made it very clear to herself what she wanted.

A female member of the staff put her hand on Hayley's shoulder. 'Off. Get offs me,' Hayley ordered.

They asked her to sit down. A second member of staff snatched at her arm, but she yanked it away, shouting, 'Fucking touchy weirdos, get off!'

All eyes were on her. Her concrete eyelids were back. She smacked her own face. 'Wake up, bitch.' Eyelids slammed shut again. She crashed against the bin, sending trays flying across the floor. 'Stupid fucking place, this is, arshholes.' Stumbling forward she tried gain focus with her constant blurred vision. That's when it happened.

That shirt, those buttons, those sweaty armpits. Those fucking teeth.

Only now, his buttons were done up and a friendlier smile adorned his face. He held out a bottle of water, and she took it. She could hear him telling the staff to leave her alone, that she was having a rough time recently, that she was just letting off steam, and that *she* was his girlfriend, that *he* would get her home safely. 'The fuck you will, horse face.' They didn't hear her. Did she even say it out loud? It didn't matter, they believed him and ignored her. Trying to speak again, nothing would come out the way she intended. In her head, she was telling them he wasn't her boyfriend, but that didn't leave her mouth. Her rambling was that of a crazy person. 'Teeth, perv, sweaty twat.'

'Please, just take your girlfriend home. She's upsetting the customers.'

Her actions and slurred speech appeared comical to bystanders, a group of teenagers held out their phones, the bright lights shining in her face adding to her confusion.

The ceiling was whiter than hers, no light bulb directly above her. The back of her throat felt scratchy, her eyes heavy. She put her hand to her stomach as the sickness rose to her chest. She sat upright sharply to counter this. Looking across to her right, she expected to see her en suite; it wasn't there. The sick feeling was rising again from the pit of her stomach. All she could see was a small window, four walls, and a closed door. A feeling of dread rose from her stomach, no time to be sick anywhere appropriate as the vomit poured into her lap. Choking, she fell to the floor and continued to be sick. Satisfied it was over, she wiped her mouth. Sitting back up on the bed, she looked down at her bare legs and saw blood, some of it dry but not all. There was more on her underwear.

One more bout of sickness surfaced. This time it was just yellow liquid. As she heaved for the last time, nothing would come out. She lay back down, her head spinning. Rolling onto her side, she could see her dress carelessly thrown into the corner.

She never left her clothes like that. They would always be neatly folded or hanging correctly.

She struggled to stand as she panned the room for more clues. Her shoes were on the other side of the room, the room that wasn't hers. She needed to get out, out of this strange room. That's when her first flashback hit her. Clapping her hands over her ears, she held her eyes closed tight as she remembered. Different faces, all-male, laughing at her. Her eyes shot open. Moving a few feet forward she stumbled into a wall. Using her hand to balance herself, she clutched her dress and put it on, pain radiating from her body. The worst of it between her legs. She touched her face. Her cheek felt swollen, sore to the touch. She could taste acidic copper through the vomit.

Her clutch bag was on the floor. The muscles in her legs tensed as she bent down to retrieve it. Inside was her phone. It was dead. In her purse was a single twenty-pound note, maybe enough to get her home. But from where? She was supposed to have caught the last train back to Dorking. That was a plan before it went wrong, before she got tired, before the fast-food place, before…him.

From the small window in the room, she could see daylight outside. Last night was Friday. It must be Saturday. Her thoughts turned to her friends. How could they let her go off alone in that state? Where were they? She put her ear to the door and listened. She couldn't hear anything. Pulling the door open, she peered out and could see a half-naked man sleeping on the sofa. She inched her way out. Another man, wearing jeans and a shirt was asleep on the floor. More flashbacks. He was the one crushing her legs, laughing at her before turning angry and slapping her. She closed her eyes and grimaced; she felt that slap all over again; she touched gently at her face.

There was a glass coffee table with empty beer bottles and cigarette packs. They had pushed her head on to that table; she grabbed at her hair at the thought of her face crashing against the glass, and the white lines of powder. 'Snort it, bitch,' they shouted. Her hand went over her mouth.

Deep breaths, she knew she had to get out. It was a large apartment all on one level. The décor was modern, expensive. She tip-toed towards the door. Her escape was in sight. She looked across to a bedroom on her left. The door was open. Two more men were crashed out on a double bed. Beer bottles were scattered around the room, together with several tiny bags with more white powder inside.

She needed a phone that worked. She needed her best friend. The one person that she needed was a phone call away. This friend could make this better. She was safe. She was home. From now on it would be nights in with her friend like she used to, go to the cinema, a meal, a show, anything is better than drunken nights that ended in blackout.

The man on the sofa moved. His eyes remained closed as he turned to face the other way. Another flashback. He was the one who forced her underwear into her mouth, making her choke. She needed to go right now. This was her chance. She arrived at the front door and turned the handle slowly. It wouldn't open. She turned harder, noticing the bruises on her wrist. She felt light-headed, remembering the man on the floor. He was the one holding her wrist so tight she thought it would break. It was all flashing back through her mind like a film on fast forward. The man in the club with the teeth. And then him again in the fast-food restaurant. The pain, the humiliation, the violence. The vile acts they performed on her.

Why? Why her?

She kicked the door.

'Fucking open.' She screamed.

An arm reached across her shoulder. 'Let me,' he said as he turned the lock. She threw herself to the ground and protected her head with her hands.

He slowly pulled open the door. She looked up and saw the huge smile through those teeth, 'There you go little birdy, free to go. No harm done. Fly away.'

Woken from her sleep after a long night shift, she answered the phone. No one called the landline anymore, hadn't for years. It was an operator asking if she was happy to take a reverse charge call. She had no idea who would be calling this early on a Saturday morning. Gripping the receiver tighter, she said *yes*.

She could hear the crying, and then a girl's voice, a voice she knew well. 'I didn't have any coins for the phone. I had to reverse the call. It wouldn't take—'

'Hayley?' she interrupted.

'Please help me, Cat. I need you.'

PART ONE

Vengeance is in My Heart

"Life is never fair, and perhaps it is a good thing for most of us that it is not."

Oscar Wilde

CHAPTER 1

Catherine Hart looked straight through her therapist, Roisin Kelly. Her tone was calm. No tears, no anger.

'I cry for no reason. I cry for many reasons. An advert on TV, a homeless person digging through a bin, my dad being dead…my mum being alive. Why wouldn't I want to leave this world? What is there? We're set up to fail from the moment we're born. There are so many stars that need to align perfectly for someone to have a good life, a fair life. I believe there are more people unhappy than happy. It isn't possible for us all to be afforded happiness. Only a few can succeed, and most of the time it's at the cost of others. To have the rich, we need the poor. For people to be good, we need the bad.'

Roisin remained silent, allowing Catherine to continue.

'I am tired, so tired. I don't want to fight anymore. They win. They can have it all. I want and need nothing. I want to be left alone to go. No fuss, no fake tears, just let me go. I don't feel present any longer. People no longer see me, and that's fine because I don't want them to.' Catherine's eyes, one sky blue and one hazelnut brown, were still vacant, but she appeared to have shifted her attention to the dark skies beyond the window.

'You are having suicidal thoughts?' said Roisin.

When answering, Catherine kept her gaze away from her therapist. 'Mum says I'm faking being depressed, unbelievable considering she's spent most of her life in the same state.'

'No one fakes depression. But people do fake happiness, fake it to hide depression. They become experts at disguising it. They can attend parties with a smile, greet a neighbour with a smile, but when that front door closes and they're back with their own thoughts, it's back.'

'I know how I'll do it,' Catherine said.

'Would you mind sharing that with me?'

'I'd rather keep it to myself.' Catherine looked back in Roisin's direction but still avoided eye contact.

'I dreamt I was gone. It was so vivid, so perfect, one of those dreams you have where you wake up angry, where you try to get back to sleep to carry on the dream. It was a deep, beautiful feeling of freedom, and I wasn't in pain. There were many faces, but none I recognised. They were happy for me. I was happy for me.'

Roisin looked down at her notes and then back at Catherine. 'You look tired. Are you getting enough sleep?'

Catherine attempted a smile. 'All the time. That's all I want to do. The minute I get home I put my electric fan on. Not for the cool air, but for the noise. That constant whirring drone helps kill the thoughts. Complete quiet sets off the noises in my head. And then once I've switched off all the lights and I have the darkness, I'll fight to clear what's left in my mind, then I sleep.'

'And food? Are you eating regularly?'

'I'm rarely hungry. I drink coffee, some snacks maybe.'

'All your symptoms are—'

'Of someone who is depressed, miserable, feeling sorry for themselves. Suicidal. I know. Google told me all I need to know. Google – the answer to everything.'

'Being here with me is brave. The fact that you're here shows you want to—'

'Live. You think I want to live like this, in this world? I don't. But what choice do I have? She needs me.'

Roisin Kelly hesitated before leaving her office, gazing at the seat where Catherine sat less than an hour ago. Her concentration was broken by her phone. The display flashed the word *husband*.

'Hi, you, I'm just leaving the office.'

'No problem. Just wondered if you wanted me to pick something up? Or we could go out?'

'I think pick something up. Chinese maybe? I don't fancy going out tonight,' Roisin said.

'Everything okay? Has something happened?.'

'Do you ever wonder what our girl would have looked like? As she got older, I mean.' There was a brief silence before Roisin continued. 'I'm sorry. I'm just being silly. Having a moment.'

'All the time, Roisin. Every day,' her husband replied.

'I've met someone today. She…oh I don't know, maybe it's her age as she would have been the same around now. It's been some time since it's hit me this hard.' Roisin held her hand against her chest.

'I love you, Roisin Kelly. I'll pick up the food and a bottle and see you at home. We can talk more then.'

"A mother's love endures through all."

Washington Irving

CHAPTER 2

THREE MONTHS LATER

Catherine pictured her mum dying.

'If she died tomorrow, I'm fine with that,' Catherine said, maintaining her ice-cold stare.

Roisin Kelly stopped making her notes and sat back in her Chesterfield leather desk chair. 'I can understand your anger towards your mum but—'

'I'm not angry with her anymore.' Catherine cut her off. 'I feel nothing. I won't cry a single tear when something happens to her, and it will happen. She will die soon. She's killing herself.'

Roisin shifted her chair forward a few inches. 'I would never try to tell you how you feel as only you know that. All I would say is, despite your mother's behaviour towards you in the past, she is still your mother. You may find your reaction is different when the time comes.'

Catherine shook her head in disagreement. ‘I won’t. When I was young, say six or seven, she would creep into my room through the night and tell me how ugly I was, tell me that I shouldn’t have been born. Can you imagine that? I never told my dad, he had no idea. Once she’d leave the bedroom after one of her sick rants, I’d sit there for hours holding my bear, waiting for my dad to wake. Dad thought it was nightmares keeping me up, but the nightmare was laying in his bed and he never knew.’

‘But despite these feelings, you still choose to live with your mum. You both have the resources to live alone. You paint a picture of two people who despise each other, yet you stay.’

‘It’s my dad’s house. It’s all I have of him. Why should I go?’

‘Or, and I’m not suggesting it is the case, you care for your mum. If you move out, she’ll be alone.’

‘It’s not that, believe me. Those nights where she tortured me with her words, I would pray that one morning, dad would come in and say that my mum didn’t wake up. And I still feel that way.’

‘She’s still your mum. People love who they love despite the wrongs they have bestowed upon them, however painful.’

‘How could I love someone who did that to me?’ Catherine turned her head away from Roisin and dabbed a tissue at her eye. ‘Love? Love that woman? Never.’

Roisin leaned forward. ‘I’m not trying to upset you. The reason I’m saying this is so you don’t judge yourself if you ever do feel differently. Go with your emotions and don’t be too hard on yourself. You've been through so much. You've been coming to me for several months now. You've come so far.'

'I have. And you've helped me come to terms with my father's death. That's what I needed. He's been gone half my life, yet there isn't a day goes by that I don't think about him. I still get angry that cancer took him so young. But, since I've been coming to you, I now think more about the good memories I have of him, and less about the time when I lost him. Just like you told me to.'

'That's good. It's a huge achievement and you've got there yourself. You should be proud. And I don't want anything to set you back. This darkness in your heart towards your mother threatens your happiness. It may manifest itself in other ways.'

Catherine smiled. 'It won't. I won't let it. Thanks to you, I'm now focused on my life away from my mum. I now know what I want to do.'

'This sounds positive. Would you like to share with me?'

'Victim Support. I'm volunteering for them. My dad believed in helping others in his own way. I could do similar,' Catherine said.

'What does it involve for you?'

'If someone's been a victim of a crime, it can leave them affected, you know, mentally, or they may just need practical help. It's mostly being there to listen and help where we can, point them in the right direction for extra support. I know it'll be tough. It's a lot of training, and mentally it might trigger me. I'm aware of that, but I want this. I want to help others. I start with helping support people of lesser crimes, mostly burglaries and minor assaults.'

Roisin's emerald-green eyes glistened. 'They're lucky to have you.'

'Thank you,' Catherine said, her cheeks turning red.

There was a long pause. Catherine pushed her blonde hair out from her face.

'My life's been good recently. I enjoy keeping busy. It makes me feel more positive. I don't like what's in my head. It can be a dark place and I like to get away from it. Along with volunteering, I'm still working at the care home. I'd miss the residents too much if I left. On top of all that, I'm training at the gym several days a week.'

'Training? Is that where that came from?' Roisin pointed to Catherine's eye.

Catherine touched her face. 'Oh this. I got caught in sparring. My own stupid fault for dropping my guard.'

'Boxing?' Roisin asked.

Catherine's smile lit up her eyes, eyes of different colours, one sky blue, one hazelnut brown. Proud that Roisin had acknowledged her bruised eye, that was now a bright mixture of green and purple. 'Mixed martial arts. Last night was boxing. Tonight, it's Jiu-Jitsu.'

'Oh wow, that sounds tough. I know a bit about boxing. When I say I know, what I mean is, I know someone who boxes. What is Jiu-Jitsu?' Roisin asked with genuine curiosity.

'It's a bit like wrestling, grappling. It involves takedowns, and once on the ground, we use a number of techniques to force our opponent to submit, to tap out.'

Roisin raised her eyebrows. 'To tap out?'

'It's not as bad as it sounds. Once I have my opponent locked in a position that they can't get out of, they tap to let me know they submit. I then let go.'

'Your face changed the minute you started talking about this. You enjoy it, I'm happy for you. This is all positive.'

'It gives me confidence, not just in how I could handle myself, but in everyday life. The people there are amazing. We train hard together. We may beat each other up physically, but the respect between us all is huge. Tony owns the gym. He's been great to me. When I first joined, he didn't always charge me. I was in my teens, and he knew my mum wouldn't give me any money. He'd simply wave me through with a smile.'

Catherine shifted in her seat. 'You said you knew a boxer. Anyone I know? If they live locally, I may train with them.'

Roisin shook her head. 'I can't say their name. It would be unprofessional of me.'

Another long silence. Catherine focused her gaze on a tall, thin woman walking past the window. Maybe a patient, a doctor, or just a visitor. By the lost, pained look on the woman's face, Catherine concluded she was a patient.

'Catherine, we don't have to go there today, but I would like to talk about when you first came to me. You had some very dark thoughts, and you've not mentioned them for a while. Have they become less frequent?'

Catherine exhaled and bit her lip before replying. 'They're still there. My anger is better. People still bother me, but I try to do the right thing. I'd like to do more to them. I can't stand bullying in any form.'

'Do more to them? There are other ways of dealing with situations. Talking or walking away.'

'Personally, I think it depends on the situation. My dad taught me that. Don't let anyone bully you. Strike first, that sort of thing.' Catherine held her stare with Roisin longer than usual.

'Is there someone in-particular who's bothering you? Is there something you want to tell me? Is anyone in danger? Are *you* in danger?'

Catherine shrugged. 'No one's in danger. There's a problem at work.'

'At the care home?'

'Yes.' Catherine tapped her feet up and down and nodded to a beat that wasn't there. 'One of the residents is having some trouble. I'm not sure what's going on. He's not been himself for some time. Bullying of any kind upsets me. He had a mark on his head. He said he slipped, but I'm not so sure.' Catherine gritted her teeth before continuing. 'I think it's his son. He's always moody with his dad when he visits. He just sits there glued to his phone when he should be talking to his dad.'

Roisin moved forward. 'You've told management? I assume that's procedure.'

'I don't have proof. But I will, then I'll deal with it.'

'Catherine, this is the behaviour we talked about before. It's not on you to protect everyone. Tell your manager. Don't confront this person yourself. It could lead to problems for you.'

Catherine casually nodded her head. 'There won't be a problem. Not for me.'

The following morning, at eight o'clock on the dot, Catherine arrived at Pinehurst Rest Home. She was never late. She'd set up a hidden camera the day before, knowing Bill's son was visiting. She started her regular rounds, making tea and coffee for several residents, listening to their stories, and helping them with their breakfast. It was time to go and see Bill. As she walked into his room, she could see he'd returned to his bed.

'Good morning, Bill. Time to get up and dressed.' Catherine peered over at Bill's tray. 'You haven't touched your breakfast. Your cornflakes are all soggy. And you've not even opened your yoghurt. Is everything okay?'

Bill had his back to her. When he rolled over to face her, Catherine could see his eyes were red. He'd clearly been crying.

Her eyebrows drew together as she bit her lip. 'What happened, Bill? You need to tell me. Was it him? That bloody son of yours.'

'No, no. He wouldn't. He's a good boy. I swear it's not him.' Before he could continue, Catherine went over to the cabinet where she'd hidden the camera. She moved the clothes to one side, the ones she'd strategically placed around the camera to conceal it.

'Bill, I'll be back soon. If you want a fresh bowl of cereal, just let me know. Please eat your yoghurt, and when I come back, we can have a chat.'

Catherine went to the staff office and plugged the camera into the laptop. She found the file and started watching the footage. She sped it up until she saw the son arrive.

'Here we go. I've got you now, you piece of shit.'

She watched as the son leaned over and kissed his dad. She frowned as she watched them in deep conversation. Bill looked happy. The son looked engaged. He went on his phone several times but that was all, then he left the room briefly before coming back for more time with his dad. In all, he was there for over an hour before he kissed his dad again and left. Catherine shook her head in disbelief. She'd just witnessed Bill's son being like any other caring child. She sped it up again until she saw her colleague, Nick, enter the room. Catherine was about to whizz past this when she saw Nick look out into the corridor before closing Bill's door. She let the video play and stood back in horror as she saw Nick going through Bill's wallet.

'No. Not you. You arsehole, Nick.'

Nick was a quiet lad in his early twenties. He rarely spoke to the other staff, but he appeared to work hard, so he was left to it. Catherine had two options. Tell her manager, and show her the video, or deal with it herself. She knew what Roisin would tell her to do, what she should do, but Catherine chose option two. 'Fuck you, Nick.'

She went back to Bill's room and held his hand. 'I know everything now, Bill,' she told him. 'And I'm so sorry for suspecting your son. There's no need to be afraid anymore. I know who hit you and I promise you it'll never happen again.'

Bill had tears in his eyes as she left to work through the rest of her shift. She was due to leave at four o'clock, but she didn't go anywhere. Nick had to pay.

She waited in Bill's room until Nick entered. He gave her a weak smile. 'Hi, Catherine. Shouldn't you be off home? I'll take care of Bill.' He winked at the old man.

'Take a seat, Nick. I'd like a quick chat.' Catherine pulled a chair out for him. 'I don't want you to say a word until you've watched the video that I'm about to show you.'

Nick sat down. The colour in his face had drained. 'What video? What's going on?'

Catherine put her finger to her lips. 'Shh. I said, not a word.' She pressed play and showed him the footage. He sat there wide-eyed before his complexion changed to bright red.

'You've been recording me, you bitch.'

Bill started crying. 'Catherine, call someone for help. Pull the alarm cord. I don't like this.'

'It's okay, Bill. Nick isn't silly. He knows he's been caught. And now he's going to sit and listen to what I have to say.'

Nick was fidgeting in his seat. His fists clenched. 'You don't understand, just fuck off, Catherine. Give me the video and I'll leave.'

Catherine pulled herself closer to him, close enough for their knees to touch. 'You're going to leave this job, and you're never going to work in care again. Do you hear me? You have until tomorrow to bring Bill back all his money. If you don't come back with it, this video goes to the police.'

She sat back, waiting for Nick to decide, and then leaned forward again. 'Oh, and one more thing.' Catherine punched him across his jaw, sending him sprawling backwards, smashing his head on Bill's tray knocking a cup of pills flying across the room.

'Sorry, Bill. I'll pick those up in a minute,' Catherine said as she stood over Nick. 'I'll see you back here tomorrow with Bill's money.' She stamped on his groin. 'How could you? Taking his money, worse still, hitting him. You're a vile piece of shit.'

'I didn't mean to hit him,' Nick pleaded as he rolled on to his side.

She turned to Bill. 'We'll have your room spick and span in no time.'

Bill sat up. 'Don't hit him again, that's enough. The lad knows he did wrong.'

Nick got to his feet and ran out of the room.

'How much money did he take, Bill? I'll get it back for you.'

'Don't you worry about the money. It wasn't a lot. I don't keep much here. There's no point. What would I spend it on?' Bill slowly got to his feet. He came forward and hugged Catherine. 'You're a good 'un you know, Catherine. Thank you for caring. But do you think you needed to hit him? You'll get into bother with the police. He's just a bit of a thief, not worth you getting in trouble over.'

Now it was Catherine's turn to have a tear in her eye. 'Whatever he is, he won't touch you again.'

"Fear makes the wolf bigger than he is."

German Proverb

CHAPTER 3

Wednesday was sparring night at Spartans gym, lots of nervous faces as each member turned up. Lots of avoiding eye contact to stay focused on what was to come. Catherine entered the gym and gave the owner, Tony Bowman, a nod as she made her way to the immaculately clean changing room. The air fresheners strategically placed around the lockers couldn't mask the smell of sweat and hard work, though.

'C'mon you lot, quick warm up and then we start,' Tony shouted.

The fighters started off with ten minutes of stretches, then with a jog around the gym, swerving in and out of the bags that hung from the ceiling. As they jogged, Tony would shout instructions, left glove down, right glove down, knees to chest, heels to butt, go backwards, side to side, other direction, and so on and so on. Five minutes of shadow boxing followed. Warm up complete, they gathered in together.

'If you're not in the cage, hit the bags. Don't go nuts or you'll have nothing left for in here. But also, don't stand around doing fuck all, I'll notice. I know some of you are crafty and hope to step in here fresh against a tired opponent. Don't be a pussy. Test yourself. Be the fighter you can be. Right, Catherine, you looked the most nervous when you walked in, you're in first against Jose.'

Catherine shook her head. Her smile revealed her black gumshield. 'Thanks, Tony.'

'No problem. Get in there, give me one minute, then I'll change one of you to someone else. If I don't think you're giving me enough, you'll stay in until you do.' Tony grinned.

Catherine and Jose touched gloves.

'Start light, one minute, go,' Tony ordered.

Applying her make-up, she added extra concealer to hide the light bruising under her right eye. Catherine leaned in closer to the oval-shaped mirror in her bedroom and took a closer look at the bruise Jose had given her during sparring. Pausing briefly, she registered the glint in her eye. With her hair-straighteners suitably hot, she squeezed the tongs together, creating a smooth straight finish to her hair. Ready to leave for her twenty-minute journey, she tapped the front of her phone. The time revealed itself as 8.06 a.m. Her appointment was at 10 a.m.

She sat there remembering how the first few appointments had been so challenging, how she had trouble talking about losing her father at only twelve years old. To even say the word *dad* was difficult. With tears forming, she shook her head, trying to escape her thoughts. Standing up to avoid her reflection in the mirror, she started to pace around her bedroom. Her thoughts wouldn't leave, thoughts on how she'd repeatedly told Roisin how much she hated her mother, but how she was reluctant to tell her why. The truth was horrifying. Too disturbing to say out loud. That would mean it was real, that it really happened. She knew she had to 'open up' to someone, someday.

Sitting back down in front of the mirror, she tried to say it. 'My mother abused me, she…' Catherine stood back up sharply, sending her stool crashing to the ground. She turned and kicked the small grey bin next to her dresser.

'Sometimes I wonder if it was as bad as my head tells me it was. I know she wanted to scare me, and often hurt me, but the other stuff. I don't know anymore. I've never talked to anyone about this. How can I?'

Roisin gave Catherine the tiniest of nods to continue.

'It feels right talking to you. I trust you. You're like…' Catherine stopped.

'Please keep going,' Roisin said.

'Like a mum. Like a mum should be. You care.'

Silence filled the room.

Roisin opened her mouth but didn't speak. Like she had changed her mind about what she was about to say.

Catherine threw her arms up. 'I know what you're going to say. You are not my mum blah blah, and you're just here to help me. That's fine. I get it. But I can't help how I feel, I like feeling liked. I like thinking someone cares. Can you at least give me that?'

'I do care, Catherine. But what you need is for me to remain as your therapist, to keep this professional. By listening to you in a professional capacity, I can help you best.'

Catherine stood up and headed towards the door.

'Catherine, please stay,' Roisin said.

The door closed behind Catherine.

Roisin's breathing had quickened. Rising to her feet she rubbed at the back of her neck as she looked to the sky for answers.

TWO DAYS LATER

'Hi, Catherine, how are you? How have you been since our last appointment?

Catherine was scratching at her arm. 'Good, I think.' Pulling her sleeve back down, she began picking the fluff off her jumper.

'Look, I'm sorry for walking out last time. I don't know what happened.'

'It's okay, I was worried about you, that's all. I did call later that evening.'

'I'm fine, honestly. Won't happen again.'

'You did nothing wrong. From time to time, you may feel frustrated with what we talk about, maybe confused about your feelings. I just ask that you keep talking to me about those feelings. I can then address them, and we can move forward together.' Roisin glanced at her notes. 'Did you talk to your manager at work, deal with your problem?'

Catherine looked away before making eye contact with Roisin. 'It's all taken care of. The person responsible was a member of staff. They won't be back.'

'They were sacked?'

'Kind of. They're gone. That's the main thing.'

Roisin tapped her pen on her pad and her smile grew. 'That twinkle in your eye tells me you're not going to tell me the truth on this one and I should leave it where it is. Very well, Catherine, I won't ask again. Best we move on.'

Catherine nodded in agreement, and after a ten second silence, she changed the subject. 'It's my dad's birthday soon. Most days are hard without him, but his birthday is tough. That and the anniversary of when he died. Christmas is awful as well. I've never enjoyed Christmas since he died. I don't want to.

Christmas Day wasn't acknowledged in the house without Dad. No Christmas tree, no decorations, and definitely no presents. Although I used to buy Snoop a present when I could get the money together.'

Catherine picked a spot on the carpet to stare at and lost herself in her memories.

'What is it, Catherine? What are you thinking about?' Roisin asked.

'Christmas…I fucking hate it. There's nothing wonderful about it. It's the loneliest time of year. A whole month of gut-wrenching feelings of loss. Looking out of the window at happy families. The Barkers across the road having family get-togethers. Nan and grandad, aunties and uncles, all turning up with perfectly wrapped parcels. Kids running out to greet them. Every bloody TV programme portraying happiness. I couldn't wait for January. It was around Christmas I first considered…' Catherine looked up at Roisin. 'You know.'

'I'd like you to continue. I want to understand what you went through, but only if you're happy to, Catherine.'

'I wouldn't have done it. I couldn't decide how. Pills seemed the easiest way, but I had no idea how many I'd need to take. Hanging is too brutal and cutting my wrists too messy. And my dog, Snoop – leaving him with her wasn't an option.'

'And do you still have suicidal thoughts?' Roisin asked.

'Doesn't everyone? They're just thoughts, right?'

'There are stages people go through that show how serious they are. Did you make any plans around the suicide? Have you ever? When a person is serious, they'll possibly write a letter, get their financial situation in order. Another sign is driving loved ones away. Trying to fall out with those close to you as it adds to their feeling of not needing to be around.'

'I don't know. Thoughts can't be helped.' Catherine tapped her finger on the arm of the chair.

'We've talked a lot about your dad's illness, about the sadness and loss you felt when he passed away, but we haven't talked much about your dad. He sounds like he was a great father to you. You must have some lovely memories.'

'He was so caring to me. I've heard stories about him being something different, but not with me. He was gentle and loving. He always wanted to be with me, play games with me, take me to the park, the cinema, anywhere. We did so much together. My favourite memories are of just Dad and me at home. When I was young, every night he would read a different Roald Dahl book to me. His favourite was *The BFG*.'

'That's a great book,' Roisin replied.

'As the BFG got up from the table, he pulled his trousers down and showed his bum.'

Six-year-old Catherine took the book off of her dad and read the pages. 'Daddy, it doesn't say that, stupid.' She was laughing as her dad smiled back at her.

'Just checking you're awake.'

'Of course I'm awake. We haven't finished the whole book yet,' Catherine said as she lay back down.

'The whole book? You mean I have to read the whole book before you'll go to sleep?'

'Yes, Daddy, that's the rule. Promise you will, please, Daddy?' She closed her eyes, waiting for him to carry on.

'I made that promise when the books were a lot shorter, Meg and Mog, Biff and Chip, We're Going On a Bear Hunt…but a promise is a promise, beautiful,' he said before continuing. 'Putting his bum back in his trousers he…'

She chuckled and smacked his leg.

'Okay, okay, I'll read it properly.'

And he did. He read the whole book even though she fell asleep with three chapters to go.

Catherine shook her head gently. 'The thought of not seeing him again hurts so much, you know, right in here.' She touched her midriff. 'It's a sickening pain. I try to bury it, but it won't go. I can see him now. I haven't heard his voice in years and yet I hear it in the conversations I have with him in my mind. He was a good-looking man, always dressed smartly, and he was so strong.

He was stuck in the eighties. All the music and the films he watched were from back then. We must have watched *The Karate Kid* together a thousand times. I think that's where my love of martial arts comes from.' Catherine smiled, even though tears were developing.

'It was a good era for films, and music…but the fashion was questionable,' Roisin said.

'Definitely. I've seen photos of my family back then. My mum was about fifteen. She was tiny, but she had this huge perm that looked too heavy to hold up, like this giant crash helmet. And my dad, he had a mullet, wearing a grey suit with white flecks. The tie had bloody piano keys on it.' Catherine laughed, briefly.

'If we went out in the car, he'd have Queen or Spandau Ballet blasting out. He'd sing along to the words, shouting Gold stupidly loud. My mum didn't like that. She'd get embarrassed and say, "Eddie, you're not impressing anyone." He'd carry on, and I'd laugh. She'd stare at me with those eyes, those cold, dead, shark-like eyes. I knew what she was thinking. I knew what she wanted to do to me. But she couldn't do or say anything. Dad would always take my side, and she knew it.'

'Your dad sounds like he was a lovely man,' said Roisin.

'Are you taking over the front room again? All for a bloody football match?' Patricia asked sternly as she pointed to the sea of claret and blue around the room.

'C'mon love, it's only one match. It'll be done and dusted in two hours.' Eddie pecked Patricia on the cheek.

'Grown men running around a field kicking a bit of leather, pathetic,' she said as she left the room.

A seven-year-old Catherine Hart breathed a sigh of relief, reached forward for her cup and took a swig.

'Cherryade okay for you, beautiful?' her dad asked.

'Perfect,' she said as she smiled, revealing a red ring around her mouth, made all the sweeter as she was currently missing a front tooth.

'There's salt and vinegar in that one, ready salted in there and best of all, pickled onion Monster Munch in that one.' Eddie pointed to the three bowls before picking up a can of Fosters from his icebox.

'Cheers,' he said, reaching out his can and tapping Catherine's cup.

'Cheers, Dad.'

'Quarter bloody finals and we had to get this lot. With the Russian money they've spent, they should beat us. It's wrong that's what it is. Bloody Chelsea, load of —'

'Eddie, that's enough,' Patricia barked.

Eddie shot a look over his shoulder. 'Sorry, love. I didn't know you were back in the room. Here, come and park that perfect bottom of yours next to me. You might even enjoy the game.'

'Unlikely, and don't be so crude. I'll be upstairs. The minute the final whistle goes, she's off to bed, and I want the soaps back on.' Patricia pointed at Catherine before leaving the room, this time slamming the door.

'Could be extra time, Dad. She'll be so mad.'

Eddie smirked. 'Let's hope so. I love her when she's mad.' They both laughed.

The game had kicked off, ten minutes gone, and they were two nil down.

'Of all the poxy players, that sodding Lampard has to score. He plays for England and does bugger all. Him and Gerrard can't string a pass together. Every bloody time he plays against us, if it's a penalty, he scores. A free kick, he scores. He can't miss. Why did we sell him to them? It's the chairman's fault. Kick him out I say.'

'Hold on, Dad. Here we go. Noble's in the box.'

'Ref, you arsehole, that's a penalty, you blind—'

'Dad, he's given a penalty.'

'Legend. Quality ref this geezer. I've said that all game. Get in there.'

Catherine grinned. 'Will Noble score this, Dad?'

'Does a bear plop in the woods? Of course, he will.'

They both stood up, put their drinks on the coffee table, and waited as a young Mark Noble ran towards the ball. He struck it perfectly into the bottom left-hand corner of the goal.

'Yes, bloody get in there,' Eddie shouted as he picked up his daughter and danced around the front room, her head flopping from side to side as she laughed and cheered.

The game ended with Chelsea winning, and Catherine going to bed smiling from another great night of fun with her dad.

'We had so much together, including football. He was West Ham mad, and I followed.'

'Special memories. You'll always have those,' Roisin said.

'Going to the stadium was amazing.'

'Your dad took you to a live match? I bet that was fun. Did your mum go with you?'

'No chance. She hated football, and she hated that my dad took me. She would say football is a lower-class sport played by thugs and supported by hooligans. Hateful bloody woman. She hated most things. The only sport she'd watch was the tennis once a year. Wimbledon in the summer.' Catherine looked around the room, the hate for her mum written on her face.

'But you enjoyed going to the football? You and your dad.'

'I loved it. I loved the people up there. The whole day was great.'

Eddie held his polystyrene cup of tea with two generous sugars in one hand and tucked his newspaper, he'd just purchased at Dorking train station, under his arm. He bought Catherine her usual can of Coke, a magazine, and some sweets.

On the train to London, Catherine, with her nose pressed against the window, watched the world go by, looking into people's gardens from Surrey to London. Her dad read the paper but would occasionally peer over the top to check she was okay. His little winks or smiles meant the world to her.

'Big game today, beautiful,' he said. 'West Ham and Man U at Upton Park, lets av it.'

Their train arrived at Victoria Station with three hours until kick off. Her dad left his paper on the seat for the next passenger, just as he always did. As the doors opened, Catherine could hear the singing from the fans. Not just West Ham fans, but all the teams playing in London that day. And then on to the Underground. Catherine would peer down the giant escalator before holding on tightly and plucking up the courage to step on. On the train, they were packed in like cattle, rocking side to side, only held up by each other. It didn't always smell great, but she had never cared. Her hand was firmly in her dad's giant bear paw.

When they got off the train and entered Green Street, the stench of cigarettes and takeaway food hit her. Grown men randomly shouting, 'Come on, West Ham' or 'Come on, you irons' like they had some kind of West Ham Tourette's. Her dad still held her hand tightly as they were herded in tight formation by the police. Every so often he'd look down at her, another smile or wink to let her know she was safe. And she was. And then he said, 'Hats, scarves, and badges' as they crossed the street by The Queen's pub. Seconds later, they heard the shout, 'Hats, scarves, and badges,' and there he was – the same man standing on the same old milk crate. They both smiled. It was all part of their routine. The weathered-looking man was selling his football merchandise, hung from the side of an old telephone box. He was wearing a grey flat cap and smoking a terribly rolled cigarette, which looked super-glued to the side of his mouth.

Her mother would have hated all of this. And for that reason, Catherine loved it even more.

Catherine forced a smile, but she couldn't hold it. She blinked as a single tear ran down her cheek.

Roisin remained silent, waiting for her to speak.

Catherine rubbed away the tear and said, 'We'd enter the Bobby Moore Stand and, as we came out to our seats, we'd hear the roar. There it was. That pitch. Those fans. The players would be warming up, giving the occasional wave to us, the fans.' Catherine was becoming more animated the more she remembered, but she suddenly stopped.

'Catherine, please carry on.'

Taking in a deep breath, she replied, 'One match, we were leaving the stadium and the away fans, Spurs, came towards us. My dad said we'd be okay coz fans don't touch kids. But one of the fans bumped into me and I fell. My dad helped me up and called them back. One stepped forward and swore. He hit this man three times before the Spurs fan hit the floor. The first punch was enough, swear he was already unconscious, but the next two landed lightning quick. The other Spurs fans backed up. Everyone backed up. I watched as my dad loomed over the man. The look in my dad's eyes was something I'd never seen before or since.'

'That must have been hard to witness.'

'No. That's the thing, it wasn't. Dad explained to me after that it was justified. He had to pay. You don't hurt children. Bullies do that and bullies get dealt with.'

'I don't think that's quite right for a parent to teach any kind of violence, he—'

'Why? Surely it depends in what world you're brought up in. Some may never see or need violence. But life isn't as simple as that for others. Violence is their only way out.'

'Was your dad arrested?'

'No. No police involved. He was applauded by the West Ham fans. They sang 'I'm Forever Blowing Bubbles' while patting him on the back as we walked up Green Street. Some chanted his name, they knew his name.' Catherine sat tall in her chair. 'That was my dad. I loved those days. just Dad and me. I miss him so much. I don't feel I'll ever know love like that again. Sometimes I think I had so much love from my dad that I used it all up in the twelve years I had him.'

'I don't believe that, Catherine. I believe we're all capable of giving and receiving love our whole lives. It may not always feel like it, and there may be times when we must work harder to be loved, but it will come. I also believe we must give love in order to receive it.'

'I'm not sure about that.' Catherine's foot was tapping up and down. 'My mum is incapable of love. She is, and has always been so miserable…God, I hate her. My dad would sing to her in the kitchen, like when a slow song came on the radio. Dad would often belt out a bit of Phil Collins. He would put his arms around her waist and sing to her, and all she could do was tell him to stop. I think she hated being happy.'

Catherine clenched her fists, knuckles turning white. 'Why do you think he married her? A man like that choosing someone like her. I've seen photos so I know she was very attractive in her day. I get that, but surely there needs to be more than that. Behind that once pretty face, it is all venomous hate. He loved life so much, and he lived with a smile. Even towards the end, in his darkest hour, when he was in pain he would try to smile. Maybe that was for my benefit.'

They had their own room at a private hospital, a tastefully decorated room with its own television, but that familiar hospital smell filled the air. 'Money can't buy everything,' her mother moaned.

Catherine's dad lay there, his eyes sunken and dark. His haunted expression was of someone who knew what was coming. His dry mouth was constantly open, taking in his last breaths. His once beautiful, thick black hair was now gone, replaced by a handful of weak-looking strands that lay on his yellowing skin. To ease the pain, he had one arm above his head holding on to the frame of his bed, holding on to the last hours of his life. The only food he could take on board was a tasteless jelly, and the only fluid was from ice lovingly wiped on his lips by his distraught daughter.

Behind Catherine, her mum sat in the only seat in the room. She wasn't crying. She hadn't spoken for over an hour. Catherine was left to ease her father's pain with words that should have been coming from an adult, not a twelve-year-old.

'It's okay, Dad, I'm here for anything you need. Keep fighting, Daddy. I don't care what they say, I know you can beat this. You're the toughest person in the world. Nothing can beat you.'

Her dad blinked. It took every effort to give that to his daughter.

'That's it. Enough of this. They should be helping him pass,' Catherine's mum declared, rising to her feet.

Catherine let go of her dad's hand and turned to face her mum. 'Shut up, just shut up. He's not going anywhere.'

The rage in her mum's eyes lasted a split second as her attention was diverted to Eddie's lifeless body. Catherine didn't need to turn to know why her mum's expression had changed so dramatically.

'Help, help us,' Catherine screamed as she went back to her father's side.

Two nurses entered the room. Catherine watched as they checked Eddie for any sign of life.

Catherine wiped her face again, but this time the tears wouldn't stop. She stood up and walked towards the window. 'Life is so fucking cruel. When he died, my whole world changed. Mum blamed me for everything. She blamed me for him dying. On the day of his funeral she said, "Your dad was always so fit and healthy, and then you came along and the stress of having you caused his cancer." She would loom over me and snarl, "If you hadn't been born, he'd still be here."'

'That's awful. It must have been very upsetting for you to hear,' Roisin said. 'I'm so sorry, Catherine.'

A month after Eddie's death, Catherine's mum was becoming more and more bitter and twisted. Catherine had been awake no more than ten minutes. She entered their front room to a venomous, vicious rant. 'You caused this, he had to give up his old life, our old life, the stress of having you, to comfort you when you cried non-stop as a baby, always so needy and demanding of your poor dad.'

A twelve-year-old Catherine braved a reply. 'How can someone catch cancer through being a parent?' Catherine knew she'd gone too far saying that, but a month of continuous insults had built an anger inside her and, on this morning, it had got the better of her. She didn't care. Whatever the repercussions, she thought it would be worth it to say what she truly felt. 'If Dad's cancer was caused by stress, then he caught it because of you.' Catherine jabbed a finger at her mum's contorted, spiteful face.

The recent smacking was a new thing since Eddie's passing, but the smack she received then was new. This was different. It was a vicious punch from her mother's clenched fist. She had never felt such a pain. Catherine could hear the ringing in her ears, and when she blinked, lights flashed. She closed her eyes tight and shook her head, but she couldn't make it go away.

Her mum hadn't finished with her. Catherine felt her collar being pulled from the back of her neck. The front of the collar tightening against her windpipe. She could hardly breathe. She grabbed at it, getting two fingers in, just enough to ease the pressure. Her mum put her mouth to Catherine's ear and whispered, 'Never back chat me again, you stupid little girl. I'm all you have, and all you'll ever have.'

Catherine tried to reply but couldn't get her breath. She pleaded in silence, her eyes doing all the talking as she looked desperately at her mum, begging to be released. Begging for her life. Feeling herself going limp, she mouthed the word sorry.

Her mum eased her grip, and shouted, 'Just fuck off to school. I want you out of here.' And then she turned away from Catherine and started looking around the room for the TV controller, like nothing had happened.

Catherine got her breath back. 'But it's only seven o'clock. It's too early for school.'

Her mum screamed, 'I want you out of here now. It makes me sad to even look at you. I want to watch the television in peace. Just go.'

Catherine stood up and instinctively ducked, just in case her mum threw another punch. Going into the kitchen, she wiped away her tears so that she could see clearly in the mirror. She needed to check her neck. She didn't want her teachers seeing the marks. Her collar hid the worst of it.

'My dog, Snoop, was always a source of comfort to me, especially after the many incidents within the house. I remember bending down to give Snoop a hug before I collected my school things together. I opened the front door and shouted, "Bye, Mum. Bye, Snoop." There was no answer from the front room, but a single bark came from the kitchen.'

'Where did you go at that time of the morning? I assume you couldn't go into school until nearer nine?' Roisin asked.

'I went to the local woodland park in Dorking, known as The Nower. From that day on, I went there every morning before school. In the winter months, it was still dark. The Nower was close to our house and only five minutes from my school, Sondes Place. There was a bench there I always sat on. It had a gold plaque with the words, *Rest in Peace, Jessie. Love Jim* and then three *Xs*.'

'You must have been scared? Twelve years old is very young to be sitting in a wooded area alone,' Roisin said.

A familiar face stopped in front of her – a lovely older man who had recently introduced himself.

'Morning, Catherine, how are you today?' Catherine hid her tears and told him she was okay. She wasn't scared of him. She trusted him.

He told her things would get better, maybe not today or even tomorrow, but they would get better. Catherine shrugged and didn't reply. His dog brushed up against her leg. The man pointed his stick in Catherine's direction. 'Dobby likes you. He doesn't like everyone.'

'He shouldn't. I'm not a good person, so I'm not sure why he likes me.'

'Nope, I'm not having that. You must be a good person. Dobby doesn't get it wrong. Never has. Same as when someone is a bad egg, he barks at them non-stop. Good people always get rewarded eventually. My wife always said that to me. Whenever I got stressed at home, she would touch my hand softly and remind me to calm down. She'd say life was too short to be angry. She'd say I was kind to everyone but myself, and she was right. She was always right. And Catherine, you should be kind to yourself too.'

'Your wife sounds lovely.'

'She was. Eight years she's been gone, and I miss her every day.'

'I'm sorry. What was her name?'

With his walking stick, he tapped the plaque on the bench. The bench Catherine had chosen to sit on each morning. It wasn't just any bench. It was Jessie's, put there by Jim in his wife's memory. For so long, she had sat there with no idea that this bench was for his late wife.

'It's no mistake you sitting here each morning. Jessie will watch over you.'

Catherine grinned. 'I hope so.'

Jim pointed to Catherine's face. 'Your eyes. Heterochromia, they call that. Eyes of different colours. Jessie's were the same. Would you believe it?' Bill said with surprise. 'Beautiful, kind eyes, both of you. Thank you for sitting here, and Jessie thanks you too.'

They said their goodbyes and Catherine watched as Jim walked into the distance, every so often turning to check she was okay.

Catherine dug deep into her pockets, searching for a tissue. 'There was a man who walked his dog there. He would talk to me most days. He was kind. And then one day he stopped coming. I never knew where he lived. I never thought to ask him, so I couldn't find out. I wanted to check on him.'

'That must have been sad for you, too.'

Catherine shrugged. 'It was…but everyone leaves, don't they? I feel that whoever I care about will leave. So, I now think it's easier not to care so much.'

'Do you think you push people away on purpose? Because you're scared they'll leave you?' Roisin asked.

'Maybe…I don't know. I have people I care about – a few at the gym, but we're not friends outside of there. I don't want anyone too close. Hayley is my only friend. I trust her and care about her. I hated her at first. She used to bully me.'

Catherine arrived just before the bell was due to go off. The normal pack of girls were there, sitting in their same spot as they were every day. Catherine had no choice but to walk past them. She had heard Hayley call her every name going over the last year, and each time the group's laughter would add to the misery. Normally, Catherine wouldn't look up, but not today. Angry from her mum's abuse she decided to fight back. Catherine stopped next to Hayley, took in a deep breath, and pushed forward with her hand on Hayley's chest, driving her into the wall.

'Fuck off, Hayley. Find someone else to bully or this will go very wrong for you.' Catherine kept her stare firmly on her, waiting for a reaction. The group laughed nervously, waiting for Hayley's comeback. But there wasn't one. Hayley didn't even move. For once, she didn't have a smart comment to throw back. Catherine turned and walked away. She kept walking desperate to look behind her, but that would have killed the performance. It looked better if she walked away as if she didn't have a care in the world.

The payback would come, Catherine was certain of it. The first lesson had finished, then break time. No retribution so far. Lunchtime was always the same for Catherine, sitting alone on the steps reading. That day she was reading *The Hunger Games* by Suzanne Collins. She loved the main character, Katniss Everdeen. She was brave and fought for her survival. She dog-eared the page she was on, tucked the book away in her bag, and went to the toilet before the bell went off. While she was washing her hands, the door opened. Looking in the mirror, she could see who it was. Hayley Flashman and two of her friends, grinning.

'Keep an eye out and hold the door shut,' Hayley said. Catherine carried on as she was, but was waiting for something to happen. She didn't have to wait for long. Hayley came up behind her and grabbed a fistful of her hair. She yanked her head back and whispered, 'Don't ever chat back to me again. Do you understand? You thought you were tough earlier, didn't you? Telling me to fuck off. I wonder how funny it would be if I drove your head into those taps?'

Catherine reached up and grabbed Hayley's hand, trying to release the pressure on her hair, but she caught her reflection in the mirror and something changed. A switch in her mind had been flicked. 'Hayley, I don't care anymore. Go on, do it.' Hayley's reflection in the mirror showed Catherine that her smile had gone. She let go of Catherine and stood back. The atmosphere in the room had changed, had darkened. 'I've had enough of people like you, and people like my mum.'

Hayley inched back further and waited.

'What is it you want to do?' Catherine said. 'Ram my head, you say? Let me save you the job.' Catherine thrust forward, head-butting the mirror, shattering it into tiny pieces. Shards of glass rattled on to the porcelain.

Hayley stepped forward and held her before she could do it again. Blood dripped down Catherine's face and into her eyes. Hayley's friends ran out…but she stayed. 'Stop it, Catherine. Stop this. I didn't want this.' Hayley was crying, begging her. She started grabbing handfuls of cheap school tissue to hold against the cut.

Catherine looked Hayley in the eye. 'It's okay, I won't tell the teachers. I'll say it was all me.'

Hayley shook her head. 'I don't care about that,' she said as she carried on wiping Catherine's face.

'I just want to be left alone,' Catherine pleaded.

Hayley held Catherine against her. 'I know. I'm sorry, it won't happen again. I promise. Not by anyone.'

'We had a falling out one day, a bad one. I cut myself on purpose to scare her, blood everywhere, and in that moment, she changed, like she saw something in me she wanted to care for. I had opened up to Hayley. I told her about some of the abuse. And then she told me about her parents, and how her dad could be nasty when drunk, how he came and went from her life. We promised we wouldn't tell each other's secrets to anyone else. And we didn't. We started clearing up the broken glass and as we did that, I felt a warmth toward her. I can't explain it. Hayley and I had connected in a way that didn't feel possible between friends. I'd not had that before. Hayley left the toilets before me as I got more tissue to hold against the cut. It wasn't that bad. The door re-opened. Hayley came back in and hugged me.'

Roisin smiled. 'You needed each other?'

'We did. At the end of school that day, I left as normal, with a stupid huge plaster on my forehead. Head down, I was making my way through the crowd when someone called my name. I was embarrassed and wasn't used to people knowing me. I looked around and saw Hayley waving me over. As I approached, she was telling two boys to piss off for staring at her, and they did piss off. She was so confident, and so funny. Hayley smiled at me and said, "I'm going for a cigarette up The Nower. Wanna come?" I'd never been asked to go anywhere with a friend. We went to Jim's wife's bench and just sat and talked. And since that day, Hayley has been the one person I can talk to…the one person I would do anything for. She's the closest thing I have to family.'

TWELVE YEARS EARLIER

Hayley knocked on the door, after a short wait and no answer she tried again, this time using her fist in a hammer motion she hit the door three times until she heard a voice the other side.

'Who the fuck is hitting my door? If you're a Jehova, piss off you religious nutcase.' The door opened and Catherine's mum stood there, her expression changed from anger to an unnerving smile.

'Hello dear, you okay?'

'Is Cat there?'

Catherine's mum looked behind and then back at Hayley. 'She's in her room love, having a sleep. Best not bothering her.'

Hayley held her stare firmly on Mrs Hart. 'I want to see her. She had bruises on her yesterday and then she wasn't in school today. I'm not going until I see her.'

Mrs Hart stepped toward Hayley and pulled the door too. 'I said she's asleep. And as for the bruises, probably football at school or some other silly game. Clumsy she is. Always has been.'

Hayley drew in a large breath, exhaled, and stood tall. 'I know it's you, she tells me. Mrs Hart, you disgust me. She's your daughter. Leave her alone. She's been through enough.'

Mrs Hart raised her hand. Hayley didn't flinch as continued speaking, 'Go on, I'm not scared of you. I've been hit by a man with your ways. Do you think you can do any worse?'

Mrs Hart returned her arm to her side. 'You're a confident one, aren't you? Best you go before I do something I regret.'

'I'm not going until I see my friend, you stinking piece of piss, get out of my way. Where's my friend?'

As Hayley went to enter the house, she heard Catherine call out, 'It's okay, Hayley, I'm fine. You go home, I'll see you tomorrow. I promise. Please, go home.'

Hayley stood back. 'Cat, are you sure? I'm not scared of her.'

'Please, I'm fine, it'll be fine,' Catherine said.

'You heard, she's fine. Now run along little girl,' Mrs Hart said as she motioned with her hand.

Hayley stood face to face with Mrs Hart. 'One day your daughter is going to fight back. I've seen it in her eyes, seen what she's capable of. She has something in here,' Hayley touched above her heart. 'Something others might think dark, something to be scared of. Something you put in there.' Hayley poked at Mrs Hart's bony cold chest. 'I'd be scared if I was you. When the time comes, and it isn't far off, she's going to pay you back for every smack, every punch or kick, every sickening word you've used against her. And I can't fucking wait.'

'It's all lies. I haven't touched her.'

'Save it. You tell yourself that. You don't need to convince me of anything. I know what you're about.'

Mrs Hart turned her back to Hayley and went to walk inside. Hayley grabbed her shoulder. 'Trust me, it's coming, and you deserve it all you cunt.'

Mrs Hart threw Hayley's hand off. 'Get away, don't ever come back here.'

'It's coming, you wait.'

"Success is not final, failure is not fatal, it is the courage to continue that counts."

Winston Churchill

Chapter 4

The H.G. Wells centre in Woking was the venue for Fight Night 64, an MMA southern fight league. And second on the fight card was Catherine Hart v Suzie Butcher. Three, five-minute rounds of mixed martial arts. Butcher was known locally for her knockout power. Catherine had trained to keep away from Butcher's right hand.

'Circle away to your right. Do not walk on to that right hand. If she lands that, you're in trouble. Feint with the jab and go for the takedown,' Tony said.

Catherine was steely eyed. 'Okay.'

'C'mon, Cat, smack her.'

Catherine looked cage-side. The rather brutal instruction had come from Hayley. Catherine gave her a thumbs up before looking back at Tony.

'No Catherine, don't smack her, take down.'

Catherine smiled nervously.

Round one commenced. The fighters met in the middle of the cage. A left kick landed on Catherine's thigh, leaving a red mark. Unfazed, she moved back a few inches to keep out of reach. Butcher landed a jab, Catherine threw one of her own, but missed.

'Find ya range, Cat. Stay calm,' Tony shouted.

Butcher threw the next jab and followed it with that overhand right that missed Catherine's head by millimetres. Catherine threw a feint jab and went low, taking a double leg. Using her weight, she lifted Butcher and threw her to the ground.

'That's the one. Now take her back,' Tony commanded.

With Catherine's full body weight on top of Butcher, she started raining down hammer fists. Butcher wriggled side to side to avoid being hit, and that's when she made a mistake of turning onto her front. Catherine used her feet as hooks to spread Butcher's legs out flat, she then got her arm under Butcher's chin and the choke hold was on. Squeezing tight, the ref looked closely as Butcher's face went bright red, unable to breathe Butcher frantically tapped Catherine's arm.

'That's it, it's over,' the ref said as he separated the girls.

Catherine hugged her opponent. 'Are you okay?'

Butcher nodded. 'Fuck, my coach said you'd do that.' She punched the canvass out of frustration.

'Yes, Cat,' Hayley screamed.

The fight lasted forty-eight seconds.

'Took ya time, didn't ya?' Tony said with a huge grin as he pulled Catherine in for a cuddle. 'Good, girl. Exactly as planned.'

With a warm smile, she entered Roisin's office and sat in her usual spot.

'How have you been this last week?' Roisin asked.

'I'm good. Won my fight. I'm enjoying work. All the residents have been happy and well. No one died this week. That's always a plus. My volunteering at Victim Support has really got going.'

'You look happy, and no bruises, so I assume you won well.'

Catherine grinned. 'It went okay. It's the Victim Support I'm happy about. I'm not quite on my own yet, as I've had a manager shadowing me, but I'm about to have my first case. It's a burglary. All the training I've been doing is paying off. They think I'm ready. I can't wait.'

'You must be doing well to be working alone this early in your volunteering. I knew you'd be a great asset to them.'

'I'm going to meet a family tonight and see how I can help them.'

Roisin nodded. 'I'm pleased for you. They'll be lucky to have you helping.'

Roisin shifted some papers about on her desk before continuing. 'Today, I was going to ask if you feel ready to talk about your mum and what happened when you were younger. We agreed it would be when you were ready, so I'm just asking. We don't have to. I don't want to change how you feel today. If you're feeling good, maybe we should leave it. What do you think?'

'You're right. We always said we'd talk about it when I was ready, and I think I am. Let's do it. The quicker you know all about my mum, the sooner you can help me.' Catherine shrugged.

'I don't want to stop your progress. You're doing so well. So, if at any time it feels too much, we stop.' Roisin relaxed in her chair, giving Catherine her full attention. 'How about we start at when things changed at home, when you stood up to her? Are you able to talk about that?'

Catherine's smile had gone. She cleared her throat and nodded. 'I'm ready. I can tell you exactly when she last hurt me physically. That's when things changed.'

Roisin reached out with her hand but didn't touch Catherine. 'When you're ready.'

'It was always late at night. Bad things are always worse at night, aren't they? She started her usual hammering on the bottom step. I lay there frozen with fear, but as I heard the next few bangs, my fear turned to anger. I was no longer a helpless little girl. The hate I felt for her empowered me. I was older and ready to stand up for myself. Earlier that day, Mum had kicked Snoop. It's strange, isn't it? She'd kicked me a thousand times, but that day she'd kicked my Snoop. I wanted to hurt her. Kick her exactly the way she kicked him. I'd dreamed of fighting back for so long and suffered far too long at the hands of the one person who was meant to love and protect me. In my head, it would play out perfectly. I'd strike her once – a punch, a kick, anything hard enough to inflict pain, but nothing too bad. Just enough to stop her. In my dreams, Mum would then cry and apologise for the years of abuse. And then maybe, just maybe, I could have the mother and daughter relationship I wanted.'

'The relationship you deserved,' Roisin said.

Catherine's mum continued to thump the steps. The thumps grew louder. She was near the top. It was now or never. Catherine pulled back her covers and tiptoed across her room. With her ear to the door, she could sense her mum on the other side.

The whispering started. 'Catherine, Mummy wants to see you.'

She closed her eyes, maybe she could talk to her, beg her to stop, ask her to get help. They could go together. Catherine knew that wouldn't work. She'd tried that before. Her mum was beyond help.

As the whispering continued, Catherine felt the hatred surging through her chest. Her arms shook. Not from fear. It was adrenaline running through her veins. She closed her eyes and pictured her mother kicking Snoop. She was a lit fuse waiting to explode. The wait was over. She pulled open the door. Her pathetic looking mother was on her knees unprepared for what she was about to encounter. She didn't get the chance to stand up. Catherine planted her left foot firmly on the ground and kicked with the right, her stronger foot from years of striking a football at school. She caught her mother on the nose, sending her spiralling backwards down the stairs.

Catherine watched in bemusement but also in fascination at the sight of her mum falling.

'I hit her so hard, she flew backwards down the stairs.'

'That must have been very traumatic for you.'

Catherine didn't answer Roisin.

Her mother called out in a weakened voice, '"Help me. Call an ambulance. My back. You've broken my back.'

Catherine stepped backwards slowly into her room, and gently closed the door. The monster in her life was now a weakened wreck, begging her for help.

'You'd think kicking someone in the head would hurt your own foot, but it didn't.

'I kicked her with everything I had, and it felt…good.' Catherine nodded slowly.

Pacing around her bedroom, Catherine thought about helping her mum, but then changed her mind.

'You kicked Snoop. That's for kicking him. Hurts, doesn't it?'

'Mum deserved to be in pain, but I didn't want to be like her. I opened the door and peered out. All I could hear was my own breathing. I tried holding my breath but couldn't. It made me feel as if my heart was coming out of my chest. I pulled the door fully open and looked down to the bottom step. There she was. Lying there helpless and silent.'

Catherine stopped talking and lowered her head. She was waiting for Roisin to speak, but when she didn't, Catherine continued. 'I made my way down and crouched over her body. I could see the beating pulse in her neck. She was still alive. I reached forward to wipe her hair from her face.'

As Catherine brushed her mum's hair back, her mother lashed out with her arm, screaming, 'You evil little bitch.' She caught Catherine in the face with her flaying arm.

Catherine stood back. It hadn't hurt, and she wasn't scared. She knew her mother couldn't hurt her anymore. As her mum went to stand up, Catherine put her foot against her backside and pushed forward. Her mother's head rebounded off the wall, and she flopped back, flat out on the floor. Catherine could hear

Snoop barking in the kitchen. She shouted at her mother to stay down, telling her she didn't want to hurt her any more than she already had, but she would if she needed to.

Her mother didn't like that. Looking up, she said, 'Don't lie, bitch. Of course you want to hurt me. You nearly killed me. I can see it in your eyes. You have the same look your father used to have when he lost his temper.' She struggled to her knees.

Catherine warned her. 'Don't talk about my dad, and if you come near me, I'll kick you again, and I won't stop.'

'After I threatened her, I hoped that was it. I wanted it over. Mum sat, leaning against the wall, and said, "Look at you, all big and tough. Pathetic."

'Maybe she was right.' As tears started to run down Catherine's cheeks, Roisin reached for the tissue box and held it in front of her. Catherine took two out. 'Thank you.'

Catherine covered her face with her hands and screamed, I'm not nothing.'

Her mother sneered. You're no daughter of mine. Look at you. You're ugly. You'll amount to nothing.' The laughter was sickening. She'd used it on Catherine regularly.

Catherine put down her hands to stare at her mother. 'How can any one person be so twisted? You're a sick, lonely old woman. How can you hate your own child the way you do? What kind of person does that?'

The laughter stopped. 'It's easy. Hating you is easy, has been for years. I never wanted a child. He wanted you.' She gestured to a picture on the wall of Catherine's father. 'I wanted him and me. We were so happy when it was just the two of us. Then you came along with your persistent screaming, so pathetic and needy, needing attention day and night.'

Catherine looked directly at Roisin and shook her head.

'Do you know something? She never wanted me. She told me that, and she meant it.'

'I'm so sorry, Catherine.'

Snoop was scratching at the door. His barking became more desperate. Catherine noticed blood on her mother's teeth. It didn't stop her from torturing her daughter with her words. 'Of course, I didn't want you. Your father and I had money. We had fun. We went out for meals most nights. We would get drunk and dance together. Then you came along. And all he wanted to do was stay at home with you. He was obsessed. And from that moment on, he hardly looked at me. And then he got cancer and left me. And I was left to look after you.'

Catherine let herself fall back against the wall, sliding down until she was sitting with her legs pulled up. She watched her mother wipe the blood away from her nose. She spat more from her mouth before carrying on with, “I never wanted a child, especially one like you.” Standing up, she walked towards Catherine. She went past and started walking up the stairs as if it was finished.

But Catherine wasn’t finished. She screamed, “I’m more than you think I am. I know that now. You’ve destroyed so much of me and I let you…but no more. It ends tonight. I’m stronger than you physically. I have been for some time. But now I know I’m mentally stronger than you, too.”

Her mother turned. The horror in her eyes was clear to see – a horror that turned to tears as all the control she ever had over Catherine started to float away. Catherine looked at her father’s picture on the wall. She now felt very much her father’s daughter. She could see herself in him.

Catherine wiped away more tears.

‘I told her I was stronger than her in every way. That I wasn’t scared anymore, and I could see in her eyes that she knew it. And then she changed. She came back down and sat in front of me. She said, “Don’t speak to Mummy like that”, and she started stroking my hair. For a brief moment I felt something close to being loved. It was beyond amazing to have Mum touch me affectionately. In that moment, the years of abuse were forgotten. My chest ached. I wanted to hug her and, for a split second, to forgive her… but then I felt the pull, and the pain of my head being yanked sharply.'

'Oh, Catherine.' Roisin sat back in her chair, her hands covering her mouth.

Catherine was taking deep breaths to control her emotions. She was reliving every second of her pain. 'I screamed, but Mum wouldn't stop. All I could see were her veiny, disgusting white legs in front of me. I kicked her shin as hard as I could. She let go instantly and fell to the floor. She lay there screaming, begging not to be hurt. Clumps of my hair were in her clenched fist. And that's when I hit her with everything I had. All the years of abuse were returned with the kicks and blows I rained down upon her.'

'That was the last time you touch me,' Catherine yelled.

Her mother put her hands up to defend herself and begged not to be hurt.

Catherine stood over her, her eyes bloodshot, teeth clenched together. The hatred was so strong. 'I want to finish you, to kill you. I want to stamp up and down on your head. Who wants to do that to their own mother? Look what you've turned me into. I've become you.' Catherine put her foot on her mother's chest. 'I am not going to physically hurt you anymore. I'll make you suffer in different ways. My happiness will be me pitying you. My happiness will be when I have my own family and you never get to see them. My happiness will be in the laughter of my children. Children you'll never meet.'

Catherine was breathless as she screamed out, 'I fucking hate her. I wanted to kill her.'

Roisin touched her hand. 'Catherine, have a break if you need to. Let's take a break.'

Catherine nodded, but she continued. 'Her eyes were so wide. She called me a bitch, started telling me she'd given me a life, a roof over my head. I told her, You're my mum. You're supposed to do those things. And that's when I said it. That's when I bought up the sexual abuse. I called her disgusting and evil. I told her she should be in prison with the other monsters.'

Catherine took her foot off her mother's chest and allowed her to get onto her knees.

Her mother reached out to her. 'Those things are in your head. I've never touched you that way. Hit you, yes, you deserved it.'

Catherine grabbed her hand and twisted it. Her mother pleaded with her to let go. Putting her mouth to her mother's ear, Catherine hissed, 'You don't deserve to be called Mum. You're nothing. Not a mother. Not a friend. You're not even human.'

Catherine shook her head and wiped away more tears.

'I twisted her arm harder. I told her if she ever touched my Snoop again, I'd kill her, that I would burn her and the house down. I made it clear that she never speaks to me again. Never. I let go of her arm and she crawled up a few stairs, out of my reach. I opened the kitchen door, and Snoop's attention was only for me. He started rubbing himself against my legs. He jumped up and licked my face as I stroked him. I told him it was okay, that she wouldn't ever touch us again. I loved Snoop so much. He died a few years later. I never wanted another dog. Snoop couldn't be replaced. He helped me through so much. I miss him. Like I said, everybody leaves.'

Roisin wiped a tear from her eye and placed her hand on Catherine's. Catherine's tears had stopped. She was pale and had a haunted look on her face. Leaning forward, she rested her head on Roisin's chest.

'All I want is to be happy. That's all I want.' Catherine sobbed. 'I don't like feeling this violence within me. She said I get it from my dad, that I had never seen what he was capable of, but that I had that same streak in me, But—'

'But what, Catherine?'

'People deserve it. They have to pay. My dad taught me that vengeance isn't bad, it's a form of justice. He said no one should get away with hurting me or anyone I love. He said he always made people pay, that way it wouldn't happen again.'

Catherine left Roisin's office and made her way to the reception area. Feeling light-headed, she knew she needed five minutes before driving home. Helping herself to a coffee, she sat and let out a sigh. Looking around at the dozen empty seats in the waiting area, she realised she'd taken the only seat that was directly next to someone else. Scared to look up, instead she glanced down at their feet. They belonged to a man who smelled of expensive aftershave, a nice smell. Her sideways glance carried on up where she caught sight of his tanned hand resting casually on his knee. He was wearing a wedding ring, diamond encrusted and silver. Why did she feel disappointed that he was married? She hadn't even seen his face. The red glow in her cheeks gave her feeling of embarrassment. She needed to move seats, leave altogether, or say something.

'I'm sorry for sitting here. I honestly didn't notice you there. I don't mean I didn't notice you. What I mean is—'

The man saved her any further embarrassment by interrupting. 'Please don't worry. I get it. This place can be difficult. There have been many times when I've left here upset and had no idea how I'd even got home in my car.'

Catherine dared to look up at his face. It was only for a split second, but she recognised him and instantly looked away. Her face took on another level of red.

'My appointment's in a few minutes. I like to get here early, partly for the coffee, and to compose myself before going twelve rounds with the therapist. This is my first session in a long time.'

Catherine needed to check it was who she thought it was. Bravely, she sat up straight, took a sip of her black coffee and held eye contact as she replied, 'Why did you stop? Did you feel it wasn't working?'

'It wasn't that. I moved away. I don't come back to Surrey very often but, when I do, I like to see her. She's one of only a few people that gets me. She's one the few that tells me exactly how it is, even if I don't want to hear it.'

'Roisin?' Catherine asked.

'Yes, Roisin. Do you see her too? Sorry, I shouldn't be asking. This all meant to be very private.'

'I don't mind. Nobody knows me around here. A bit different for you, I'd imagine?' Catherine gave a wink which she instantly regretted.

'Why do you say that?'

Catherine grinned. 'I know who you are, Jack. You're Jack Stone, the boxer.'

'Ex-boxer. I'm yesterday's news.'

'You were a world champion. You'll always be famous.'

'It's peaceful where I am now. No one cares who I am down there.'

'I see your old gym is still open. I was going to go there years ago. I live in Dorking and ended up joining Tony Bowman's MMA gym instead.'

'Tony's a great coach. Say hello from me. He used to bring his fighters over for extra boxing training. He had some good boxers who gave me some tough sparring. You should go over to my gym with Tony some time. Tell him I said you could.'

'Your gym? You still go there?'

'Not often, but I own it. After the owner died, I bought it, and now my friend Shawn runs it for me, Shawn Dunmall, I'll give you his number.'

Catherine checked herself and changed her huge grin to something far stranger – an awkward gurn that she felt made her look simple. She raised her coffee cup to hide her mouth. She watched Jack walk over to the receptionist and return with a pen and paper.

'My name's Catherine.' She wanted to smack herself. Why would he care what her name was?

He wrote the number down and handed it to her. They were then interrupted.

'Jack. When you're ready.'

Catherine and Jack looked over at Roisin.

Jack took the pen back to the receptionist before turning to Catherine. 'Nice to meet you, Catherine. Good luck with the training.'

Catherine watched Jack walk away. Once he had gone, she said quietly to herself, 'Nice to see you too, Jack Stone, ex world-champion boxer who smells nice but is happily married.'

"Helping others, you will learn how to help yourselves."

Amy San Suu Kyl

CHAPTER 5

The house was in a perfectly pleasant, typical English neighbourhood, with beautifully kept lawns, and streetlights that gave an air of safety. The thought of this family home being burgled left an uneasy feeling within Catherine. Approaching the front door, she took in a deep breath. This was her first solo appointment, and she was beyond keen to help. Her hand shook as she pressed the doorbell. She took a step back and squeezed her hands together in an effort to keep them still. Seconds later, the door was unbolted. A lady held it half open and invited Catherine in. Introductions were made, and the children were asked to go to their rooms.

'You have a lovely home. I'm so sorry we're meeting under these circumstances. What happened to you and your family is awful. It must have been devastating.' Catherine knew she was rambling.

Mrs Adams looked to her husband. He shook his head and rolled his eyes. This was followed by an awkward silence.

Catherine was hoping they would discuss the break-in without being prompted. 'Are you happy to talk about what happened?' she asked nervously.

'Will it do any good? I mean, what's the point?' Mr Adams replied.

Catherine dropped her head and looked through her notes. This wasn't what she had been trained for. She was a volunteer. She didn't expect to be made to feel like this, so unwelcome and useless. 'It sometimes helps to talk about what happened,' she said softly.

'Will that get my money back? Will my kids sleep at night not worrying about some scumbag coming into our house?'

Mrs Adams reached out and touched her husband's leg. 'That's enough, Gary. The lady is here to help. She hasn't done anything wrong.'

'It's okay, Mrs Adams. I understand you both being upset. This kind of thing can stir up all kinds of emotions.' Catherine swallowed hard. 'Mr Adams, I can't get your money back and I can't promise your children will sleep peacefully, but I'm here to help the best I can. We can offer advice on home security. We can supply window alarms if that would help in some small way. They are free. And we can also help with advice on other sources of help, talking therapies, etc.'

Mr Adams stood up. 'Talking therapies? Have a day off, will you? This is pointless. I'll be upstairs.' He marched out of the room.

'I'm sorry,' said Mrs Adams. 'He's angry with everyone since it happened. He blames himself, wishes he could have caught them. I'm glad he didn't. He'd be in prison for murder.'

Catherine half smiled, but she wanted to leave. 'I wish I could do more. Have the police said if they have any idea who did this?'

Mrs Adams nodded. 'They have fingerprints and are confident it will lead to an arrest. They said it wouldn't be their first time, so they're probably on record.'

'That's great news.'

Mrs Adams didn't smile. 'I suppose it's something, but the police warned us that we wouldn't get anything back. The burglar took our holiday money. We were saving to go abroad in the summer. Nowhere fancy. Spain or Greece. Fifteen hundred quid we had in that tin. They took the lot.' Her shoulders started to shake and tears ran down her face.

Catherine moved forward. She had been warned in training about physical contact. She was supposed to keep her distance. But this wasn't training in a classroom. This was in a family home where they had had their dreams dashed, and where they now felt unsafe. Catherine put her arms around her and comforted Mrs Adams until she pulled away.

'I'm so sorry. I shouldn't cry like this. It's the money and the thought of them going through my children's toys. They took so much.' She rubbed her eyes and braved a smile. 'Thank you for coming round. We really do appreciate it. And I am sorry about Gary. He's usually nice. Please don't judge him.'

'Honestly, don't worry. I'd like to see you both again, and maybe next time will be easier for him.'

'Why? Why do you want to help us? We both know nothing will come of this. The police have other priorities.'

'Because I care. Because my dad taught me you don't take what isn't yours. You don't hurt people without good reason. And most of all he taught me that life is hard enough without bullies making it worse and getting away with it. A price has to be paid.'

Catherine stood nervously watching Mrs Adams size her up.

'You want a cuppa?' Mrs Adams asked.

Catherine stayed for another half hour, listening to Mrs Adams and letting her get out any anger or frustrations she had. She talked about how her husband wanted to move house now. Catherine offered to attend court if it went that far, to support the family.

Once she left and was alone in her car, she sat in silence and stared vacantly ahead. The tears came from nowhere. Breaking down was so unexpected, but she felt so helpless. She had volunteered, hoping to make a difference, but Mr Adams had made her feel the complete opposite.

With her head on the steering wheel, she thought about what she could do to help. But before she could make any plans she had to check in with her manager.

After any visit, she had to call and say she was safe and well, and to advise Victim Support of any problems. She made the call and said it went perfectly well.

That was the first of her lies to her manager.

"Friendship is born at that moment when one person says to another, 'What! You too? I thought I was the only one.'

C.S Lewis

CHAPTER 6

The sun in Catherine's eyes was causing her to squint. Roisin pulled the curtains together, making her office instantly cooler. 'That's better,' she said.

Catherine watched as Roisin picked up her notes and tidied them into a neat pile with her gold pen placed perfectly in line with her papers. 'After our last session, I made a note to talk to you about the period after the physical abuse stopped. Are you okay to talk about that today?'

Catherine clasped her hands together and gave the slightest of nods. 'I don't mind.'

'We don't have to. We can talk about how things are now, about your volunteering. We could talk about that?'

'Honestly, I'm fine.'

Catherine knew from Roisin's prolonged silence that it was on her to start so, after a long deep breath, she did. 'Once I stood up to her, that was the last time she laid a finger on me. We barely spoke for a couple of years. We passed each other like strangers in a subway, neither of us looking up, both afraid to make eye contact. There was forced interaction. I had to ask her for money for school most weeks, but I'd do that from the other side of the door. She never made it easy, but what choice did she have? If she neglected me, the school would have been on to her and arranged a home visit through the social, and my mum is many things, but she's not stupid. She wouldn't want them finding out what she did to me. She isn't built for prison.'

Catherine stared down at her hands, hoping Roisin would take over, but she didn't. Feeling the need to fill the silence, she continued. 'At home I was so lonely. I was glad the abuse stopped, but the loneliness was almost as bad. I had Snoop. I felt sorry for him because I'd sit with him for hours, desperate for his attention, when he probably just wanted to lie in his bed alone.' She let out a small laugh at the memory.

'It's crazy. Mum no longer hit me or abused me. She simply ignored me, and somehow that felt worse. I got nothing from her. I think in her head I was dead to her. She couldn't bully me around anymore. Instead, she despised me. She barely acknowledged my existence.' Catherine held her hands out, palms upward.

Roisin gave nothing away in her expression as she said, 'You were still technically a child. Feeling that way must have been so hard for you.'

Catherine could feel the stinging in her eyes, tears imminent. She blinked hard to fight them back. Moving forward in her seat, she stared at Roisin. 'Fuck her. I'm not getting upset over her anymore. I'm sorry, but fuck that frail old…I'm sorry, I didn't mean to…'

'It's okay, Catherine. You can show emotion, whether it be anger or sadness. It's safe here to say how you feel. And swearing is not a problem. I'm from a large Irish family and have three older brothers. I know every cuss word ever invented.'

Catherine sat back. Roisin's kindness took out her defence against tears. She let them fall. 'I fucking hate her. Why couldn't she get fucking cancer? What kind of God gives a beautiful man like my dad, cancer, and not her? If there is a God, he's an arsehole. And if there isn't, he's an arsehole, anyway.' Catherine pulled her sleeve over her hand and used it to wipe her away her tears. 'I'm sorry, I shouldn't bring God into this if you believe in religion. I didn't mean to—'

'Catherine, please don't worry. You have every right to be angry at the world. Your childhood was cruel in the worst way. Questioning one's faith is common in troubled times.'

'I've never had much faith but, like most people who don't believe, I have a tiny worry there is something that will judge me one day, possibly because of the crap my school used to spout at us. All those prayers in assembly and the visits from the weird local priest who would rub his hands together the whole time he was speaking. My dad taught me not to trust religion. He said it caused nothing but problems and that most wars were born out of religious indifference. He said religious people were afraid to face reality. They were uptight and lacked a sense of humour.' Catherine grinned.

'Some maybe. Not all,' said Roisin.

'Mum would sit there all day in her own filth, fuelled by black coffee and hate, and then from around six o'clock the alcohol would come out. She would go into the kitchen and take a whole bottle of spirits, usually gin, into the front room. That would save her going back and forth to the kitchen. By midnight I'd find her, glass in hand, slumped over the side of her chair. I'd stand inches from her, watching. Sometimes I hoped she wouldn't wake up. Other times I'd help her. I'd gently put her head upright just in case she was sick and swallowed it.'

'You cared for her?'

'No,' Catherine snapped and glared at Roisin.

'There's nothing wrong with admitting you care. You are a good person. No matter what your mum did to you, it didn't change the type of person you became.'

Catherine bit her lip. 'It did. It has changed me. I'm not always a good person. I have thoughts of hurting my mum. I have thoughts of hurting other people, but I justify it by thinking it's for the right reason.'

'What reason would justify it?' Roisin asked.

Catherine folded her arms.

'Catherine, we're just talking, and these are just thoughts. You can tell me. When we're depressed, we naturally see more of the darkness in the world. We can't help our thoughts. Tell me what you see.'

Catherine relaxed, swallowed, and lowered her arms. 'I don't like cruel people. I don't like bullies. There's so much injustice going on all around the world. You see it every day on the internet, in the papers, on the news. I see it, and unlike most people I want to do something about it. Take some form of revenge. Real revenge. Not put them in a cosy prison cell and then send them back to the streets to repeat their past behaviour.

'The police do all they can. I don't blame them, but even some of them are bad. They'll turn a blind eye, take a bribe here and there. Look at that policeman who pretended to help that poor lady in London. What did she do wrong? Nothing. She trusted him and look what that bastard did. I'd like to get my hands on him. Dad said rapists should be hung by their bollocks, and he was right. I hope someone in prison already has gone to work on that man. Fuck him. And fuck the people running this sick country.'

Catherine's breathing got short and sharp. She shifted from side to side in her seat.

'Even when the police do their job, they get let down by British courts giving out inappropriate punishments. The sentences are a joke. These arseholes get away with it, or they get a slap on the wrists. I watched a true crime documentary. I watch them all the time. There were these boys in their late teens who attacked a young woman. They beat her and attempted to rape her. In court, they didn't even get a real prison sentence, just because they were under eighteen. It's disgusting. It doesn't take a genius to work out they'll do it again. I'm sorry, but if you commit an adult crime, you deserve an adult sentence. Instead, they went to some cushy kids' home for a year, and then that's it. Out on the streets to do it again.'

Catherine raised a clenched fist. 'One bloody year and they'll be back out to ruin someone else's life. Someone's mother, their sister, their child. What about the victim, eh? How does she move on? She doesn't. If I could get my hands on them…'

Catherine looked at Roisin and stopped talking.

'What, Catherine? What would you do?'

Catherine shook her head. 'Nothing good, that's what.'

'This really upsets you, doesn't it? I'm concerned this will eat you up from the inside if you don't manage your emotions on the subject. You can't save everyone. You need to care more for yourself first. It's noble that you care for others, but, unfortunately, the world isn't perfect. I'm concerned you're taking on other people's problems as well as your own. You can't be responsible for all the bad in the world.'

'Well, who is responsible?' Now both of Catherine's fists were clenched. 'The government? They do fuck all, apart from line their own pockets. All those rich Eton types born with a silver spoon. What do they know about the real world? Protected all their lives, not one ounce of common sense between them. They have second homes, holiday homes, abuse their expenses, cheat the tax system, cheat on their partners, they have second and third jobs that pay them fortunes for doing nothing. What is it they called it once? Cash for questions. Money and greed, that's their only concern. That and their dodgy sexual habits that appear in the press from time to time.'

Roisin stayed silent.

'There's just so much that's cruel in the world, and there's far more bad than good on this planet. Something shitty happens, people just stand by and watch. Not their problem, is it? Or they get their phones out and record it for social media. The bullying that goes unpunished and then gets uploaded on to YouTube is disgusting.'

'I have to ask, Catherine, do you see that your anger about injustice in the world comes from what happened to you? It's understandable that you feel like this. Nobody stepped in to help you. You were a child. It wasn't fair what you had to go through.

There could be a connection. You could be projecting your own feelings of helplessness. You want to help them. You want to save them…save yourself, maybe?'

'I don't see it like that. I believe it should bother everyone. We should all stand up for what's right. My dad taught me that. If you go around in life hurting people, you deserve it back.'

'You're a good person. But I worry you'll end up in trouble by getting too involved. You could be putting yourself in danger. I want you to be safe and to move forward with your life. I don't want you hurt or arrested.'

'I'll be okay. Something inside tells me I'm here to help others. What else is there?'

'Your own happiness, for one. That's the goal here. And you may find happiness helping others. I'm not saying you won't, but it has to be done in the right way – through your volunteering and the way you are trained.'

'I want to do it that way. I'm trying, but what if that's not enough?'

Catherine avoided eye contact by choosing a spot on the carpet to look at. There was silence again and, this time, she was determined she wasn't going to be the one to break it.

'Catherine, can we go back to your teenage years? Did you have other friends at school, other than Hayley, the girl you spoke about last time? Did you stay in touch?'

'She's my closest friend, my only friend. We've worked together, and often been on holiday, just the two of us.'

'That's nice.'

'As I got older, I would go to Hayley's house most evenings. I was happier there.'

'And you work with Hayley? At the care home, I assume.'

Catherine started laughing. 'Worked. She left after an incident.'

'An incident? Sounds like an interesting story.'

Mr and Mrs Roland were the only married couple living together in the nursing home. A couple truly in love and inseparable. Mr Roland was ageing rapidly. He was less able to care for himself and was becoming very forgetful.

One morning he forgot to wear a belt. A simple mistake, but one which would prove to be a costly one. Hayley and Catherine were helping him get dressed for breakfast. Mrs Roland was up and ready, smiling away as she did, waiting in her armchair as her husband stood from his bed. He used his walking frame to steady himself. As he stood up, his trousers fell to his feet. Hayley was behind him, Catherine at the front. Hayley was laughing in silence as they both bent down to pull his trousers up.

Her laughter was about to be a distant memory.

As they got higher, they were both met with a view of poor Mr Roland's vitals. It wasn't just his belt he'd forgotten to put on. He had forgotten to wear his usual white Y-front underpants.

Because Catherine was at the front, she had the pleasure of his bits and bobs inches from her face swinging like a pendulum on an old grandfather clock, which Hayley found wonderfully amusing. For Catherine, this was an occasional occurrence within her role at the care home, nothing new, and it never fazed her. She remained professional and didn't laugh, but Hayley was always full of mischief. Catherine bit her lip as she could hear Hayley's growing giggle. However, it was at this point Mr Roland…had an accident.

Catherine wiped laughter tears from her eyes as she explained to Roisin what had happened. 'It covered Hayley. I can still see her now. It was everywhere. Initially she stayed calm. She didn't scream or yell. She simply said, "Screw this," and left the room with one eye closed and her arms well away from her body.' Catherine started laughing so hard she was holding her stomach, and by now Roisin was rubbing away her own tears of laughter.

'It's nice to see you smiling, Catherine. I'm glad you have Hayley.'

Catherine composed herself to carry on. 'Hayley had to finish her shift, but she had no spare clothes. We had to borrow some from Betty. Hayley looked so funny in that floral dress. Every few minutes she'd ask me if she still smelt of pooh and I'd lie and say no. And every time she caught me looking at her, she would smile and say, "Oh, fuck off, you." That was her last night. She resigned the following morning. I think her final words to our boss were,

"I'm not being shat on by anyone for eight pounds an hour." Despite being pooed on, they were good times. I miss working with Hayley. She's working in London now, got a proper career. It changed things for us, long hours for her. The socialising that came with it meant less time for us. But it doesn't change how much I care for her.'

"The axe forgets, but the tree remembers."

African proverb

CHAPTER 7

Catherine's phone rang just as she was serving Betty her favourite pudding. Catherine gave it a glance, saw that the number was withheld, and put it back in the tight pocket of her jeans.

'Come on, Betty Ramsden, let's eat it all. If you finish it, I'll make sure we put your boxing on later. Actually, I'll go one better than that. This weekend I'm on nights and the big fight is on Saturday. It'll be in the early hours of Sunday morning, so management won't approve, but no one needs to know. We can watch it together.'

Mrs Ramsden smiled. 'Bugger management, miserable sods.'

Betty had early signs of dementia. Her memory was getting worse, she would get confused midway through the simplest of daily tasks, and her behaviour and language could be unpredictable. But the one thing that had not changed was her love for boxing. Her husband had been a boxer in his younger days. She could remember so much about his boxing and yet she could forget she'd had dinner earlier that evening. When the boxing was on, she would sit there waving her fist at the screen, her language becoming beautifully industrial.

At the end of her shift, Catherine checked her phone. Another missed call, but this time there was a number. She immediately called it and was greeted by her manager at Victim Support.

'Hi, Shirley, is everything okay?'

'Hello, Catherine, I'm not sure. We've had a call from your case. Please could you call Mrs Adams? She left a message with us and sounded upset, but she only wanted to talk to you.'

'I'll ring her straight away and come back to you after.'

Mrs Adams explained to Catherine how the case was being dropped. They'd arrested a man and his fingerprints matched those found at their house. However, the evidence had gone missing, been misplaced, and couldn't be found. They were terribly sorry, but they no longer had the proof required. He gets off free and we get nothing. I don't even have any insurance that covers the money he took. I have a household cover of sorts, but they said it doesn't cover cash kept at home.

Catherine held the phone against her chest and mouthed the word, *shit*. She put the phone back to her ear. 'They can't do that. He was one hundred per cent guilty. They had his prints.'

'That's what my husband said to them, but they said sorry and there's nothing more that can be done. He's furious. We have the man's name, and my husband knows him, knows his address. I'm worried he'll do something silly.'

'How did you get his details?'

'The officer told us his name once he'd been charged. They asked if we knew him. His address wasn't hard to find through local friends. My husband knows most people in this area. The man's name is Richard Terry. He lives locally and is a career criminal type. He's got a nice house. We thought he'd be some homeless druggy. It turns out he's even got a wife and kids.'

Catherine thought about her dad. What would he do? 'What did you say his name is?' Catherine asked.

There was silence for a few seconds before she answered.

'Richard Terry. He lives at 32 Hawksmoor Drive, Ashtead.'

Catherine made a note of the address. 'Are you in tonight? I'd like to pop round just after eight. I won't stay long.'

'I'll be in. My husband will be at work. I'm glad because he'll probably take it out on you. I don't want that. I know it's not your fault, but he's angry at everyone.'

Catherine called Shirley to let her know everything with Mrs Adams was fine. Another lie.

She arrived at Mrs Adams' house five minutes after eight o'clock.

'Hello, Catherine. Thank you for coming. Please…' Mrs Adams gestured for Catherine to enter her home.

Catherine looked behind before answering. 'I can't stay. I just wanted to give you something and say I'm sorry for what you've been through.'

Catherine handed her a creased envelope. Mrs Adams looked inside. 'What's this?'

'It's just over a thousand pounds. I thought you could put it back in your family holiday pot.'

Mrs Adams smiled briefly before frowning. 'But where did this come from?'

Catherine couldn't look her in the eye. 'It's from…from a fund we keep at Victim Support. We have donations come in and we use the money for times like this.'

Mrs Adams looked beyond Catherine and then moved towards her. 'I'm not sure I believe you. I'm grateful, I truly am, but wouldn't this money have to come from the courts after conviction? And even then, I thought we'd be lucky to get anything as he wouldn't pay any fines handed out.'

Catherine put her hands in her coat pockets. 'Look, please don't worry about where it came from. And please don't tell anyone else you were given the money, just…'

Before she could finish her speech, Mrs Adams put her arms around Catherine. 'Thank you so much. You have no idea how much this will help us. My kids will be so happy that we can still go away.'

Catherine remained stiff with hands in her pockets. 'I'm happy I could help. I mean, happy Victim Support could help.' She took one hand out of her pocket and awkwardly touched Mrs Adams on her shoulder. She then stepped backwards. 'I'd better go. Please take care and if you need me, give me a call.' She handed her a small piece of paper with her private number on it. Another breach of the rules.

Mrs Adams' two young children came running to the door. 'Who is it, Mummy?'

Mrs Adams smiled at Catherine. 'It's Catherine, Mummy's friend. She's helping us go on holiday. We need to call Daddy and tell him the exciting news.' The children jumped up and down in happiness.

'I'll leave you to it. Take care.'

Catherine walked back to her car, feeling content. A happy, warm feeling was in her stomach. A feeling like no other. She looked up at the stars and smiled.

Hawksmoor Drive was a nice, respectable road. Oak trees lined the street. There were only a couple of streetlights and they hadn't come on yet so, to avoid drawing any unnecessary attention, Catherine was quick to turn her headlights off and stay in darkness. The front room of number thirty-two was brightly lit. With a quick look to make sure no one was around, she opened her car door and walked tentatively towards the house.

Holding out the palm of her hand she could feel rain gently landing on her skin. She lifted the hood on her black top. Peering in from a distance, she could see a man on his phone, laughing, with not a care in the world. Catherine could return another time when he wasn't home and take his belongings. With rain peppering her face, she dismissed her thoughts and returned to her car.

As she went to turn the key in the ignition, she gave one last look at the house. The front room had switched to darkness. She waited. The front door opened. Catherine sunk into her seat, awkwardly low but still able to watch the man's movements. He closed his door behind him and walked towards her car. She ducked lower, her knees in the footwell. Her breathing was heavy. Once enough time had passed, she knew he wasn't coming for her. She looked up and could see him walking away, a black rucksack on his back. Once he was a safe distance, Catherine started the engine and, keeping it in second gear, followed him with her lights off. Panicking, she pulled over feeling she was too close and, grabbing her gloves from the passenger seat, she followed on foot. The man headed down an alleyway with overgrown branches hanging from both sides. She sped up, not wanting to lose him. He turned right as the alleyway forked into three different directions. She picked up her pace to a casual jog. It was pitch-black, the terrain unpredictable. As she turned the corner, she felt a hard blow to her face. She went down, clutching her nose.

'Who the fuck are you? Why are you following me?'

Catherine lay still with the rain hitting her face. She rubbed her eyes and dabbed the blood coming from her nose as she got to her knees. 'You dropped something. I was just trying to catch you up to give it back. You didn't need to hit me.'

He looked her up and down. 'Well?'

Catherine looked at her gloved hand and could make out the blood. 'Well, what?'

'Give it to me then, what I dropped, you stupid cow.'

Catherine put her left hand in her pocket.

'Hold on, let me find it.'

With her right hand, she threw her first punch; it was a clean contact but not powerful enough to put him down. He lunged at her. Catherine ducked and put her body into a side position before putting her arm around his neck. Moving on to his back, she hooked her feet between his legs. She positioned her right arm tight across his neck. His trachea was at the crook of her elbow. With her right hand, she grasped on to her left bicep, her left hand then went behind his head. She squeezed hard and pushed his head forward. He stumbled around with her on his back. He grabbed at her arms. She could feel him weakening as they fell backwards to the ground. Despite the hard impact, she didn't lose her grip, keeping it tight until she felt his body go limp. He was out cold. Unconscious. But for how long? She wriggled free from under his heavy body. Exhausted, she knew she didn't have much time. Frightened and breathing heavily, she went through his pockets and took the only thing she could find – his mobile phone. She took a last look at him to make sure he was breathing before grabbing his rucksack and running back to her car.

Once she'd driven home, she ran in through the front door, ignored her mother's waffling from the front room, and went straight to the bathroom. After showering, she took her clothes to the washing machine and washed everything she'd worn during the fight. She was reliving the incident, questioning herself. Did she do the right thing? Did he deserve it? And then simply said two words before making herself a coffee. 'Fuck him.'

Sitting at the kitchen table, she put her mum's unused washing-up gloves on and opened the rucksack. Inside was a crowbar, a roll of tape, a *Rambo* style knife, and some black gloves. With a smile, she threw the phone back into the bag and said, 'You're done.'

"It's never wrong to do the right thing."

Mark Twain

CHAPTER 8

'Is that a four-leaf clover?'

Roisin peered down and touched her pendant before replying, 'Yes, a friend bought it for me.'

'I've noticed you always wear it. Other pieces you wear come and go, but not that. Was it a special gift?'

'It was,' Roisin said before changing the subject and pointing at Catherine's face. 'Is that from martial arts again? It looks nasty.'

Catherine touched her nose. 'It was my own fault. I switched off and got caught. It looks worse than it is. The fight ended in my favour.'

'It looks painful. Both your eyes are black, your nose looks broken. Are you meant to hit each other that hard in training?'

Catherine replayed the blow that caused the damage. 'Like I said, it looks worse than it is. I'm fine.'

Despite Roisin's smile, Catherine knew she didn't believe her. Catherine was aware Roisin could read her better than anyone.

'I want to say one more thing, and then I promise we'll move on. If you are ever in trouble or in danger, you would tell me, wouldn't you? I'll always do all I can to help you.'

Catherine nodded. 'I would.'

'Can I ask about your martial arts training? You mentioned before about them making you feel like a family. I can see why that's important to you.' Roisin looked down at her paperwork. 'And Tony, he runs the gym?'

'Tony's amazing. He's built like a silverback, shaved head and tattoos, and yet he's so nice to everyone and so kind.'

'Like a father figure?' Roisin asked.

'I wouldn't say that. Do you think I've been looking for one since losing my dad? I don't need a replacement.'

Roisin nodded. 'Father figures can enter our lives at any time. It doesn't mean you're replacing your dad. It's just nice to know you feel protected, and maybe you can talk to him in times of trouble.'

'I can talk to Tony. He always listens. He kicks my butt too, once we're on that mat, or in the ring. He doesn't mess about. We laugh and joke afterwards, but during training we have to be focused.'

Catherine started picking a small piece of thread off her jeans as she continued. 'The first day I walked into that gym he came up to me and shook my hand. I could hardly get my tiny hand around his. His grip was so strong. But he beamed that rare smile of his and said, "Welcome to the madhouse." I knew right away it was a safe place. My safe place.'

'You weren't intimidated at all?' Roisin asked.

'Not one bit. I looked around and could see a boxing ring, a cage in the shape of an octagon, cardio machines, weights, and punch bags hanging all around the gym, most of them swaying about as they were being hit by punches and kicks. It was dark and dingy and smelled of old clothes left in a gym bag for far too long, but I loved it. A few of the fighters stared at me, but not long enough to make me uncomfortable. I grew up receiving worse looks. They just went back to what they were doing. I've had plenty of people look down their noses at me over the years, but not one of them there did that.'

Roisin stayed silent, so Catherine continued. 'The posters on the walls displayed fighters I hadn't heard of – Chuck Liddell, Tito Ortiz, and then I could see the fighters I knew – Michael Bisping, Ronda Rousey, Jon Jones, and Conor McGregor. The noise in the gym was thrilling. Not much talking, just plenty of heavy breathing, grunts, and groans. Above Tony's front desk, there's a giant crest – a Roman soldier's helmet with two crossed hammers in front of it. There were only two other girls in the gym, the rest were all men. I decided this was a good thing. In general, I get on better with men.'

'It was very brave of you to go there, especially alone. I don't think I could do that. In fact, I know I couldn't.'

'I didn't go alone. Hayley came with me, but she didn't get past the reception.' Catherine laughed. 'Hayley isn't a fighter. She won't even watch it. She said there was no way on earth she was joining some smelly, sweaty club to get punched, kicked, and thrown around the place.'

'I think I'm with Hayley on that one,' Roisin joked.

'It's not for everyone. But there's something special about knowing I can defend myself. It gives me confidence. When I walk around in everyday life, I don't fear people like I used to. I don't want a fight and would never go looking for one, and I'm more aware of what people can do since I've learnt to fight, but I like knowing I can if I need to. I remember the first time I watched Ronda Rousey fight in the UFC. She was amazing. At the weigh-in, she was pretty and glamorous, but on fight night in that octagon, she was brutal, and she earned the same respect the men were given.' Catherine's face reddened. 'I should stop going on about the gym. I could bore you all day about it.'

'Not at all. I love how passionate you are. Thank you for sharing with me.'

'My mum has never asked about my training. I'm not even sure she knows I go.'

'Do you mind if we change the subject to your mum? Can I ask how your relationship with her is going?'

Catherine pictured her mum sitting in the same old chair in the front room. She could see the back of her mother's head. These days, that's all she saw of this woman she called Mum. Whatever time of day Catherine came home, her mum wouldn't turn around and say hello. There was no concern at all for her welfare.

'It is what it is.' Catherine shrugged.

'Do you talk to each other? Make each other a cup of tea? Is there any interaction at all?'

Catherine shook her head. 'No, and I'm happy that way.'

'Can I ask why you choose to still live there? You have money to buy your own house.'

Catherine sat back with her arms folded. 'As much as I hate her, it's still my home. It's the home I shared with my dad. The only home I know. For all the bad memories she's given me, I have ten times that in good memories from him. And if I'm honest, I'm waiting for her to go so I can live there alone.'

'Where's she going?' Roisin asked.

'I mean when she dies. If you saw her, you'd know she isn't going to make old bones. She hardly eats, she takes painkillers like they're sweets, and she drinks a large bottle of gin every single day. Her insides must be screaming for her to give up.'

'But she could go on for years. Some people get lucky.'

'Then I'll enjoy ignoring her for even longer.' Catherine's grin was fake. She waited for Roisin to respond, maybe smile back at her, but she didn't.

After a long pause, Roisin tapped her gold-plated pen on her notes. 'Do you go out socially? I know you have your friend Hayley, but do you…?'

'I don't have a partner. I've dated, but I don't want a relationship.'

Roisin remained silent.

'I had a boyfriend once, that was enough. I knew he wasn't the one for me. He told me he loved me on the Tuesday, but on the Wednesday he stole my Penguin bar from my lunchbox. The little arsehole thought I wasn't looking.'

Roisin chuckled. 'How old was this romantic thief?'

'Seven, maybe eight.'

They both laughed.

'I don't trust anyone enough to let them in like that. I don't believe there are many good ones out there. I'm safer alone,' Catherine said.

'I understand you thinking that way. Relationships can hurt. But they can also be worth the risk. Having someone to share your day with, having someone who you know will always look out for you, no matter what—'

Catherine interrupted. 'Having someone who cheats on you, having someone who lets you down, having someone who judges you, controls you? No thanks.'

'It doesn't have to be that way. I'm not saying you need to settle down now. I'm saying, when the time comes, I don't want you regretting not taking a chance. Not everyone is bad.'

'I think everyone is capable of being bad. They just need the right reason,' Catherine replied as her phone started ringing. 'I'm sorry. I normally turn it off,' she said as she took her phone out and pressed mute.

'That's okay. We're nearly finished. If you'd like to call them back, I don't mind. It could be one of your cases.'

Once Catherine was back in her car, she prepared herself to return Mrs Adams' call. Catherine's car was one of only a few luxuries she afforded herself with her dad's money. It was the same model he'd driven. Her mum sold his after he died. Catherine longed for those days when he would take her for drives to the coast. A 1977 MG MGB GT, white with tan leather seats. The only thing modern inside was the Apple CarPlay stereo. The bodywork was immaculate. The pristine leather seats and wooden interior trim sent her back twenty years with a single waft of the car's aroma.

Mrs Adams answered and thanked Catherine for calling back.

'No problem. How can I help?' Catherine asked.

'We can't believe it ourselves, but they've rearrested Mr Terry. New evidence apparently.'

'That's good.'

'Good! It's unbelievable. They found his bag in the bushes at the back of our garden and the CPS said it was grounds for trial as the new evidence was compelling. His prints were all over everything in that bag. They'd searched that whole area the day after the burglary but must have missed it.'

'Well, everyone has an off day. Even the police,' Catherine said.

'Maybe, but my husband wouldn't have. He was out there for hours, and he would have found it.'

'He was stressed at the time. I think you should stop worrying about how and when they found it and enjoy the fact that he's been caught properly this time.'

'Oh, I know, you're right. In his bag, there was a huge knife. Who knows what could have happened to us? Anyway, the police told us the knife would add some weight to his sentence. They also informed us Mr Terry was unfortunately attacked. Said it was a random attack by strangers. He told the officers he was minding his own business while out on his evening stroll, and a group of men attacked him. It was quite serious. They left him unconscious.'

Catherine sniggered. 'That sounds very scary for him. It'll teach him for going out alone at night. Probably best he stays in of an evening.'

Mrs Adams laughed. 'Poor Mr Terry.' Once she'd composed herself, Mrs Adams continued. 'They even asked where my husband was on the night, thought he may have been out for revenge. It was a good job he was at home with me.'

Catherine looked out of her window. A chaffinch was delicately resting on the thinnest of branches, his head bobbing side to side, and then stopping, staring directly at Catherine. 'I should go. You take care, Mrs Adams.'

'Catherine, I've got to ask. The money? I know that didn't come from Victim Support. It wouldn't have been in cash if it had. And then Terry getting attacked, and his bag ending up in our garden. It was you, wasn't it?'

Catherine was still staring at this beautiful bird with his blue crown and pinkish-brown breast. She tapped her steering wheel. 'It's the right outcome. He got what he deserved, and so did you.'

'What do you mean?' Mrs Adams asked.

'Revenge,' Catherine said.

'Justice. You mean we got justice? Revenge sounds like we're doing something wrong.'

'Revenge. Justice. The line is blurred.'

The little chaffinch quickly disappeared when Catherine started the engine. She put her seat belt on. 'Mrs Adams, I really must go. I'm running late.'

'Catherine?'

'Yes, Mrs Adams?'

'Thank you.'

Catherine hung up and allowed herself a moment as the warm feeling in her chest sent a shiver through her body and goosebumps appeared on her arms. She put the gearstick into first and pulled away, feeling proud. She hit the brake as her phone rang.

'Hi, Maggie, how are you?' Catherine asked.

'Catherine, whatever you said to Mr and Mrs Adams, it must have worked. They've contacted head office and sung your praises. If you're around this evening, you could tell me more. Could you join me on tonight's home visit?'

'I could. I mean I can. I'm not up to anything.'

'It's a domestic abuse case I've taken on. You could come along and shadow me. You won't need to say anything, just be there with me and observe. I'll call Mrs Whitaker and let her know you'll be with me. I'll text you the address. Meet me there fifteen minutes before the seven o'clock appointment and I can give you a brief summary of the case.'

'Sounds good. See you there.'

"Friends are those rare people who ask how we are and then wait to hear the answer."

Ed Cunningham

CHAPTER 9

Catherine accepted the charge from the operator and took the call.

She could hear the crying, and then a girl's voice, a voice she knew well. 'I didn't have any coins for the phone. I had to reverse the call. It wouldn't take—'

'Hayley?' she interrupted.

'Please help me, Cat. I need you. I'm bleeding. I'm not sure where it's coming from.'

'We need to get you to a hospital,' Catherine replied.

'No,' Hayley replied sharply.

'How bad is it? If it's serious, you need to go.'

'I don't care. I just need you to take me home. No hospital.'

'I'm leaving right now, but if it gets worse call for an ambulance. Where are you?'

'I'm not sure. The houses look expensive, like town houses. Ah fuck, there's a man coming towards me, no.'

Catherine could hear her crying. 'Hayley, stay strong. It's going to be okay. I will be there as soon as I can, but you need to tell me where you are.'

She could hear Hayley's deep breaths. 'That's it, relax. Look around, is there an address on the phone somewhere, look for a postcode, anything.'

Through her tears, she replied, 'He's gone, went straight past. I'm in a bad way, Cat. They raped me. All of them, I think. They…'

Catherine's body shook. She caught her reflection in the mirror, teeth clamped tight as she stared in anger.

The line went dead. 'Hayley, Hayley,' Catherine yelled.

With no number to return the call, all she could do was wait for Hayley to call back. Catherine stared at the phone intently willing it to ring. 'C'mon, for fuck's sake.'

Just under five minutes passed before Catherine got her wish. She interrupted the operator. 'Yes I do accept the call. Please put her through.'

'Cat. I'm at a station. I can't see the fucking name. Hold on, Richmond. Richmond Station. Should I just jump on a train? I don't know what to do. People are staring at me. Blood, they can probably see the blood, it's…'

Catherine interrupted. 'I'm coming. Stay where you are. Is there somewhere you can wait?'

'There's a Costa. I could go in there if they'll let me. I need to wash. I'll use their toilets to clean myself up.'

'No, don't,' Catherine insisted.

'Why not? Why can't I wash myself?' Hayley's panicked voice grew louder.

'I just think it's best you don't. Not yet.'

'Oh god. You don't want me to because of the police. What are they going to do with me?'

'Hayley, I don't know, but it's best you don't wash away any DNA that those bastards may have left.'

Catherine held the phone to her chest as she felt herself about to break down. She composed herself the best she could before putting the phone back to her ear. 'Hayley, I'm on my way. Please stay in the Costa. I'm leaving now. It will be okay, I promise. I love you. I'm going to look after you.'

'Costa, I'll be in there,' Hayley said.

As Catherine pulled up outside the station in Richmond, Hayley came running out. Catherine put the car in neutral and got out. She embraced her friend like she never had before. Both were in tears, not wanting to let go.

'I'm so sorry. It's my own fault,' Hayley said, as her tears rolled from her face on to Catherine's shoulder. 'I drank so much, too much. I'm not sure if it was more than normal but I hadn't eaten since the morning. It must have been that. I'm fucking stupid.'

Catherine leaned back so she could look into Hayley's eyes. 'Don't you say that. It wasn't your fault. Those fucking animals.' She pulled Hayley back in close to her. 'I've got you now. I'll look after you. Where's the pain? How bad is it?'

Hayley just nodded. 'I just want to go.'

Catherine squeezed her tight. 'I am so sorry. They'll pay for this. One way or another, we'll make them wish they never came near you.'

Catherine helped her into her car before getting in herself. Using her phone, she looked up the nearest police stations, it suggested Twickenham. It was only two miles away. She put the address into her satnav and reached across to hold Hayley's hand. Clutching it tightly, she said, 'It's going to be okay.'

Hayley did not respond with affection. Instead, she freed her hand and began pulling the hem of her skirt lower as it was bunching up beneath her.

'This fucking skirt, it's too short. I shouldn't have worn it. I look like a slag. A slag that sleeps with a bunch of men in one night.' Hayley started punching her own legs. 'A fucking slut. Look at me.'

'Stop, Hayley, it wasn't you. It was them.' Catherine reached again for her friend's hand.

'I'm not doing this. No police. I'm not being prodded and poked by them in there. They're not sticking anything inside me.' Hayley gestured towards the police station. 'And I'm not having the world know those men raped me. I'll be judged forever. Damaged goods.'

Catherine pulled her in close and held her tight. 'I'm not going to make you. I'll do whatever you want to do.' She could feel Hayley's tears on her shoulder. 'But if we don't go in there, and we go home, you won't have all the evidence you might need. I want you to realise what that means. In a day, a week, a month, you may change your mind and you won't have the evidence. What kind of friend would I be if I didn't try?'

Catherine let Hayley go as she sat back.

'I can't do it. I'm sorry,' Hayley said.

Catherine thought about the men and what they had done. She pictured her best friend being passed about by those animals. Her body shook in anger. Looking across at the bruises and cuts on Hayley's knees made her feel sick. She looked up at Hayley's face where there were more disturbing marks. Reminders of the torture they'd inflicted.

'Hayley, if we're not going to the police, I'd like to know more about what happened and find out who they are. Where did it happen?'

Hayley shook her head. 'What do you mean?'

'Where did they take you? Have you got the address? A road name?'

'I can't go back. I won't.' Hayley turned to stare out of the window.

'I'm not asking you to. I know you, Hayley. You would have noticed as you left. Can you remember the road name or anything?'

'Maybe I don't want to remember. I just want to go home.'

'We are going home, but the address, Hayley. I know you know it. Please tell me?'

'Marlborough Road. It was Marlborough Road. An apartment building. Grove House.'

'Number?'

'Twenty-two. Number 22. On the third floor.'

Catherine took out her phone and typed it into her notes. 'Good. That's good. And you're sure you want to go home?'

'Don't, Cat. I definitely want to please.'

'Okay, I'll leave it. I'm sorry.'

As Catherine pulled up at Hayley's house, she looked across. Her best friend was sleeping. She left the engine running and sat back, not wanting to wake her. She looked her up and down imagining what she'd been through. Catherine's forehead was moist with sweat, she wiped it away with her arm. She took deep breaths to control the anger within. Someone should pay. Her dad always said you have to look after your own. They should always pay. She punched the steering wheel.

Hayley jumped. 'What's happening?'

'I'm sorry. It's fine. We're home.' She touched Hayley's leg.

Hayley sat back, closed her eyes, and exhaled loudly. Catherine knew she was reliving the ordeal. Sleep had given her a small window of solace. Now that she was awake, she was back in her nightmare.

'I'll come in. I'm not leaving you alone.'

Hayley didn't answer as she opened the car door. Walking down the path to the house, Catherine took her hand and stopped. 'Are you going to tell your mum? She's going to know something's happened.'

Hayley was quick to reply. 'No. She doesn't need to know. No one does.'

Catherine stared at her. People should know who and what those fucking animals were.

Hayley inched forward and tugged at Catherine's hand. 'Promise me, no one.'

Catherine tapped the steering wheel with her fingers. Then, she slowly turned her head to face Hayley. 'I promise.'

Once inside, they made their way to the bathroom. Catherine helped Hayley start to undress. With every movement, there was a different pain. 'I'm sorry, am I hurting you?'

Hayley didn't respond as she removed her underwear. Catherine could see the blood at the top of her thighs. 'Oh god, Hayley. Those bastards.' More tears fell from Catherine, but not from Hayley.

Catherine turned the shower on before picking up all of Hayley's clothes.

'Can you leave me alone for a bit, just while I shower?'

Catherine attempted a smile through her tears. 'Of course. Call me if you need me. I'll be in your room.'

Catherine found a bag and put Hayley's clothes in. She paused and looked at the contents. Checking Hayley was still in the shower, Catherine ran out to her car and put the bag in the boot. On her return to the bedroom, she peered into the bathroom. Hayley was sitting in the corner of the shower, shaking with her legs pulled up to her chest, the blood washing away down the drain along with her tears. Catherine closed the door and left her. The anger was in her stomach, rising to her chest. 'Bastards, those fucking bastards.' Desperate to hit something, someone, anything, she laid face first on Hayley's bed and screamed into a pillow.

Catherine went through Hayley's drawers and found some underwear, some loose-fitting tracksuit bottoms, and a baggy hoodie. She lay them out on the bed and went back to check on Hayley. As she opened the bathroom door, she could see Hayley standing in front of the mirror, aggressively combing her hair.

'Here, let me.' Catherine took the brush from her and gently put it through Hayley's blonde locks.

'Cat, I'm tired.'

Catherine led her to the bedroom and helped her get dressed.

'I'd like to lie down, get some sleep. You can go,' Hayley said.

'I'm staying with you. You can sleep. I'll call in sick and not go to work tonight.'

'No. I need to be alone. I'll be fine. I just want to sleep. Come back tomorrow if you like.'

'Hayley, I can't leave you.'

Hayley lay on the bed. 'Please. I just want to sleep. I won't do anything silly, if that's what you're thinking.'

That's exactly what Catherine was thinking, but she lied. 'I didn't think that. I'm just worried about you.'

'Before you go, please can you turn the television on? I don't want the silence.'

Catherine turned it on and sat next to Hayley. 'I'll go once you're asleep. But promise me you'll call if you need me.'

'I'll call. I promise.'

Catherine stroked Hayley's head until she fell asleep. She didn't leave. She leaned down and kissed her forehead and whispered, 'If someone hurts you or anyone you love, you never let them get away with it, they pay twice the price, Dad taught me that, and he's right.'

"One always measures friendships by how they show up in bad weather."

Sir Winston Churchill

Chapter 10

Betty Ramsden was throwing punches along with Tyson Fury. Every time he had his opponent against the ropes, she would shout, 'Go on, son, smash his bloody face in.'

Catherine sat there in silence. Normally she'd join in with Mrs Ramsden, but not tonight. The only thing on her mind was the welfare of her best friend. Catherine was anxiously looking at her phone, waiting for Hayley to call, regretting leaving her alone. Catherine could feel Mrs Ramsden staring at her. She'd stopped her shadow boxing.

'You all right, love?'

Catherine didn't answer.

'Catherine, what's wrong, dear?'

Catherine forced a grin. 'I'm okay. How are we doing? Is he winning?'

'Of course, he's winning. But don't lie to me about being okay. I know you all think I'm crazy, but I still know when someone's upset, and you're upset.' Mrs Ramsden's long skinny finger was now in Catherine's face.

Catherine anxiously rubbed the back of her neck. 'My friend got hurt. She got badly hurt, and I don't know what I can do about it.'

Mrs Ramsden took a sip of her tea, leaving bright red lipstick on the rim of the cup. 'This friend of yours, is she a good friend?'

'The best. I'd do anything for her.'

'And is someone responsible for her pain? Did someone hurt your friend?'

'Yes.'

Mrs Ramsden put her cup and saucer down. 'And you want to hurt them back, don't you? I can see it in your face.' The finger was inches from Catherine's nose.

Catherine didn't take her eyes off the television screen. 'Yes. I do. They deserve it.'

Mrs Ramsden nodded as she replied, 'I completely understand. Sometimes I want to hurt Pat. Bloody woman will eat anything that's not nailed down.'

'Betty, don't say that. What has she done to you?' Catherine asked.

Mrs Ramsden narrowed her gaze, her drag queen styled blue eye shadow highlighted her wrinkles as she pointed again.

'She's fat, for one. Big and fat. Fat Pat I call her. Have you seen her legs? They're the same shape from the top to the bottom. She hasn't even got knees. Who doesn't have knees? Or ankles. What a state to be in. I've seen better legs on a snooker table. And on top of being fat, she cheats when we play cards. Maybe she's French. They cheat.'

'Betty Ramsden, you can't say that. That's a terrible thing to say. And I'm sure she doesn't cheat…and she can't help being overweight.' Catherine tried not to smile, but could feel it brewing.

Betty raised her arms. 'I've said my piece.'

'Come on, Betty, be nice.'

Betty went back to watching the boxing as she replied, 'Of course she can help being a fatty. She needs to stop filling her fat face.' Betty blew her cheeks out to demonstrate before continuing, 'Have you seen her at lunchtime? After her lunch, she sits there shovelling in one biscuit after another until the packet is empty. I've seen her do a whole pack of HobNobs before now, straight after her dinner, greedy pig. She even shakes the crumbs from the packet into her porky face, can't waste any, oh no.' Betty shook her head and continued, 'So fat. Like a hippo, a hungry one. Remember that game, Hungry Hippos, that's her. And cake, Mavis had her birthday last week, we all had a small piece, you know, to be polite. Not Pat, three pieces, eating it like a toddler she was, throwing it at her fat face hoping it would hit that hole in the middle of her giant head.'

Catherine looked away to hide the growing smile on her face. She knew Mrs Ramsden talking like this was mostly down to her condition, she hoped it was. 'That's not funny. Come on, Betty. Pat is a nice lady. I think you're being a bit nasty.'

'Yeah…well I think she's being a bit fat.'

Catherine sniggered before Betty continued, 'And you would say I'm being nasty because you're nice to everyone. It'll get you nowhere, being nice.' Betty's long skinny finger was back in Catherine's face. 'Stop being so nice. Look after yourself. This world is a cesspit full of shithouses. Take what you can from it, and fuck 'em all.' Betty stuck her middle finger up in the air.

'I'm not always nice, Betty, not nice at all.'

The next round started. Tyson Fury came out knowing the knockout was inevitable, jab, jab, and then he unloaded with a right hand. His opponent was down.

'And fucking stay down,' Betty shouted as she jumped to her feet.

Catherine allowed herself a full smile for the first time today.

Mrs Ramsden took another sip of her tea. She then put the cup and saucer down and without looking at Catherine, she continued, 'Do it then. If they deserve it, do it.'

Betty stared intently at Catherine. 'Titus Adronicus, Vengeance is in my heart.' She touched Catherine's chest. 'Death in my hand.' She touched Catherine's hand. 'Blood and revenge are hammering in my head.' She tapped Catherine's head before returning to the boxing.

'What did you say?' Catherine asked.

Tyson Fury had won. The ref raised his hand.

'That's my boy,' Mrs Ramsden called out. 'Look at him. All that muscle. If I was fifty years younger, he'd be in all kinds of trouble.'

Catherine touched Betty's arm, 'Betty, what did you say, that about vengeance?'

'Sorry love, what?' Betty said.

Catherine knew Mrs Ramsden would forget their conversation by the morning, but what did she mean about vengeance being in her heart?

Once Catherine had calmed Mrs Ramsden and got her to bed, she spotted the books on Betty's shelf, Shakespeare's Titus Andronicus was at the front. She flicked through before taking a seat. The reality of what Hayley went through was hitting her hard. A mixture of anger, grief, and sadness was boiling inside. It had been two days since Catherine took her home that morning, and Catherine had only left Hayley's side to attend work. She sent a text to Hayley asking if she was okay, asked if she wanted to talk. To her relief, her phone started ringing.

'Thanks for calling. I just wanted to check in,' Catherine said on answering.

Hayley spoke softly. 'I just keep sleeping. My mum came up. She thinks I have a cold or flu, so I left it at that. She's been great, though, making me eat and drink something.'

'That's good. Hayley, can we talk a bit more about it? Can I ask about what happened? I mean, I won't if you don't want me to.'

'Like what?'

'You said you remembered him in the club and then at the fast-food place. What was the name of the club?'

'Ciros, in Leicester Square. I was okay when we went in. I was a bit drunk but nothing too bad. An hour or so later I felt awful, blurred vision and tiredness. I remember needing air.'

'Ciros, Leicester Square,' Catherine said as she made a note.

'I think there were four of them.'

'Would you recognise them if you saw them again?'

Catherine waited for Hayley's reply, worried she was pushing it too far.

'I remember two of their faces, the main one with his big white teeth, and the other one that was on the floor in the morning. The rest is all flashbacks…one of them was filming me on his phone. I can't remember his face, just that he was tall.'

Catherine wrote this all down.

'And…they all, they all raped you?' Catherine asked before saying, 'I'm sorry. I shouldn't have said that.'

'I think so…they were all over me, all of them. The ginger one, the one on the floor. He used something on me. He forced it in and wouldn't stop.' Hayley's words came out fast, 'I screamed, but the main one put his hand over my mouth. I couldn't breathe, so I bit down on his hand. One of them punched me or maybe kicked me. My head was ringing, and I couldn't focus.' Hayley grabbed at her hair.

Catherine looked to the ceiling, hate filled her mind as she imagined what she would do to them.

Hayley relaxed her hand, strands of hair pulled from her head revealed themselves. 'I woke up in that bedroom. I don't know how I got there. Hold on.'

'What? What is it?'

Catherine waited. She could hear Hayley fiddling about with something.

'I've charged my phone. The photos. I remember taking photos. They'd, they had finished with me, they weren't looking my direction, I took a pictures, at least one. And then it died.'

'Photos of what?'

'I'm sending them over.'

Catherine's phoned pinged. She opened the message and there were two photos from the apartment.

'I knew I was in trouble.'

Catherine stared at the photo. Four men, a mixture of ages, thirty to forty years old, sitting at a table. There were beer bottles everywhere.'

'Hayley, you were so brave to take these. You should be proud of yourself. We could show these to the police?'

'No,' she shouted. 'No police. It's not going to happen, Catherine…I think I need to sleep some more. I'm going, I'll see you soon.'

'I'm sorry. No police, I understand. I'll be around after work in the morning, before I go home.'

'Cat, thank you, you've been a good friend.' Hayley said before hanging up.

Catherine smiled, and as quick as that smile arrived, it disappeared when Catherine went back to the photos.

Catherine finished her shift and sped to Hayley's house. Hayley's mum let her in while Catherine was pretending it was just another normal visit. Hayley was asleep. Catherine sat with her for a while before leaving a note asking her to call her. Catherine rubbed at her stinging eyes. She needed sleep, but every time she tried to forget, she could see her disgusting version of what happened to her friend. Could it be even worse than she pictured?

She got a solid five hours of sleep, which was good for Catherine. She would regularly have broken sleep from her recurring nightmares. She now had new nightmares to join the old. Lack of sleep was also one of the downsides of working night shifts. Hayley stirred and once awake, Catherine stroked her hair until she fell back asleep.

'I'm going now. It's time,' Catherine whispered. She kissed Hayley's head and left with revenge on her mind.

She opened the satnav on her phone and typed in the location, 22 Grove House, Marlborough Road, Richmond. It said it was twenty-one miles, and would take fifty-two minutes. She clicked on the directions tag and sat her phone in it's holder.

She parked a short walk from the apartment block and looked over both shoulders nervously. Walking towards the entrance of the building, Catherine kept her head down, avoiding eye contact with several passers-by. Once outside the front door, she pulled the handle, but it was locked. Panicking she looked up for any sign of cameras, none were visible. She took out her phone to act casual, like she had a right to be there. She needed a code to get in. Becoming impatient, she looked at the numbers and started guessing, *1234*, of course it didn't work.

'Shit.' *4321*. 'Bollocks.'

Below the numbers was a button that said *trade*. Could it be that easy? She pressed it, the door buzzed, she pulled, she was in. Within the small reception area, there were numbered mailboxes for the residents. Some of the larger envelopes were poking out. Box twenty-two was one of these.

After a quick look around and happy she was alone, she pulled it out. It was addressed to Bryce Bellfield. For now, that was all she needed, she had his name and address. Back in her car, she looked him up on social media. There were several Bryce Bellfields, but only one who lived in Richmond. It read, *see Bryce's about info*.

'Okay, don't mind if I do.'

Work was at the top of the page, *headteacher at St Johns School*. Catherine nodded in disbelief.

'A fucking headteacher.'

A job of authority, of trust, and care of children, yet he was a rapist scumbag.

Education was blank.

Places Lived was blank.

Family Members, he had a daughter.

Catherine's right hand covered her mouth.

'How could he?' This rapist had a daughter. There were no recent posts of him with a partner. Maybe he was divorced, either that or he wanted to come across as single. From his pictures, he looked respectable and well-travelled. He had nothing on his profile that was political, no affiliation to any clubs, not even a photo that showed which football or rugby team he supported.

Catherine went into her notes app and typed, Rapist Number 1 – Bryce Bellfield – Headteacher.

What she typed next was the price he would pay.

"To exact revenge for yourself or your friends is not only a right, it's an absolute duty."

Stieg Larsson

Chapter 11

Bryce Bellfield arrived home every day around 6 p.m. He parked his six-month-old BMW 5 Series in the underground car park of his attractive apartment block, just as he did any other day. He exited his car with his brown leather satchel in hand. Inside was his laptop, wallet, and paperwork. Bellfield locked his car. Again, just as he did any other day. But this wasn't like any other day. The constricting grip around his neck was new, the squeeze against his windpipe forcing his airway to be blocked was also new. He tried to fight, but the chokehold was in tight, and correct, he had seconds before darkness would arrive. He moved his bodyweight, along with his attacker, backwards into the car parked next to his, but they didn't let go. Vision blurry, feeling weak, he grabbed at the arm that if held there long enough would snatch his life from him. His hands fell to his side as his body went limp.

As he regained consciousness, he coughed, causing a small dust cloud. His face in the dusty tarmac, he spat out the debris that was stuck on his tongue. With no idea how long he'd been out, he was about to get up, but that's when he realised his hands were cable tied. And then she spoke.

'Stay still, and don't say a word. If you do, I will push this knife into your spinal cord. It won't hurt for long. Seconds, probably. The pain will only be gone because you're paralysed…would you like to be paralysed?'

'No, no. Who the fuck are you?'

'Do not swear at me, I don't like it. And it doesn't matter who I am. I know who you are though, Bryce Bellfield, Mr Rapist Number One.'

'Bollocks, get the fuck…'

The blow to his head caused his skull to bounce up off the tarmac. 'You really must stop swearing. When I tell you to, you're going to get in the back of your car. And when I'm satisfied you've cooperated sufficiently, I'll let you go. But, for now, all I need from you is your laptop password.'

'What? Fuck off, no.'

She tutted before standing up straight and stamping on the side of his face. He screamed out in pain. Blood poured from his nose as she kept her foot against his face.

'I said don't swear. Your password. Now…let me guess, is it, *I'm a rapist*?' She kicked him in his back. 'Or is it, *I gang rape women*?' The next kick was in the base of his spine. 'Is it…'?

'Ahh, stop, that's enough. It's *lizzy2010*, all lowercase,' he said as he spat blood out.

'Is that your daughter's name?' Catherine asked.

'How the fuck do you know…'

Another kick, this time to the back of his neck.

He attempted to raise his cuffed hands, 'Yes, that's my daughter.'

She crouched down and put her mouth near to his ear. 'What would you do if someone raped your daughter? A group of sweaty drunk men raping her over and over again?' Catherine's mouth was now touching his ear as she whispered. 'The sweat from their brows falling on to her as they laughed and mocked her. Raping her until she bled? And you know where the blood would be coming from, don't you? Your precious daughter, laying there calling for her disgusting daddy. Picture it, you fucking…'

He screamed out as his tears fell. 'I'd fucking kill them, and I'm going to kill you.'

'Yes. You would, wouldn't you? So would I. You just swore at me again.' She pushed her knife against his back with minimal force, not quite enough to enter his body.

'Please don't, I'm sorry. The girl was drunk. We were drunk. We—' His wasted plea was interrupted.

'Save your lies, Rapist Number One. You need to remain silent, or I will put this knife inside of you.'

'Okay, whatever you say.'

She grabbed a fistful of his hair and yanked his head back. Blood transferred from his locks on to her gloves.

'Get to your feet. Do not turn around, do not look at me. If you look at me, it's over. I'll stab you, and it will be your fault. I'll simply go whoopsadaisy, and push it in.' Catherine pushed the knife two millimetres into his skin.

'No, no, no. Don't, please don't. I'll do as you say.'

She picked up his keys and pressed the button on the fob to open the car. Once he was on his feet, she pushed him in. He kept his eyes closed as promised. She slammed the door shut and then got in the front of Bellfield's car.

'What are you looking for? I'll tell you whatever you want to know. Are you looking for my friend's names and addresses? I'll give them to you, I promise.'

'I know you'll tell me, but I'd rather find them myself. Because you could be a big fat fibber,' she said in the same way an adult talks to a toddler. 'Anyway, I'm nearly done here. Five more minutes, and I'm off. Now, shut up and keep your eyes closed.'

'Please let me go, please.'

'Do you want me to stab you? I can. In fact, I'd like to.'

There was silence long enough for Catherine to approve. 'Thank you, Number One.'

Catherine carried on using the laptop until she'd done what she needed to. Typing in gloves wasn't easy. She'd intended on the letter O and got a P, she'd type an E and get an R. 'Sodding stupid laptop.'

Once satisfied she'd got what was necessary, she closed the lid and made her way to the back of the car.

'You better have your eyes closed, Mr Rapist. If not, I'll put this shiny knife through them.'

'I promise, I'm facing away,' he pleaded.

She watched her victim as she opened the door. She leant forward to look at his face. His eyes shut tight like a child pretending to sleep. The laptop hit him as she threw it in.

She wasn't quite finished. She had what she needed, but he still needed to realise what he'd caused. He needed to know, to feel pain. Pain close to what Hayley felt. Catherine's dad would have made sure he paid a real price. He'd get even. What was even? Would he have killed them? She lifted Bellfield's shirt and, using the sharp silver blade, she pushed down and dragged it deep within his skin. He screamed out.

'Number One. You now have a number one on you for life.'

'No more, please, that's enough.'

She kept the knife against his body as she ran it down the small of his back.

'I'd like you to confirm the names of your three friends. I need three names, then I'm done with you, for now. I might be back, I might not. I haven't decided.' She pressed the knife into his backside, piercing through his expensive suit trousers. Then, with more force, she went through his underwear and into him.

'No, don't do it, please. I'll give you the names, I promise.'

'I know you will,' she replied.

He spoke fast. 'Tristan Bridger, Ian Whiting, and David Worboys. There you go. That's it. You've got the names. You said three names. I've given you three names, I can go, right?'

She reached into his pocket with her free hand and took his phone. 'Code for your phone, now.'

'Twenty-two, twenty-two,' he said.

She went through his phone and looked up the names, one by one. Placing the knife momentarily on top of the car, she punched the names and numbers into her phone.

'Rapist Number Two, Tristan Bridger, where does he work?'

'What?'

Retrieving the knife and pushing back inside him, she could hear her dad's voice in her head ordering this man around. With venom in her veins, she shouted at him, 'Not *what*. *What's* no fucking good? What does he do? Tell me what he does?'

He started talking even faster. 'Wine. He sells wine or something. Expensive, snobby shit.'

'Where? Where does he work?'

'He doesn't. He's all over the place, travels anywhere he can sell it.'

She forgot her dad briefly and calmed down. 'Okay, that will do. Thank you, Number One.'

Then she saw her dad again. He'd make them pay through pain. She pushed the knife far inside him. He screamed out in agony.

'Oh, come on, Number One. You think it's okay to put things inside a woman, don't you? You put your penis in a woman when she didn't want you to. What's the difference with me pushing this inside you?'

'I'm begging you. You're going to kill me. I can give you money, whatever you want.'

She laughed at him sarcastically followed by a golf clap. 'Money. This isn't about money, Number One. This is about what's right. What price you should pay?'

With her mouth now back against his ear, she continued, 'Hurts, doesn't it? Intrusive, isn't it? You wait until the morning when you're SHITTING BLOOD.'

She gave the knife a twist before pulling it out and cutting his hands free. He howled in pain as he clutched at his backside. As she walked away, she smiled at his whimpering.

The night had been torture. Bellfield didn't sleep, he spent most of it in the bath trying to ease the pain. The minute he sat in the soapy water, it turned bright red. He couldn't go to the hospital. How could he explain to the NHS staff what had happened?

It was now 8 a.m., and he had to make his way to work. Before putting on his underwear, he put as much tissue as he could between his cheeks. The pain was inside. He couldn't see it, but he knew it was bad. He grimaced as he put his suit on. He cried as he tied his tie. He looked in the mirror, now hating the man in front of him. Why did they do it? He promised himself he would never do it again; she was the last. He believed that. He didn't want to see his friends anymore; he was done. From now on he would concentrate on his job, be the best teacher he could be. He would give every weekend to his daughter instead of the pub. From now on, she was his life. No more cocaine or alcohol. No more prostitutes. He wanted to change.

The drive to work was painful. Several times, he pulled over to check the amount of blood on the tissue before changing it. Each time, it got a little less, but the pain did not. He made it to school and walked uncomfortably to the front door. Doing his best to disguise his pain, he made it to his office, his place of sanctuary.

The first hour went by fast. He was brought his usual cup of coffee and exchanged pleasantries with other staff. At 11.02 a.m., the knock on his office door was firm and loud.

'Come in,' he said.

A smartly dressed man and woman entered the room.

'Hello, Mr Bellfield, we'd like to talk to you regarding some allegations that have been made against you. I'm Detective Haddon, and this is Detective Marsh.' He pointed to his colleague.

Bellfield assumed this was about the rape. He had his story ready. She was there by her own choice. She wanted to have sex with them all; we were all drunk. It was one of those nights, etc.

'I didn't do anything. What am I being questioned about?'

'We'd like you to come with us, and we need your laptop. We have the paperwork right here explaining why we're taking it.' Detective Haddon held the paper in the air.

The laptop. Through all the pain he felt in the night, he forgot to check what she did on the laptop. What had she done? He had to let them have it and face the outcome. His gut knew this was going to be bad, but he had no idea just how bad until Detective Haddon spoke.

'I'm arresting you on suspicion of downloading and distributing indecent images of children. You do not have to say anything, but it may harm your defence if you do not mention when questioned something which you later rely on in court. Anything you do say may be given in evidence.'

"If you're feeling helpless, help someone."

Aung San Suu Kyi

CHAPTER 12

Hayley's mum looked drained and dejected as she opened the door to Catherine. She welcomed her in but asked if she could have a chat before she went upstairs to see Hayley.

'She hasn't spoken for days. I've known her to be upset before, but nothing like this. I take her dinner up, and she doesn't touch it. Sometimes I lie with her, and she doesn't say a word. Has something happened?'

Catherine hated lying. She was in an impossible position, protect her best friend's secret and lie or come clean, hoping it may help Hayley if her mum knew.

'Not that I know of. Would you like me to have a chat with her?' Catherine replied.

Hayley's mum let out a heavy sigh. 'You can try, but I don't think she'll talk to anyone. Something's happened. I know it has. I'm not the best mother in the world, but I know when my girl's in pain.'

'I'll go up now,' Catherine said as she went to walk past.

Hayley's mum blocked her path.

'You will tell me, won't you? I can't help her if I don't know. I can trust you, can't I, Catherine?'

Catherine couldn't maintain eye contact. 'I'll find out, I promise.'

Catherine could tell she wouldn't be able to lie after today. She needed to convince Hayley to talk to her mum. She made her way to Hayley's bedroom and gave a knock before entering. The curtains were drawn. It was dark and musky and in silence. Hayley was fully clothed, lying on top of her duvet. She didn't turn to face Catherine when she called her name. Catherine walked around and crouched in front of her.

'Hey, you. How are you feeling? I was hoping you'd come out for a coffee somewhere. Get some fresh air.'

Hayley didn't reply. Catherine watched a single tear leave Hayley's eye. It rolled across the bridge of her nose and joined tears from her other eye. She didn't blink. Catherine put her hand on her shoulder and then moved it up to Hayley's head as she stroked her hair.

'Come on, you. It's going to be okay. We can get through this. How can I make it better?'

Hayley didn't move.

'Shall we go to the police? Would you feel better if they're arrested? Now you've had a bit of time, maybe now you'd like to press charges. They shouldn't get away with this.'

A gentle shake of the head told Catherine enough. She looked to the ground in despair. The anger inside was palpable. *They all had to pay*. Her best friend is in front of her, and she's broken. They've taken all her happiness away in one night of brutality. Was she too easy on Number One? Should she have done more to him? Number Two was going to get worse.

'Hayley…do you want me to hurt them?'

Catherine looked to the sky, surprised by what she'd just said. She didn't want Hayley to know what she'd done to rapist number one. She didn't want her to be held accountable in any way if the police found out.

Hayley's eyes no longer looked *through* Catherine. She was looking *at* her.

Catherine continued, 'I can get to them. I can get to them all. I know who they are, all four of them. It won't come back on you.'

Hayley gave the nod and turned her back to Catherine. Catherine had her answer.

'I'll stay for a bit. I'll be right here,' Catherine said as she lay on Hayley's bedroom floor.

"Revenge is an act of passion, vengeance of justice."

Samuel Johnson

CHAPTER 13

Catherine had the next four days on day shift, the nights were hers. It was time for Tristan Bridger to meet his fate.

Rapist Number Two, real name Tristan Bridger, was a wine expert from Surrey. Age thirty-six, divorced with two children. He had no fixed address for his place of work as he travelled around Europe buying and selling expensive wine. Catherine knew from social media that he had some connections to the Wine Estate in Dorking, all courtesy of Facebook. The plan was to follow him each evening until the timing was perfect. He was a scumbag like the rest of his friends, and she was confident she could lure him in, but she needed help from an unlikely source.

Catherine found Nick's address through the employment files at the care home. After what he did to Bill, he was the last person Catherine wanted to see. Nick Jameson lived on the Goodwyns Estate in Dorking. Catherine entered the lift and pressed the button for the eleventh floor. As the door was about to close, a young girl with a pushchair was in sight. Catherine held the lift for her. 'What floor?' Catherine asked.

'Five, please. Thanks for holding the lift. Most round here don't bother.'

Catherine smiled at the toddler in the pushchair, he was staring back at her and let out a huge grin that made Catherine feel warm inside. These moments were welcome gifts that reminded her not everyone is an absolute bastard in this world.

They got to the fifth floor, and Catherine gave a nod of goodbye. The doors closed and Catherine re-focused on the job at hand.

She rubbed her sweaty palms together and took in a deep breath before knocking. Nick answered the door and stared at her; his top lip curled. 'Nah, bitch. Fuck off.'

Catherine put her foot in the door, stopping him from shutting it. 'That's not very nice is it? I've not come to hurt you. I need something…I'll pay you.'

He peered through the foot-wide gap. 'Like what? I ain't got nothing you need. I haven't even got a job thanks to the busy cow with her foot in my doorway.'

'Oh, it's my fault you're a robbing scumbag, is it? *You* lost your job, so shut up, stop feeling sorry for yourself, and listen. I need ketamine, and don't tell me you can't get it. You'll find a way. I'll give you whatever it costs you.'

Nick didn't answer, but did open the door fractionally wider.

A loud voice came from behind him. 'Nicolaus, who is it?'

Catherine attempted to look past Nick.

'Fuck off, nosey, don't worry about her,' Nick said as he blocked Catherine's view.

More shouting, this time louder and more needy. 'Nicolaus, please, I need to go.'

Catherine saw the pained look in Nick's eyes, his anger extinguished. She couldn't tell if he was embarrassed, sad, or if he was being impatient at being called for.

'If you need to go, I can come back,' Catherine said.

Nick shook his head. 'It's fine. My mother, she's unable to walk without me. Along with her manners, she's lost full use of her legs.'

'I'm sorry.'

'What, like you really care? What does it matter to you?' Nick snapped.

Catherine looked down. 'That's not fair, Nick.'

'I have to wipe her arse as well. How about that? Twenty-three years old and I'm wiping my mum's arsehole. You can have a good laugh now, can't you?'

Catherine couldn't look Nick in the eye. 'I would never laugh at your mum being unwell. Can you get help? Some assistance from the council?'

'We get some, but not much. People like us don't count.' Nick leaned into Catherine. 'Now you know why I'm a bit of a robbing bastard. Why I sell a bit of gear. I pay for a bit private care when I can. At the moment, I can't. Life's shit, always has been, always will be.'

'I honestly had no idea. I'm sorry. If I can—'

'What, help me?' Nick butted in with sarcasm. 'Would you like to wipe my mum's arse? Carry her to the toilet? No, of course you wouldn't.'

Catherine stayed silent.

'Look, I don't blame you. I'm sorry for being a prick, but people don't realise what others are going through. I get judged by people all the time, especially in here. They call me a druggy and all that. I don't even take drugs, just sell a bit. And not to kids, I wouldn't do that. Just sell a little here and there, enough to get by and help Mum.'

Catherine afforded Nick a look of concern.

'I can get what you need,' he said.

'If you're sure?' Catherine held out the money.

'Give me a day. Come back tomorrow. Pay me then.'

'I'll be back late morning. And, Nick, I need the real stuff, strong.'

He opened the door wider. 'Are you sure? Ketamine. You don't want to play about with that shit, you know that, right?'

'Don't worry about that. It's not for me.'

Nick chuckled. 'Fair enough. I didn't take you for the date raping sort of girl.' He gave her a cheeky wink.

'I'll see you tomorrow, Nick.'

The next morning, she wasn't sure if Nick would try something silly or maybe not even respond when she knocked on his door, but he answered with a grin.

'Morning, Catherine, I've got you enough to put someone out for the count, 200mg. Assuming it's a normal sized adult male. I'm assuming male, of course. If you use much more than that, it could cause overdose.'

Catherine didn't answer.

'You don't want to cause an overdose, do you?' Nick asked.

'Of course not, 200mg is all I need. There you go,' she said as she handed over two hundred pounds.

'It's in liquid form, nice and easy to slip into a drink. You're not trying to kill off one of the old boys at the nursing home are ya? You in for some tasty inheritance?' He laughed.

Catherine was staring at him intently. He looked at the money and then back at Catherine. 'That's too much,' he said as he held out four fifty-pound notes and attempted to give three back to her.

She took the small bottle. 'Keep it, bit extra for you to keep quiet.'

'I'd have kept quiet anyway, but that's very kind of you. Mum's the word.' He winked again and closed his door.

The door re-opened. 'Catherine, if you need more…'

She was at the lift doors and didn't turn around as she gave her answer. 'I won't. Goodbye. And, Nick…'

'Yeah,' he replied.

She turned to face him. 'I'm sorry I hit you. I should have talked to you first. I have a bit of a temper when I'm protecting someone I care about. My therapist says it comes from my dad.'

Nick put his money in his pocket. 'I deserved it. Robbing from the old guy was a fucked-up move. I really liked him. I just figured he didn't need it…but it's no excuse…I never meant to hurt him, ya know? I caught him by mistake. He came up behind me and I turned. Next thing he's holding his face, I felt awful.'

'Bill's okay,' she said as she got into the lift.

She synced her phone with his Bose stereo and pressed play, 'Don't Speak' by No Doubt started. She increased the volume until he started to stir. She loomed over him and whispered into his ear, 'Tristan Bridger, Rapist Number Two, please wake up.'

As he opened his eyes, she grinned. His eyes were that of a wounded animal. They widened as he tried to speak. And as he choked, her grin grew larger.

'I wouldn't bother. It'll be weeks, maybe months, before you can talk,' she said.

He tried again, this time blood exited his mouth, falling on to his chin. What he'd tried to say was inaudible.

She shrugged and went back to her phone. 'I have no idea what you're saying.' As she searched for a new song to play, she turned to face him. 'Are you telling me to fuck off? Sure sounds like it.' She walked over to him, knelt down, and poked his nose playfully. 'Mr Rapist Number Two, I'd be very careful if I were you. Your pal must have warned you I was coming. And Mr Rapist Number One. Your rapey little friend. He kept swearing at me, and it didn't end well for him.'

With his hands behind his back, he thrashed from side to side in desperation.

She slowly pulled her skirt up her thighs and straddled her victim. She threw a hammer fist violently into his chest. The thud was sickening. The impact caused Tristan Bridger to emit a mist of blood into the air. She leaned back fast to avoid being hit.

Once he finished choking, she leaned forward. Her face inches from his. 'Stay still, little man.' She stood up and went back to her phone and scrolled through. 'Oh, I haven't heard this in ages. She pressed play on 'Rapture' by Blondie. 'My dad loved her,' she said as she swayed delicately side to side. 'I was worried I'd given you too much. I didn't think you'd wake up.'

She stopped swaying. 'I wonder if you put more in my friend's drink than I put in yours?'

Bridger shook his head and spoke something inaudible.

'Ketamine, did you use the same? I bet you did.'

Once back at her prisoner's side, she put her foot on his chest. 'Soon, I'll explain what I did to your mouth during your little nap. But first I'll let you know why you won't be able to escape. I've cable tied your hands. I've used those extra-long ones from B&Q,' she said mockingly as she demonstrated how long they are. 'You have no chance of breaking them, not with those matchsticks you have for arms.' She leant down and squeezed his bicep. 'Gym, that's what you need. Bicep curls would do you the world of good.'

She stood and walked away. The sound of her heels became lost to her victim. He tried to scream, more choking, more blood. Once he'd finished spitting out what he needed to, he could hear her heels against the hard floor as the sound grew louder on her return.

'Mr Rapist Number Two, is this wine any good? It looks pretentious and a bit shit, perfect for a wanker like you.'

She held up the bottle, and in her best French accent she read out the label, '*Domaine Leroy Richebourg Grand Cru*. I personally prefer Mateus Rose, a tenner from Tesco. And if you were being honest, you'd admit that this shit I'm holding tastes just like any other.' She then violently threw the bottle against the wall. A sea of red spread across the room.

Again, Tristan Bridger rolled side to side, frantically trying to escape.

'Oops, clumsy me. Was that worth a lot of money? What a shame,' she said in a child-like voice as she turned on her heels and left the room again.

Bridger's pain and anger had turned to tears by the time she returned a few minutes later.

'Now, here we go. These two look reeaalllly expensive.' She grinned as she held up two more bottles of red wine.

He attempted to speak but just like last time, blood blocked his throat causing him to cough, blood splatter landing on his chest.

Catherine circled him like a lion waiting to pounce on it's wounded prey.

'Poor Mr Rapist Number Two. You have blood on your shirt. What a mess you're in. You look terribly upset. Do you know who else is upset?'

Bridger closed his eyes.

'I forgot. You can't speak, can you? I'll answer for you but let me change the music first. Let's have some fun.' She found 'Red Red Wine' by UB40 'Here we go, another song my dad liked. Now, let's play.'

Catherine removed both corks and held up the first. '*Domaine de la Romanee-Conti*. 1990, that's quite old. It's a good job I'm here. It's out of date by years and years. Here, I'll tip it away for you. Save you getting sick. Once something goes off, you should get rid of it.'

She slowly poured the wine onto Tristan Bridger's face, laughing as he coughed and spluttered.

'Look at you, feeling sorry for yourself, crying. Hayley is the only person that has a right to be upset, not you and your rapey gang.' Catherine's tone changed, no more jokey voice, no more mocking her victim. 'I bet you didn't even know her name. You don't care, do you?' Catherine kicked him in his ribs.

She held up the other bottle of wine. 'You didn't like the first one? Strange, as you chose it. Okay, let's try this one.' She cupped his chin and tipped it into his mouth. He threw his head to one side. 'Fussy little boy, aren't you? You don't like that one either? Not very good at buying wine are you, Number Two? Your friend told me you were an expert. That it was your passion.'

Catherine turned away from him and went to the dining table and pulled out a chair. 'That's better. These bloody heels are killing me, I prefer a nice pair of Air Force Ones, but you men are suckers for a blonde in heels.' She winked at him. 'How do you think I got you here?'

The next song came on by chance as she hit *shuffle* on her playlist. 'I'm quite schizophrenic when it comes to music choice. We could get anything next.'

'Linger' by The Cranberries. Her head dropped, her eyes glassy. 'My friend and I love this. We used to sing it when drunk.' Tears formed as she bit down on her lip. She moved towards him and kicked him in his ribs. She meant that kick with every fibre in her body.

This time, there was silence. He didn't cough; he didn't move. He couldn't. All the air within his lungs had been kicked from his body. He stared at her as she watched with interest.

'Don't die, Number Two. I haven't finished.'

Ten seconds had passed before he gasped, searching for air.

'Rapist Number Two, you're back with us. That's good.'

She waited until he calmed down.

'Have you quite finished? Good. I'll now explain the problem in your mouth. While you were having a nap, I had a play with the little cheffy blow torch thing I found in the kitchen. Originally, I was going to just use a lighter I bought at the petrol station, but that proved awkward. The flame kept burning my thumb as I tilted it into your mouth. I had a look about, and then I saw it, your cute little flame thrower. I bet you use it for a nice crème brûlée, to go with your poor taste in wine. Anyway, I couldn't resist.'

Tristan Bridger's eyes were filled with horror as he mumbled another attempt at talking.

Catherine pulled her chair nearer to Tristan and bent down to talk to him. 'I had to think hard about you.'

Next song came on. 'Dream Catch Me' by Newton Faulkner.

Catherine looked to the ceiling before going face to face with her prisoner. 'Another song that reminds me of her and I having fun in better times. God, I want to kill you. I really don't fucking like you. I want to hurt you so bad.'

She backed off. 'But the good news for you is…you're not going to die. She isn't like that, so I'm not allowed to. No police either. I made a promise.'

She changed the song, pressing shuffle. She turned the volume down as Adele's 'Someone Like You' started.

'Did you know that thousands, tens of thousands of rape victims decide to not involve the police? They feel, somehow, responsible for what happened. Ashamed of themselves, scared of what people will think of them. Some don't want to get the person responsible in trouble. Can you believe that? The victim has done nothing wrong, and yet they blame themselves. That upsets me. People like you walk away scot free.'

Thoughts of what her dad would do ran through her mind. *He must pay a price*. She wiped away her tears and pointed at Bridger. 'You are going to pay. You all are.'

Picking up the blowtorch, she approached Bridger. He shook his head side to side. Using her left hand, she grabbed his jaw and squeezed hard. 'Open your fucking mouth.' She used her index finger to press the shiny red button. Bridger's eyes reflected the beautiful flame that shot out with force.

The flame was an inch from his right eye. 'I found out what you do for a living from your friend, and with some help from social media. You really love wine, don't you? Travelling around

Europe. Living it up. Mr Big Time. But the truth is, you and your little pals are nothing more than rapists.'

She moved the flame around to his ear. She started at his lobule. He produced a deafening scream that continued as she got to his antitragus. Smoke rose into the air. She removed her finger from the trigger. Bridger shook his head violently, his breathing becoming shallow, he tried to spit out more of the blood that was continuing to appear in his mouth, running down the back of his throat.

Catherine moved back to avoid being spat on. 'That's disgusting. Stop it, you animal.'

She wiped her leg and continued, 'I googled how to lose one's sense of taste, and it's been proven you can still taste without your tongue, so that changed my plan from cutting out your whole tongue. I never knew we could taste through the roof of our mouth. Well, *you* can't. Not anymore.'

Tristan closed his eyes as he fathomed what she'd done to him. As he opened them, he cried aloud and begged for mercy.

'Oh, stop moaning. I only cut out half your dirty tongue. But between that and the little fire we had in the roof of your mouth, unfortunately, you'll need to find a different job.' Catherine pointed at his face. 'With that messed up mouth, you won't taste a thing, maybe a hint of burning.' Catherine gave Bridger a wink and a smile.

She couldn't understand him when he tried to speak. 'Shut up, stop whining. You took away her dignity. You abused her for your own entertainment. It's only right that you lose something. I decided it would be your career…and your tongue. I know strictly speaking that's two things, but fuck you.'

He started banging the back of his head against the floor. The thuds grew louder until she towered over him and pressed her foot down on his forehead.

'Stop it. Stop feeling sorry for yourself. This is nearly over. You can cry as much as you want when I'm gone.' She removed her foot.

'And, as your wounds start to heal, and your ego takes over, the anger will kick in, but don't even think about coming for me. That won't end well. I have all I need to put you in prison for years. And, Mr Bridger, you are not built for prison.' Catherine kicked him again in the ribs, taking the wind out of his body for a second time. As he lay there wheezing, Catherine's attention was drawn to his wrist. She studied the watch and knew from it's make that it was worth thousands. She undid the clasp and slid it over his hand. She wiped it on his shirt to remove any blood spots. 'I know who needs this,' she said before she reached into his pocket and found his mobile phone. It took her a few minutes to get the correct security code out of Bridger. He couldn't pronounce the numbers clearly. Eventually she got him to nod yes as she said each correct number. 1989 worked.

'I'll keep this as well as the watch. I bet you film all the girls you do it to, don't you? You and your dirty little mates, high fiving between rounds. You disgust me.' Another kick, the same ribs causing the same lack of air for Tristan Bridger.

Her bloodied victim's forehead creased as he stared at her as she turned away. He rolled into a foetal position and cried. Music was still playing. The current song was 'White Flag' by Dido.

Catherine turned and came back towards him. 'Ooh, good song,' she said.

Again, he started banging his head against the floor. He wouldn't stop. The thuds were getting louder. Catherine was about to kick him in the ribs when her attention was broken at the same time as Bridger stopped. He let out a cry as his beautiful white feline friend walked delicately through a puddle of his blood on the floor.

Catherine called the cat over. 'Hello, kitty cat. What's your name?' She then tried the universal language for a cat hello, using her top row of teeth against her lower lip and sucking in repeatedly. The cat started trilling as it walked towards her, but then it stopped. The cat had seen something. Something it wanted. It gracefully walked towards its prize, leaving bloody paw prints on the floor. The half-tongue. Catherine looked at him, then at the cat, then back at Tristan. 'It wouldn't,' she said.

She watched in wonderful amazement as the cat picked up the half-tongue in its mouth and crept off, leaving more perfect bloodied paw prints on the floor. Bridger was silent as Catherine tilted her head to watch the cat leave down the corridor. She smiled at Bridger. 'I'm not even going to say it. I feel like I should. But I won't.'

Bridger lay there a broken man. Shock had kicked in, no fight left, all dignity gone. Catherine stared at him, and now satisfied her job was done, she got to her feet and took one last look around.

'Okay, Mr Rapist Number Two, as fun as this has been, I need to go. Tell the other two I'm coming for them.' She bent down and untied Bridger. She knew it was safe to. He had nothing to offer. Not just broken physically, but also mentally. She knew he wouldn't attempt to fight back once untied. He didn't even make a sound.

She left the room, closing the door behind her.

"Regret is the only wound the soul does not recover from."

Sarah Ban Breathnach

CHAPTER 14

Tiny specs of dust danced about in the golden rays that beamed through her open curtains. She rubbed her eyes and last night's violent events ran through her mind. Her adrenaline had departed. She sat upright and caught sight of her dress carelessly left on her bedroom floor.

Flashbacks to the horror of last night were raw and vivid. She drew her hands to her face, but the visions became stronger. As she lowered her arms, she could see the blood under her fingernails. Throwing back the covers, she rushed to the bathroom. The sickening feeling had moved from her stomach into her chest, and with no time to lift the toilet lid she was sick into the bath. Turning the tap, she put her hand under the cold water and cupped as much as she could; she used the water to wipe her face before letting herself drop. Slumped against the bath, she pictured last night's victim crying in fear.

What had she become? Is this what she is now? A violent vigilante. At the time, it seemed right. For what they did to Hayley, they shouldn't even be alive, but should she be the one handing out the punishment?

Last night now felt like someone else had taken over.

She stood slowly and ran the hot tap. She used her hand to start cleaning the sink.

A suffocating feeling came over her.

She reached for her throat; her breathing became abnormal. Each gasp of air felt stolen. A dreadful, heavy feeling on her chest.

She screamed out, and a reply came from the other side of the door.

'Catherine, what are you doing in there?'

Catherine didn't answer, she couldn't. She stood up, opened the small bathroom window, and desperately gasped for air.

'Is it drugs? Are you on drugs in there? It wouldn't surprise me,' her mum said.

Catherine got her breath back. She looked to the sky in welcome relief.

'Piss off. You, of all people, I don't need you.'

'You were the one calling out for help. Pardon me for being concerned. Through the night as well. In your dreams. I could hear you shouting.'

'You're concerned? Yeah right. Your first thought is that I'm doing drugs. Just go away.'

Catherine waited for a reply, but it didn't come. Did her mum just show some form of concern for her? Catherine dismissed the thought and decided it was more likely her mum was being interfering and rude. She sat on the side of the bath and thought about how scary it was losing the air in her lungs.

She remembered she had Number Two's phone.

She started going through the photos. She could see the four of them sitting there laughing. As she swiped, they got even worse. Pictures of them on top of Hayley. Through repulsion, she threw the phone across the bathroom. More deep breaths before throwing her fist at the door. She needed to make herself feel better and had an idea of how she could do that.

He answered the door and watched the lift doors as they were closing. He could see an elbow before the doors fully closed. Poking his head out further he looked around.

'Who is it, Nick?' his mum called out.

'It must be those bastard kids again, knocking on our door and pissing off. Knock down ginger or whatever they call it. Little pricks. Probably that Skinner lad and his arsehole mates.'

'Skinner! Knock down ginger! What arsehole?'

'No, Mum, don't worry about it.' He grinned at his mum's response.

Closing the door, he could see the envelope at his feet. He reached down, picked it up, opened it, and read the words.

Nick, this watch is genuine. Research it and get the right price, at least £25K. It'll give you some respite. Some extra care maybe? Treat your mum. And STOP dealing. You're a bit of a dickhead, but you're the only dickhead your mum has. You'll be no good to her in prison.

"It is never too late to be who you might have been."

George Elliot

CHAPTER 15

'You've been here nearly ten minutes without speaking. I don't mind if you want to remain silent, if that's what you need to do, and you're happy, then I'm happy. But I feel there's something you need to discuss with me. You don't look yourself. You look tired, and your attention isn't here, it's somewhere else. What are you thinking about?' Roisin asked.

Catherine gave the slightest of nods and glanced away from Roisin as quickly as she looked at her.

'Please tell me. Whatever it is we can talk about it.'

'Not this we can't,' Catherine replied.

Roisin adjusted the hem of her skirt as she inched forward. 'We can. You can be open with me. This is a safe place for you.'

Their eyes met. 'But you said if someone was in danger, if it was a matter for the police, you would have to report it.'

'That's correct,' Roisin replied.

'Then we can't talk about it, can we?'

'Is it your friend? Is she thinking of doing something to herself?'

Catherine froze before replying. 'Why would you say that?'

'I'm just asking questions. It's common for women to blame themselves after going through such a traumatic event. She may have thoughts about suicide. I'm not saying she does.'

'It's not that. She's fine. It's not her, and it's not me.'

'Someone else, then. Are you going to hurt someone?'

Catherine stood up. 'I'm tired of this. All these questions. I'm not getting anywhere. I'm not happy. I haven't been since my dad was alive, not truly happy. I don't think I will be ever again. The world is a shithole, people are arseholes. They all do bad things. They lie, they cheat, they're violent towards each other. The strong pick on the weak. Why live in this world? Who would choose to be alive if they had the choice?'

'Please sit down, Catherine.'

Catherine didn't, instead she walked towards the window and looked outside.

'We all have a choice. And it won't always be like this. You won't always feel like this.'

'I don't believe you. I hate this. I hate myself. I don't blame my mum for not loving me. She shouldn't.' Catherine turned to face Roisin. She had tears running down her cheeks.

'Please don't say that. You're a good person. Your mum isn't mentally well. Don't judge love on what's coming from your mum. Judge it by what comes from your friend, Hayley. She loves you. And if you let more people in, they will love you too.'

Catherine dropped to her knees and cried. 'I think I had so much love from my dad that I can't have any more in my lifetime. I used it all up in my first twelve years. I'll never have that again, never.'

Roisin knelt down and put her hand on Catherine's back. 'You will. You will be loved. I know it.'

Catherine moved into Roisin and rested her head against her. She felt Roisin's hand stroke her hair, and she needed that. It was the safest she had felt since she was a child.

'If he hadn't died, none of this would have happened. He was meant to protect me against the bullies. He said no one would ever bully me and get away with it…and yet, she did.'

'Your mum being unwell is the reason for her behaviour. It's not because of you. Any mum would be proud to have a daughter like you.'

Catherine sat beside Hayley. 'Can I get you anything?'

'Are they suffering?'

'Who?' Catherine replied, knowing exactly who Hayley meant.

'You know who. You said you were going to do something, and I know you've started.'

Catherine inched herself closer to Hayley on the bed. Hayley was sitting holding her knees tight against her chest, wearing the same grey tracksuit she had on the last time Catherine visited her.

'Do you want me to be honest? It may be better not to know…legally I mean.'

'The only thing I don't want is what happened to me being public knowledge.'

Catherine put her hand on Hayley's knee. 'It won't, I promise. These men have nothing to gain from reporting me. They don't want the police involved.'

'Then tell me…what have you done to them?'

Catherine stood and walked over to Hayley's dressing table. A picture of the two of them laughing together from happier times stared back at her.

'Fuck them. They deserve it. I haven't got them all yet, only two so far. The other two will be taken care of soon.'

'Details, Catherine. I need to know.'

'Okay, Bryce Bellfield. I stabbed him, kicked him about a bit, and downloaded child pornography to his laptop. He's been arrested and will lose his job.'

Hayley pursed her lips and gently rocked back and forth before speaking. 'Did you enjoy it?'

Catherine shrugged. 'No. Yes…maybe a bit. He deserved it. When I'm doing it, I'm just thinking of what they did to you, then it just happens.'

'And the next one?'

'Tristan Bridger, Number Two.'

'That's his name, is it?'

Catherine nodded.

'Did you stab him too?' Hayley asked.

'Not quite.' Catherine threw her hands in the air. 'Look, Hayley, we don't need to do this. You don't need to know.'

'I do. I want to feel better, see if it takes away the pain.'

'He works in posh wines, expensive shit. I smashed up his collection.'

'No violence this time?' Hayley asked.

'I kicked him, I kicked him a lot, broke his ribs.'

'Good. I'm glad he felt some physical pain.'

'And then…'

Hayley shot Catherine a look. 'Then what?'

Catherine let out a sigh. 'I burnt his mouth. I don't want him being able to taste anymore. No more posh wine tasting, no more career.'

'Does burning your mouth do that?'

'Google said it does. But to make sure I cut half his tongue off as well—'

'Cut his tongue out?' Hayley interrupted.

Another shrug. 'Not all of it. I just wanted to make sure. And then his cat—'

'That's enough. If you've hurt his cat I don't want to know.'

'You know I wouldn't do that,' Catherine pleaded.

Hayley got under her covers and laid down.

'Number Three is next, Ian Whiting, and then finally David Worboys,' Catherine said.

'Worboys, I remember one of them saying his name. He was the one, the worst, with the teeth.' Hayley closed her eyes and pulled her cover up further.

"When people kill themselves, they think they're ending the pain, but all they're doing is passing it on to those they leave behind."

Jeannette Walls

CHAPTER 16

Catherine reached for her phone the second she heard the familiar ping. Her anxiety increased when she saw the name lit up in front of her. Hayley hadn't called or text since her ordeal. Catherine went cold. Her instincts were telling her this was going to be bad, beyond bad. She looked to the heavens before opening the message.

Catherine, you have always been my one true friend. I will never forget you. I was blessed to have such a kind, beautiful person in my life. I never had a sister, but I believe you were better than any sister I could have asked for. I love you x

'No, no fucking way. You don't get to leave me,' Catherine screamed.

She ran to her car, jumped in and turned the key. Nothing happened. 'Not now, you piece of…' she shouted as she turned the key a second time. It started. Not putting her seat belt on, she accelerated causing a wheel spin before she sped off. Breaking every speed limit between her house and Hayley's, she arrived within minutes. She didn't even take out her keys as she ran to the front door. She hit that door with everything she had and kept hitting hit until it swung open.

'Catherine, what are you doing?' Hayley's mum asked as she wrapped her bathrobe around herself. She had nothing to tie it up with, so she held it closed.

Catherine ran past her and cleared every other step as she hurried to Hayley's bedroom. The door was closed. Catherine paused for a second as she thought about what she might find behind that door. Was Hayley alive on the other side? Had she overdosed on pills or cut her wrists? She pushed the door open carefully just in case Hayley was on the other side. Hayley's mum had now caught up.

'Catherine, what's going on? I spoke to Hayley earlier this morning, and she was okay. In fact, it was the first time in a while that she smiled and had a conversation with me.'

'Don't you see, she was preparing to leave us.' She edged herself into the room slowly and looked for Hayley. The bed was immaculately made, her carpet was clear of the usual mess. The room was spotless. The door to her en suite was closed. Catherine reached for the handle and pushed the door. It wouldn't fully open. It wasn't locked, but there was resistance. She pushed harder using her shoulder, and it opened several inches. She could feel there was a weight on the other side. Catherine pushed this time with her whole bodyweight, enough to get her head in the room. Hayley was there, her face white, unresponsive.

'No, you don't. You're not doing this. You aren't fucking leaving me,' Catherine shouted as she forced her way in and started removing what looked like a dressing gown cord. She couldn't untie it; the knot was too tight. She knelt down and took Hayley's weight against her body. She had one arm trying to support Hayley's weight, with her other hand she desperately tried to untie the knot. She couldn't do it.

'Fucking help me, get in here,' she screamed to Hayley's mum.

She didn't come. Catherine could hear her screaming from the bedroom.

'Hayley, please,' she pleaded.

Catherine was alone. She knew it was all on her to save Hayley. The silver door handle had a slight bend downwards. Catherine was able to push the cord off the handle. Hayley's full body weight fell into Catherine. She laid her down and frantically started to untie the cord from around her neck. Hayley's eyes were bulging, her tongue protruding from her mouth, Catherine thought back to her training at work.

ABC: Airways, Breathing, and Circulation. Catherine used her forefinger to push Hayley's tongue gently back in. She pulled on her ankles so that she was laid out flat. With the heel of her hand placed on Hayley's breastbone, she started using her bodyweight to give chest compressions. She couldn't remember how many to do before starting rescue breaths, so after around twenty she tilted Hayley's chin and pinched her nose with thumb and forefinger. After five strong breaths she noticed a different look in Hayley's eyes.

'Oh God, please. If you are real, I fucking need you more than ever,' she said as she carried on repeating the same steps over and over.

There was no giant gasp of air. Hayley didn't suddenly sit upwards and reach for her throat. But Catherine could see the colour change in her face. Tiny shallow breaths were happening. Her eyes hardly moved, but there was life in them. Catherine screamed out to Hayley's mum, 'Call the ambulance, bloody call them now! She's alive.'

Catherine looked up at Helen, as she came into the bathroom. 'Have you called them?'

She shook her head.

'Well, get on with it, Helen. Call them now.'

Catherine talked to Hayley the whole time while they waited. 'It's going to be okay. The ambulance is coming.'

Hayley didn't move. She lay there not saying a word, not responding to any of Catherine's pleas or to the cries of, 'I'm sorry,' from her mum.

The paramedics said only one person could travel with them. Catherine had hoped it would be her, but Helen, being her mum, pulled rank. Catherine didn't argue, instead she got in her car and followed to the East Surrey Hospital in Redhill. As they arrived, Catherine watched the ambulance pull into the emergency area. She had to park in the visitor car park. Pulling up to the parking barrier, she watched as it took what felt like forever to go up. She didn't even think about the extortionate amount she would have to pay to park. Her only concern was being by Hayley's side.

Catherine ran into the emergency waiting room and waited to be called up to the reception. Several people looked at her for what she thought was longer than necessary before she noticed Helen sitting there alone. She'd aged. Catherine had only just noticed in the cruel hospital light. Her wiry hair was grey at the roots. Helen was a pretty lady but had been punished by alcohol and years of bad luck. She was still in her bathrobe and slippers.

'Where is she? Why aren't you with her?'

Helen stood up and touched Catherine's forearms. 'She's being looked after. We're not allowed in. They're worried about how long she was unconscious. Worried about her movement.'

'Her movement?' Catherine asked.

'Her lack of movement. She still hasn't moved from the neck down.'

Catherine pulled her arms away from Helen. 'It's just shock. She's still in shock. She'll be fine when she comes round.'

'Please sit down, Catherine. I'll get us a coffee.'

As Helen walked away, her dressing gown opened wide. Catherine stared at it as she sat down.

Catherine watched as Helen used the change from her purse to buy two coffees from the machine. When she returned and handed her a piping hot coffee, she had one question for her.

'Helen, do you have a cord for your dressing gown?'

Helen frowned, looked at midsection and then back at Catherine. 'I have, but it went missing a few days ago.'

'And you didn't think that was strange?' Catherine asked.

'No, why would I? I'll get another one,' she said as she sipped her coffee.

Catherine remained silent.

It was two hours before a member of staff came out to see them. In that time, Catherine had asked reception three times for information.

'Hello, my name is Charlotte Hall. I'm the neurosurgeon looking after Hayley.'

Catherine stood to greet her but didn't reply.

'Hayley is lucky to be alive, seconds later, and she wouldn't be with us.'

Helen smiled at Catherine and let out a huge sigh of relief.

'However, there are signs of brain damage. We have the results of her CT scan, and I'm concerned that she suffered from a reduced supply of oxygen. Her brain was deprived of oxygen for a dangerous amount of time. I'm afraid there are signs of cerebral hypoxia. Prolonged hypoxia induces neuronal cell death via apoptosis, resulting in a hypoxic brain injury,' the surgeon said before looking at Helen, and then gave Catherine an asymmetric smile of sadness.

'But she'll be okay. Once she heals, she'll be back to normal, right?' Catherine asked.

'I'm sorry. The signs are looking like this is a permanent state. It's very early and I won't give a final diagnosis until I'm absolutely positive. I just wanted to be realistic with your expectations at this stage.'

Catherine sat back down with her head in her hands. Helen sat beside and put her arm around her.

'You did all you could. There was no more you could do,' Helen said. A wet stream appeared on her face like rain running down a dusty windowpane.

'I've made it worse. Hayley won't want to live like this. She'll hate me,' Catherine said. She tried to talk more, but she couldn't get her breath through her heavy, loud crying.

"The best revenge is to move on happily and let karma do the rest."
Famous Quote

"Respectfully I disagree, karma rarely punishes the bad in this world, have your revenge, certain crimes deserve payback."
By The Author

CHAPTER 17

Rapist Number Three was next. It wasn't meant to be today; it wasn't meant to be this way, but the situation had changed. Catherine had changed. Ian Whiting lived in Guildford, Surrey. She drove into Clifford Manor Road and shut her engine down before opening a window. Bird song echoed around the leafy suburb.

She assumed if she was going to see Rapist Number Three, it would be on his way to work. She sat transfixed by his front door, a giant wooden door that wouldn't look out of place as an entrance to a church. The house was detached, at least five bedrooms, and was named *Millennium*.

It had a perfectly manicured lawn, and stunning trees that were shaped beautifully. The property was gated off from the rest of the world. Prior to coming here, she'd done her research. He was a business owner. Some big shot in the world of solar panels, those shiny things you see appearing more and more on people's roofs. She'd made her mind up that he probably didn't give a toss about saving the planet and using recyclable energy. Just a money-hungry arsehole cashing in on the peoples' urge to save the planet, and going by his house, he'd done rather well for himself.

Catherine had been there an uncomfortable three hours, it was now 9 a.m., so far two cars had passed her from other houses on this private road, but there was no sign of life coming from *Millennium*. Number Three didn't have any of his private life on social media. He was strictly business on there. There was plenty about his amazing company, and there was a lot of information on his LinkedIn account.

Ten minutes later the electric gate started to move. Catherine sat up straight in her seat. She could see the front door. As it opened, a lady in a full-length black coat made her way to her car. The brand- new Range Rover Sport D250 pulled out. Catherine ducked into her seat, and once the car had passed, she straightened herself out and was once again sitting upright. Catherine watched in her mirror as the Range Rover went into the distance.

'Sod it,' Catherine said as she acted on instinct. She started the engine, spun her car around, and caught up with the car at the next junction. She kept with her through the busy roads of Guildford until they were in a multi-storey car park in Bedford Road. The Range Rover stopped in a space away from other cars. Catherine parked two spaces away. She watched as the attractive charismatic lady was teetering on her heels as she walked back from getting her parking ticket.

Catherine stepped out of her car, got the attention of the lady, and pointed at her vehicle.

'I love this. It's a bit newer than mine,' Catherine said.

The lady smiled but didn't reply. She put her ticket on her dashboard and closed the car door.

'I know you from somewhere. You're Ian's wife?'

Putting her keys in her handbag, she replied, 'You know Ian?'

Catherine gave a single nod. 'We met at a business do. You know what those events are like, a bit dull, everyone being polite until the drink kicks in.'

'They sure are…Sorry, but I don't remember you. I'm normally good with faces. Do you know Ian very well?'

Catherine's fake warm demeanour changed, her jaw clenched. 'Not very well. But he knows my friend. He'll never forget her.'

The lady stepped back. 'I'm sorry, I need to go. It was nice…'

Catherine moved closer to her. 'No, don't go. I need to talk to you. Can I buy you a coffee?'

'I don't think so. I need to go. I'm late.'

Catherine grabbed her arm. 'You need to hear me out, please.'

'I don't know you. I don't want to know you. I just want to go. I'll call the police.' She reached for her phone.

'Don't. That wouldn't be good for your husband, for your family. Hear me out and if you still want to call the police, go for it.'

Catherine let go of her arm, realising she was going too far. His wife was guilty of nothing other than her bad choice in a husband. Catherine noticed the woman look at her diamond-encrusted Pasha De Cartier before she replied, 'There's a coffee shop in there.' She pointed to the Friary Shopping Centre.

'Americano, please. No milk,' she said to the barista.

'Cappuccino, with chocolate on top,' Catherine said. She also demonstrated the sprinkling using her fingers and thumb. The man nodded and smiled.

'Did you say your name?'

'Catherine.'

'Catherine who?' the wife asked.

'Just Catherine for now.'

'You clearly know who I am. I just want to know who I'm dealing with?'

Catherine didn't answer her question. 'Kerry, I found your name through your husband's social media. Do you know what your husband and his friends get up to when they go out?'

The waiter arrived with their drinks and placed them gently on to the table. Kerry didn't thank him as he asked if there was anything else he could get them.

'No, thank you. We're fine,' Catherine replied.

'My husband works in London, and he goes out from time to time for a few drinks just like anyone else.'

'Does he always come home afterwards?'

Kerry looked at the couple at the nearest table and then back at Catherine. 'On a weekend, he sometimes stays with his friends. I don't care. I don't want to listen to his drunken drivel, anyway. Gives me a night to myself. If you have something to tell me about Ian, get on with it. Are you two seeing each other? You wouldn't be his first.'

Catherine looked at the chocolate sitting delicately on the cream of her drink. She couldn't resist stirring it in.

'Your husband and his friends took someone back to a flat in Richmond.'

Catherine now had her full attention.

'Bryce, his friend Bryce Bellfield lives in Richmond.'

'Yes, he's one of them. The girl they took back was my friend.' Catherine paused briefly. 'She didn't go there by choice. I'm sorry, Kerry, but there's no easy way to tell you this.'

Kerry interrupted, 'He fucked her, didn't he? He better not have got her pregnant, stupid bloody man. He comes home and I can smell women's perfume on him. He tells me they went to a club and his mates paid for a lap dance. I never believe him. I know he's fucking about. I just hoped he wouldn't be stupid enough to bring some disease home, or get some tart pregnant, or—'

'They raped her.' It was Catherine's turn to interrupt. 'They took turns raping my friend. Bryce Bellfield, Tristan Bridger, David Worboys, and your husband Ian.'

Kerry rose to her feet and her chair screeched against the floor as it shot back.

Catherine stood up. 'Sit down, Kerry, please.'

'He wouldn't do that. He's many things, but he's no rapist. We have children. He wouldn't do it. He couldn't.'

'Kerry, I have a small piece of video of them on the night. Hayley managed to record them when they thought she was still drugged.'

'Drugged?'

'They used a date-rape drug. She remembers nothing about going back to the flat, only some of what happened once there.'

They both sat down. Kerry put both hands on the table to steady herself. 'I don't feel right. This can't be true. Drugs and rape.'

Catherine reached for Kerry's hand. 'Kerry, I'm telling you the truth.'

'If it was true, you would have gone to the police. They would have been arrested. You say have proof on a phone.'

'I can't go to the police. My friend, Hayley, she won't let me.'

'Don't be stupid, if that happened to me there's no way they're getting away with it,' Kerry replied.

Catherine let go of her hand. 'Do you know what a woman goes through if she reports it to the police? Do you realise the humiliation she feels when she's poked and prodded as they search for evidence? The doubting of her character in their questioning, making her feel like she asked for it. And what do you think happens when the public find out? Do you think they're sympathetic? Some may be, they fucking should be, but some won't. A woman worries they will judge her, that she'll be known for what happened, and not for the person she is. Or was.'

A tear appeared in Kerry's left eye. She immediately wiped it away.

'They won't get away with it, I can promise you that.'

Kerry stared at Catherine. 'Wait, is this why Bryce got suspended from the school? And Tristan was attacked in his home by masked men? They cut half his tongue out and smashed up his wine collection.'

Catherine didn't flinch. She picked her cup up and took a sip.

'Did you have something to do with all that?'

'They don't deserve to lead a good life. They deserve to be punished,' Catherine said.

'What about Ian? What's going to happen to him?'

'Well, that's up to you.'

Kerry shook her head. 'Look, if he's done this, I agree he needs to answer for it, but I'm not hurting him. I'm not some psycho.'

'I didn't ask you to hurt him physically. Do you love him?'

'I…I don't think so. Not anymore, no, probably not for years. He was nice at first, the first few years but then he became cruel, secretive and just not nice to be around.'

'Then divorce him, take him for all he's worth. This is your chance.'

'He would never allow it. I've tried. He's told me a million times if I ever left him, I would be penniless and without the kids. He'd hire the best lawyers to get rid of me.'

'What if I guarantee he was the one who left the house. That he had to give you at least half of everything without a fight?'

'I don't know. I don't know how you'd make him do that.'

'I'm very convincing. I have enough to send him to prison for years. He'd lose it all that way.'

Kerry sat in silence.

'Come on, Kerry. He's a bloody rapist. Get him away from you, from your kids. Start a new life.'

A gentle nod of the head from Kerry was enough.

'Go to a solicitor today, right now. Go to the best you can find. Ask them to draw up your divorce papers, include everything you want from him. Percentage of future wages, half of all assets, including your house. Half of his pension, full custody of the kids, and their tuition paid. Everything and anything you can think of. And then, be with him tomorrow afternoon when I call his phone at one. What I tell Ian will be enough for him to agree to sign anything you put in front of him.'

Kerry's hands were shaking.

'If you need money to pay for the solicitor today, I can help you.'

'I won't need it. I have a secret fund. I call it my *fuck Ian fund.* I knew this day would come. I knew we would separate one day. I just thought it would be when he found a younger version of me. So, I started putting cash away into a bank account. It's in the kids' names.'

Catherine smiled.

'I'm going to go now. I'll call him tomorrow at 1 p.m.' Catherine stood and reached into her pocket for money to pay for the drinks.

'Catherine, I'm sorry about your friend. Please tell her I'm sorry.'

'You have nothing to be sorry for. They do.'

As Catherine went to walk away, Kerry called her back. 'Catherine, what about David? What are you going to do to him? He's a real arsehole, wandering hands. Hands that hit women. He'll be as much involved in this as the others. Possibly the worst of them all. Be careful, he's a nasty piece of work.'

‘I’m visiting David very soon. His hands won’t wander again.’

"In the truest sense, justice is always an act of revenge, but revenge is not always an act of justice."

Jane Van Doorn

CHAPTER 18

The message was left on Catherine's phone the day before.

Hi Catherine, I'm ringing to see if you're okay? It's not like you to miss an appointment. Please contact me to confirm you got this message, and we can then re-schedule.

She'd forgotten she was meant to see Roisin. The only thing on her mind was Hayley.

Catherine was back at the hospital. As she walked onto the ward, she could see Hayley's mum crying at Hayley's bedside. Helen stood up and came towards her.

'Catherine, please. It's best you're not here.'

Catherine looked beyond Helen to see what was happening with Hayley. 'Don't be stupid. I need to be with her.'

'She doesn't want to see you.'

'Why? Why would she say that?'

'She blames you for keeping her alive. Says it's your fault she's in the state she is.'

Catherine backed up. 'I had to save her. She's my best friend. I'd do anything for her.'

'I know, but she's angry. Give her time, she'll come round. She hates me too. She wants me to help her die. She won't talk about anything else.' Helen broke down and fell into Catherine's arms. Catherine held her, but the only emotion she felt was anger. She pulled away from Helen. 'I'll call you soon. I'm sorry.'

Catherine was halfway home before she registered that she had no idea how she'd driven to this point. She focused on the road until her phone rang; she looked at the number. It was Roisin. She pressed to answer and spoke on loudspeaker.

'I'm sorry, Roisin. I was going to call you.'

'Don't worry, I just wanted to check in on you. Is everything okay?'

Catherine remained silent.

'Catherine, please talk to me.'

Roisin could hear Catherine sobbing. 'Please talk. You can come and see me today if you like. I'll make time.'

'I can't. It's all gone wrong. I tried to save her. I thought I was doing the right thing.'

'Save who?'

'Hayley.'

'What's happened to her?' Roisin asked.

'She tried to kill herself. She's alive, but she's in a bad way.'

'Catherine, I'm so sorry. That's awful what she is going through, but I'm worried about what this is doing to you. You need to look out for yourself. We spoke about this. It's not your role to save everyone.'

Catherine continued to cry. 'I don't want to save everyone. I just want to help Hayley.'

'Oh, Catherine, I know you do. But you're losing yourself. I'm worried this will end with you punishing yourself. Please come and see me after four, I am free.'

'I'm sorry, Roisin. I've got to see someone else today.' She hung up.

Closing her front door behind her, Catherine hoped her mum was asleep, or in a drunken stupor, feeling sorry for herself.

'Where have you been? You come in for five minutes, then you piss off back out. What if I'd needed you? What if something happened to me?' her mum yelled.

Catherine didn't turn to face her. 'Nothing will happen to you. Nothing bad happens to bad people. Bad things only happen to good people. You'll be just fine.'

'Don't you talk to me like that, you selfish little cow. What's wrong with you? Are you no more the centre of attention? Is poor little Catherine not getting her own way?'

Catherine turned and went nose to nose with her mum and raised her voice. 'Do not upset me right now. I don't need your crap, my best friend is in hospital. If you must know, Hayley tried to kill herself.'

Catherine waited for a sign of empathy in her mother's eyes. It didn't come.

'She's another one, weak like you. That's the problem with young people—'

Catherine's hand went to her mum's throat, she pushed her with ease against the wall. Catherine was shocked at how soft her mum's skin was, and no muscle beneath. She loosened her grip when she saw her mum's pupils dilating, and then let go all together.

'You really are disgusting. I'm not going to hurt you. You're mentally retarded. Whatever you say, I know it's not the words of a sane person. Be as disgusting as you want. I'm not listening anymore…but you need to listen to me. When you're unwell. When I find you laying in your own vomit, I'm not going to help you. I will no longer show you a glimpse of weakness. You are on your own,' Catherine said as she turned and went upstairs.

As she walked into her bedroom, she felt a stabbing pain in her stomach. Throwing herself on to her bed she allowed herself to fall asleep.

Catherine woke to the sound of the annoying alarm, still in the same position she fell into yesterday. Holding her phone to her face, she couldn't focus on the time. Squinting her eyes, she could make out the numbers 12.45. She was about to stay laying down when she remembered why she had set the alarm. She jumped up and headed straight into the shower.

At one, Catherine dialled his number and waited for him to answer.

'Hello, Ian. How are you?'

'Who is this?'

'Is your wife Kerry near you?'

'She is, and who is this?'

Catherine paused for added affect. 'Kerry is going to hand you some papers. You are going to sign those papers. Then, you have one hour to move out of Kerry's house and find somewhere else to live.'

Catherine could hear him laughing. 'Yeah, that's a good one. Have a nice day.' The phone went dead, and she instantly called back and waited for him to answer.

'If you hang up again, I'll put what evidence I have across social media. I'll also go to the police and believe me when I say it's enough to put you and your little gang away for a decade.'

'What did you say?' he replied.

'Ian, you are Rapist Number Three. You already know by now what happened to Number One and Number Two. They've been punished, now it's your turn. I decided your punishment is to let your wife go and give her everything she's entitled to.'

Catherine pinged over a picture of him and the other three sitting at the table the night of Hayley's rape.

'Ian, look at the picture. Look at yourself. I have a lot more than that. The girl you raped was strong enough to take a picture, brave enough to gather evidence without you knowing.'

'I have no idea what you're talking about. I'll fucking find you, and…' he screamed until Catherine interrupted.

'Shut up, Ian. You'll do nothing. This isn't the part where you give me the Liam Neeson speech about your particular skill set that's a nightmare for people like me, nope, this is the part where I fuck you over, so you can shove your bravery up your arse. Actually, you're getting off lightly. Your friend lost half a tongue, and the other rapist friend of yours is going on the national sex offender register, as for the next friend, he's fucked. Sign the papers…now. You have five minutes, or I go on social media. Your career, your reputation, your whole life will be in tatters.'

'I'll give you money. How much to keep you quiet?'

'I don't need your money. I have money. But, do you know who needs money? You're poor wife, Kerry, that's who. So, SIGN THE FUCKING PAPERS.' It was Catherine's turn to hang up and start a timer on her phone.

She waited five minutes before calling back.

'Now listen you—'

'Ah temper, temper, Ian. Shut up and put Kerry on the phone.'

Catherine waited, and after some inaudible swearing, Kerry said hello.

'Has he signed everything?'

'Yes, but he's threatening me.' Catherine could hear him ranting.

'Fucking right I'm threatening her. She had nothing when she met me.' He came back on the phone. 'You won't get away with this.'

'Ian. This is your last chance…actually, fuck this, I'm done with you. You need to learn. Give me twenty seconds and then go on to Facebook. Look at my account, if you don't know already, Catherine Hart.' She hung up.

Catherine went into her account and uploaded the picture of the four of them laughing and joking at the table. Above the photo she wrote, *Do you know these men? They are wanted in connection to a serious crime.* She hit *share* before calling him back.

'You've made your point. Take it down. I've signed the fucking papers.'

'Look at the photo. You boys in your pants taking drugs. How sweet.'

'Delete it now.'

'And you're not going to threaten Kerry or me again, are you?'

'I won't. I promise. Just delete it.'

Catherine went on Facebook. 'Oh, look at that, Ian, I've already had several likes, ooh and people are asking what you've done. Shall I tell the good people of Facebook that you're a gang rapist? A sick rapist who preys on young women and spikes their drinks.'

He spoke at speed. 'Take it down. I'll do whatever you say.'

Catherine spoke calm and slow. 'I know you will. And that's why you will let Kerry live her own life away from you. You will not do anything bad to her…because if you do, I'll come for you worse than I have any of the others. Have you seen your friends since my visit? The ex-schoolteacher who downloaded child pornography, and the tongueless wine expert. Put Kerry back on.' He did as he was told.

'Kerry, get the signed papers back to your solicitor today as soon as you can. And if he's not out of your house in the next forty-five minutes, call me.'

'Thank you, Catherine. Please be careful.'

"We are each our own devil, and we make this world our hell."

Oscar Wilde

Chapter 19

The next morning, Catherine had called into the nursing home and asked for another week off work. They expressed their concern, but Catherine was a valued member of staff. Her job was safe. Her volunteering role with Victim Support was a different matter. Catherine no longer felt she could volunteer when so many victims of crime were let down in the courts. She felt helpless and frustrated. All too often, she and her fellow volunteers would have to pick up the pieces after an acquittal. If the case didn't make it to court because of a technicality or lack of evidence, the volunteers would be the ones having to comfort the disappointed victims. She called her manager.

'Hi, Maggie, can you talk?'

'I'd like you to come into the office in Woking. I think we do need to talk about what happened the other evening. If you'd like to come in—'

'I understand I'm not suitable, and I know exactly why. I'm sorry I couldn't do more for the charity, Maggie. These people deserve more, and I intend on helping in a different way. I'm no good to you. I need to help in other ways. Take care, Maggie.'

'Catherine, don't go, I'd rather we—'

'Thank you for giving me the chance.'

Catherine returned home with thoughts of Rapist Number Four. She put her key into the brass chamber and twisted clockwise. She entered her house and closed the door behind her just like she had done a thousand times before, but this time Catherine knew something wasn't right. The toilet door was closed, it was open when she left, and her mum never closed it. Also, both the kitchen and front room doors were shut. Catherine stood motionless and listened. The television was never off, her mum would sit in front of that thing day and night, it certainly wasn't off in the daytime, and on the rare occasion her mum left the house, it would still be left on. Catherine pushed the front room door open slowly, leaning back slightly and choosing not to enter the room.

'Please come in and take a seat, Catherine.' It was a man's voice, a deep strong east London accent.

Catherine thought quickly. 'Get out, I've got a hammer.'

She heard him laugh before he replied, 'Catherine, we both know you haven't got a hammer. If it's the one you leave by your front door, I've got it. Now be a good girl and come in here and join me for a cuppa. Steve will make you one.'

As Catherine mouthed, 'fuck,' the kitchen door opened. Standing in front of her was a man mountain, six and a half feet of Liam Neeson muscle. He smiled at her, not the kind of smile you receive from a friend. It was menacing. His gold teeth glistened as he pointed to the front room. 'In,' was all he said.

'Don't suppose I have a choice, do I? And you really need to work on that smile,' Catherine said.

His giant hand went against her back as she started moving.

'Steve, you can stand down,' the man in the front room said.

Steve's eyebrows lowered and drew closer together. 'Hurry up.'

'Leave her alone, she's not going anywhere,' the man at the dining room table said as he looked Catherine up and down. Alexis Carver wore a light grey Armani suit, perfectly pressed, double cuffed shirt, platinum cufflinks, and an ice-blue tie with matching pocket handkerchief. His skin fade was a day old at most, the rest of his hair perfectly gelled to the left. As he smiled, Catherine could see his eyes were the same striking colour as his tie.

'Nice cup of tea this,' he said as he raised his cup to Catherine. 'Steve, be a nice boy and make Catherine a cuppa.' He looked at Steve for a split second. That was enough for him to go back into the kitchen, as commanded.

'No, thank you,' Catherine replied. It was only then she noticed her mum in the armchair. She had duct tape over her mouth and around her wrists.

'I'm sorry about all that, we didn't want to' – the man pointed to her mum – 'but she's a game old bird, she slapped Steve, and she used unsavoury words I didn't even know existed.'

Catherine remained silent.

'Don't worry, we won't hurt her. Not if you do as you're told.'

'And what am I being told?' Catherine asked.

He reached into his suit pocket and took out a square metal tin. Removing a thin cigarette, he raised it to Catherine. 'You mind if I smoke?'

Catherine shook her head.

'Thank you.' He lit the cigarette and took a long drag. On the exhale, he looked Catherine up and down again.

'It's baffling to me how you've caused so much trouble. You're what, five foot four, five foot five at a push? And you can only weigh about nine stone soaked through. Plus, you're pretty, far too pretty for the darkness you've got yourself mixed up in. So, tell me, how have you got someone like Worboys so scared he's come to me?'

'I don't know what you're talking about.'

He smiled and tilted his head. 'Come on, Catherine. We both know that isn't true. We know everything. I'll be honest, when he told me what you've been up to with his friends I was impressed. Did you really chop off his tongue? And the other one, you're getting him divorced, losing him a fortune. And then there's the other lad who you stuck a knife up his backside and made him out to be a paedo. I like you. I'd rather employ you than hurt you, but, and it's an unfortunate but for you, I'm being paid to do a job, and a job is what I must do.' He put the cigarette tin back in his pocket. 'I don't know what you have against these men, but it ends today.' His expression changed. Menacing wasn't a strong enough word to describe it. 'My job is to stop it and that's what I'm asking you to do. Will you do that for me?'

Steve came back in with a cup of tea. 'I wasn't sure, but I guessed a little thing like her wouldn't take sugar.' He put it down in front of Catherine.

'Thank you, Steve, but I said I didn't want one.'

Steve snarled at her.

'But, seeing as you've made it especially for me, two sugars, a little thing like me takes two sugars.'

'Get her the sugar, Stevie,' the man said before he leaned forward into Catherine. 'Weird little town this, Dorking. We drove in and first we see the metal sculpture of the cyclists, no one likes cyclists, entitled middle-classed twats blocking the roads. And then on the next roundabout, a bloody great metal chicken, huge. Tell me…what's that about?' He sat back.

'It's a cockerel, to do with Dorking's history.'

'Bit odd. However, driving through the town it looks nice enough. Bit too quiet for me. I own a couple of clubs in London, the type of club where men spend their children's inheritance. I also do other things for money, specialist work, which brings me to why I'm here.'

Steve came back in. He scooped out two teaspoons of sugar from a bowl and stirred until Alexis gave Steve a look; he stopped stirring.

Catherine's mum was wide eyed, trying her best to scream and shout.

'It's all right, love, I'll take that off in a minute. Catherine, once you promise me you won't go anywhere near our friend David Worboys, I'll be on my way. He's paying me a serious amount of money to stop all this. I can't say I like the bloke, but he's paying well.' He shrugged.

'I'll match it,' Catherine said.

Alexis grinned. 'Steve, did you hear that? She said she'll match it, and she hasn't even asked how much.'

Steve's gold teeth made another appearance as he smirked at Catherine, his hands held together in front of him.

'Weren't you in a *Bond* film?' Catherine joked nervously.

Steve closed his mouth.

'Good one, Catherine. But don't upset him too much, he does bite.'

Steve stood there with his hands together in front of him, twisting a gold ring on his little finger.

'Catherine, you see how Steve holds his hands like that? Out in front of him, it's a prison thing. Spent half his life in there, had to be ready at all times.'

'You don't need to intimidate me. Just tell me how much? Five grand, ten?'

Alexis stopped smiling. 'I wouldn't come south of the river for that amount. He's already paid me twenty-five grand.'

'Done,' Catherine said.

'Don't mess about, young lady. That's a serious amount of money. And, anyway, it doesn't matter. I have my reputation to consider. If I switch sides that easy, people won't use me again. I am a man of my word. A man of honour.'

It was Catherine's turn to lean forward, inches away from Alexis Carver's face. 'A man of honour? Is rape honourable? A group of men taking it in turns raping a woman, a woman they've drugged. Don't talk to me about honour. Taking his money makes you no better than them.'

Alexis shot a look at Steve. 'Fucking grab her,' and pointed to Catherine's mum.

Alexis put his finger against Catherine's chest. 'I'll let Steve snap her neck if you mess me about. Don't bullshit me about some rape. Worboys told me it was a business problem. He said they'd ripped someone off, and that you were sent to punish them.'

Catherine was shaking, not in fear, but in a rage. She bared her teeth. 'Hayley Flashman, my best friend. She's in East Surrey hospital. You can visit her if you like. I'll take you. She tried to kill herself because of what those animals did.'

Steve was growling as he put both hands around Catherine's mum's neck. 'Boss, you want me to do it?'

Catherine was close enough to Alexis to feel his warm breath touch her skin, and to see the sudden change in his eyes. His menacing look had left the room.

'No…take the tape off. And make sure she's okay,' Alexis said.

He'd changed at the flick of a switch. He went from being in complete control to someone who'd seen a ghost. Catherine noticed Alexis was looking beyond her, focusing on a sideboard.

'What, what is it?' Catherine asked.

'Steve, take off the tape. Make sure she's okay. We're done here.'

'What's going on? I want this over. I'll get you your money,' Catherine pleaded.

'No. No money.'

'There's something else. What is it?' Catherine asked as she looked in the direction Alexis Carver was looking.

'The photo.' Alexis pointed to the picture of Catherine's dad.

'My dad, what about him?'

'That's Eddie Hart. You're Eddie Hart's girl,' and pointing to her mum, he said, 'And she's his fucking wife. Steve, we've fucked up here.'

Once the tape was pulled off, Patricia started shouting incoherently until Catherine stood over her. 'Shut up. He hasn't hurt you. Sit there and keep quiet.' Catherine turned back to Alexis. 'How do you know my dad?'

'It doesn't matter.' He gave Catherine an ice cold stare, 'just leave it.'

She pulled at his arm, 'tell me, you can't just leave, not now.'

Alexis ran his hand through his hair, 'I did business with Eddie, your dad, a long time ago when I first started out. A decent man, old school. I looked up to him. I wish I had got to work with him longer, but shit happened back then. Look, if I'd known, I would never have come near you. If anything, I would have helped you for free. I owe your dad. You should have come to me with your problem. I'd happily take care of Worboys for you…for Eddie. I'd take care of them all.'

'No, I don't want you touching him. Don't touch them, any of them. I want to do this myself. Worboys is the last one.'

Alexis stood up. 'I'm sorry, but if what you're saying is true, then he has to pay from me as well.'

Catherine stood firm in front of him. 'He will, I promise. He will suffer more than the others. I'll contact you once I've finished, even send you a photo to prove it if you like. Also, on the plus side, you get his money for doing nothing. It's a win win for you.'

'I don't want it. Steve will drop it off to you tomorrow. It's done.'

Steve gave a nod as Alexis continued. 'Okay, I'll stand down on this one, as that's what you want. For Eddie. I want you and your mum to know we are sorry. This shouldn't have happened.'

Alexis Carver started buttoning up his suit jacket. 'Just out of interest, tell me what you're going to do to Worboys? Whisper it to me.' He pointed to his left ear and leant forward.

Catherine could see the crease appear in his cheek as she was telling him.

'Very nice, I like that. Are you sure you don't want a job with me? I'd look after you.'

'I'm not that sort of person. I'm only doing this because they deserve it. I have a reason to do it,' Catherine replied.

Catherine saw the glint in his eye as he replied. 'There's always a reason, Catherine, and you'll find more reasons as life goes on. Don't feel bad. People who say revenge isn't the answer haven't been asked the right question. Not many people can do what you can. It's in you, passed down from your dad. He was the same. Either that or there's something in your past that has made you this way. Whatever it is, you have it.'

Catherine shot her mum a look before replying to Alexis.

'Why do you owe my dad? Tell me more about my dad, please? I never asked him where his money came from. I was young, I didn't care. Was he a bad man?'

Catherine's mum shouted out, 'Shut up, you. You know nothing.'

Alexis raised his eyebrows and pointed at Patricia. 'Your mum, you don't like her, do you? She did something to you, didn't she? Most people would scream at the sight of their dear old mum in that state when you first entered the room. But you didn't flinch. What did she do to you?'

Catherine shook her head.

'That's a tricky one. We only get one mum. Granted, yours is a bit mad, but whatever she's done, she's your mum. My advice, let it go…there's an old saying, holding on to anger is like grasping a hot coal with the intent of throwing it at someone else. You're the one who gets burned.'

Catherine and her mum stared at each other. Catherine's glare was cold as she watched her mum look away and start to cry.

Alexis put his hand on Catherine's shoulder. 'I've always had the same belief when it comes to having children. Every parent should do what's right. Parents should make their child the centre of their world, nurture them, always be there for them, put them first before anyone else, and then when the parents pass on, they should leave their child enough security and wisdom to have a good life. If everyone in the world did that, the world would be a happier place. All any of us want is to be loved by our parents. We all want to make them proud. When a child is young, without their parent's guidance, they walk about like an unlit firework waiting to go off. If a child isn't loved, at some point that child will go off.' Alexis used his hand to demonstrate an explosion. 'My dad used to beat my mum, and he beat me. He nearly killed her once, beat her black and blue. Put her in the hospital just for staying out late one night. I never forgot the kicks and punches he gave her. When I was in my mid-twenties, my mum passed away. Cancer, lady cancer. When she was alive, she used to beg me not to fight back against that man I called my father, but then she was gone, and I could do what I wanted…and I did. Catherine, I've never told anyone this.' Alexis Carver leant forward and whispered into Catherine's ear. 'On the day of my mum's funeral, there was one grave dug, but there are two bodies in that grave.' Alexis shot Patricia a chilling look.

'You didn't need to tell me that,' Catherine said.

'I want you to know that I trust you, like I trusted your dad. And you can trust me.' Alexis straightened out his suit jacket before shooting both arms out in front of him so that his cufflinks showed. 'Catherine, my main club is in London. It's called Sapphire. If you need me, come there and ask for Alexis Carver. Come for a drink and I'll tell you more about your dad. I don't know everything. He was a private man, not the partying type. I was young when I worked with him. I was just one of the soldiers, but I can easily find out more. What I will say is your dad had a big heart, could be soft at times with money owed from certain types, but when he needed to be the other way, no one could stop him. If anyone hurt anyone he cared about, he was vicious, beyond what was necessary some might say. You didn't fuck with Eddie Hart.'

Catherine nodded. 'I get it. I'd like to know more, all of it.'

'Let's go, Steve,' Alexis said.

Catherine looked at her mum. She was shaking and avoiding eye contact. 'Not a word of this to anyone, especially the police. You don't want Alexis coming back, do you?'

Her mum shook her head and sunk into her armchair.

'Catherine, leave the past where it is. Your dad moved away from London years ago, and he did it for a reason. Leave your dad resting in peace.'

'I'll decide when to leave it. Unless you feel like giving me some answers?'

Catherine's mum stayed silent and picked up the TV remote.

"The greatest sacrifice is when you sacrifice your happiness for the sake of someone else."

CHAPTER 20

Two loud thuds on their front door got Catherine's attention. She opened the door and invited Steve in. He didn't say a word, just handed over a bag and gave a single nod before returning to his car and leaving. Just as Alexis Carver had promised, the twenty-five thousand was now Catherine's. Stacks of fifty-pound notes neatly placed inside a Louis Vuitton bag.

Catherine walked in and found her mum sitting there looking despondent, as usual. 'Here you go,' Catherine said as she put the bag on her lap. 'In case you were going to open your mouth, that should be enough for you to keep quiet about yesterday.'

Her mum looked inside. 'You have no idea. I knew the type of man your father was when I married him. I've never involved the police in any business of ours and I won't start now.'

Catherine went to take the bag back, but her mum snatched it away. 'That doesn't mean I won't take this.'

'There she is. I knew you were in there somewhere,' Catherine said as she left the room.

Catherine came back in and was back at her mum's side. 'The bag, give it. You can keep the money, but the bag is wasted on you.'

Patricia emptied the contents on to her lap and threw the bag at Catherine.

'Thank you,' she said sarcastically as she picked it up.

After receiving the call from Hayley's mum, Catherine was both scared and happy that Hayley had requested to see her.

Approaching the Ranmore Ward at East Surrey Hospital, Hayley's mum, Helen walked towards her.

'Catherine, she's been asking for you. I'll go and get us a coffee. You go and sit with her.'

Catherine hugged Helen and before she could let go, Helen whispered into her ear, 'Thank you for saving my girl. I'll make it right. From now on, I'll be a good mum. Whatever Hayley needs, I'm there for her.'

Catherine squeezed her tight.

Catherine sat nervously on to the hard plastic seat. She reached out and touched Hayley's hand.

Hayley was staring vacantly at the ceiling.

She wouldn't feel Catherine's touch, Catherine knew that, but she squeezed gently in the hope their connection would be felt.

'Thank you for coming, Catherine,' Hayley said.

'Don't thank me. I want to be here. I'm here for whatever you need.'

'Catherine, I've done nothing but think since this all happened. I need something. I can't ask anyone else. It's got to be you that does it. I can't do it myself.'

Catherine used both her hands to cup Hayley's hand. 'What, Hayley, what can I do? Just say it, I'll make it happen.'

'Help me go,' Hayley said.

Catherine let go of her and sat back. Hayley turned her head, the tears forming started to run down her face on to her pillow.

'I can't do it myself. I know you want to save me, you always have. But not this time, not anymore. Look at me. This is not a life, and even if I wanted to be around to live like this, my mum can't afford the care I need. I need to go…I want to.'

'No. No, Hayley, you can't ask me to do that. Time is what you need. Once you adjust to a certain way of life, you'll find a way to be happy.'

Hayley became agitated, shaking her head. 'We both know that isn't true. Catherine, you're the only one I can ask. Only you. Please, you have to. I've thought about how. No one would know. Visit me regularly so the nurses get to know you. They'll trust you and after a while they'll leave me alone with you for long periods. Then, when the time is right, hold my nose and cover my mouth. I won't fight it. I'll let go.'

Catherine stood.

'That's murder. No way am I doing that to you. I can't do this.'

She ran out of the ward, leaving Hayley calling out, 'It has to be you, Catherine.'

"If you prick us, do we not bleed? If you tickle us, do we not laugh? If you poison us, do we not die? And if you wrong us, shall we not revenge?"

William Shakespeare

CHAPTER 21

A shadow cast across Roisin's desk like a blanket of sadness. Catherine eyed Roisin up and down, in awe of this woman who appeared to have everything. She was elegant and spoke in an accent that was the Queen's English with an Irish lilt. Her facial features were beautiful, with stunning green eyes. Luscious lips that were highlighted with a perfect cherry red matte lipstick. Roisin always dressed so feminine with her skirts just above the knee, her soft auburn hair that flowed past her shoulders. Why do a job where she had to hear so much misery?

'Why do you do this?' Catherine asked.

'What do you mean?'

Catherine pointed at her, and then back to herself. 'You sit here listening to sad, miserable people like me. I would imagine you could do any job you choose, but you do this.'

The shadow had reached Catherine's legs. It wouldn't be long before it covered her, removing all the sunlight from her view.

'I like what I do. I like meeting new people and hopefully I help them. There are certain jobs I couldn't do. In this job, one good day outweighs all the bad.'

'Like a fireman or a nurse?' Catherine asked.

'Yes, I suppose it is. I look forward to coming to work every day. I'm happy,' Roisin said.

'Do you think I'll ever find a purpose to live, to be truly happy?'

Roisin leant forward and pressed the button on her table lamp. 'Do you not feel you have a purpose to live?' Roisin asked.

Catherine looked at Roisin in the new light and marvelled at how lucky she must be to have such beauty and intelligence. Life was for people like Roisin, the chosen ones.

'Some are so lucky, some aren't. Not everyone is meant to be happy, I'm sure of that. There are people out there worrying about where their next meal's coming from. Worrying about when the next punch will come from an abuser. Then there are the ones whose only concern is how they'll entertain their friends at the weekend. Who only worry about what show to go see, they holiday in the Alps in the winter and bask in the heat of the Maldives in the summer, their diaries are as full as their bank accounts, they grew up with two decent parents, parents that loved them. Probably bang on about being vegan and how much they care about the planet, but they also conveniently choose to not shout about how they drive their little darlings around in a giant 4x4. And they brush over the fact that those jumbo jets taking them on holiday three or four times a year blast out thousands of gallons of fuel into the oceans. Selfish, entitled pricks. Life really is for the lucky ones, the deluded ones who see no wrong in themselves.'

'Where is this anger coming from? I've not heard you talk this way before,' Roisin said.

'I don't want to do this anymore. I'm done.'

'Do what, Catherine?'

'This' – Catherine threw her arms up – 'this sick world, it's fucking vile. Why would anyone want to be here when you really think about what goes on? The happy people are the ones who don't watch the news. The ones who ignore what's really happening. I'm done with it all. I don't fit anywhere. I'm not sure I ever did. I don't even want to fit in anymore. I'm tired of trying. I'm not angry, I feel—'

'What? Catherine, what do you feel?'

'Nothing. Nothing at all. And it scares me. Feeling nothing makes me want to go.'

'I'm worried about you, Catherine. You've missed appointments recently and now you're talking differently, negatively. Not so long ago, you talked about helping others. You had a spark in your eyes. I believe you're here to help others.

That's your gift. But, like I said, before helping others, you also have to help yourself.'

Catherine tutted. 'Helping others has got me nowhere. I make things worse.'

'I don't believe that. I'm sure if I was to ask the residents at the nursing home, they would tell me how wonderful you are. If I spoke to the victims of crime you've supported, they would say you made a real difference to them.'

Catherine thought about the people she tried to help, she thought about Hayley and what was last said. Her lungs felt empty. She sat up straight and tried to steal as much air as she could.

'I didn't help them. I paid them off to make them happy. The help I'm supposed to give didn't work. The system doesn't work. And as for the nursing home, don't you see it? They help me, they're my only friends. I don't have anyone. I've got nothing.' Catherine put her hand to her throat. 'I need to go. I can't—'

'Are you okay?'

Catherine tried to exhale, but she gasped for more air to inhale. She put her hand to her chest and could feel her heart pounding. She stood up, hoping this would help. She'd read at the nursing home how coughing could help prevent an oncoming heart attack. She tried several times. The pain got worse, and no air could be found. She reached out for the windowsill as she began to feel more lightheaded. She let herself fall to the floor; her back crashing against the wall.

'Catherine!' Roisin gasped as she knelt beside her.

Catherine looked up at Roisin, confused at the concern in Roisin's eyes.

'Just relax, don't get up. Stay there until you feel ready.'

'What's happening?' Catherine asked.

'I think you're having a panic attack. Just relax and you should be fine, but we need to address why it's happened and talk about what we can do if it happens again. This is all a sign from your body. It's saying you're under too much stress.'

Catherine slowly got to her feet. 'Can I have some water?' she asked as she wiped her forehead to remove the cold sweat.

'I've never felt like that before, thought I was dying,' she said before taking a sip of the ice-cold water Roisin gave to her.

'Please tell me what's happening to you outside of this room? Has something significant happened or changed in your life?' Roisin asked.

Catherine was taking in deep breaths and once she was ready, she replied, 'Hayley. She was raped.'

'Oh, Catherine, I'm sorry.'

'They drugged her, and then used her like she was nothing.' Catherine filled her lungs with air and slowly exhaled.

'When was this? How is she?'

Catherine thought about Hayley laying in the hospital bed. 'She'll never be the same, physically or mentally. It's too late.'

'I'm sure with time and—'

'Roisin,' Catherine interrupted. 'I know you mean well, but not this time. There is no helping her. They've taken too much.'

'Have they been arrested?' Roisin asked.

Catherine moved her head slowly from side to side. 'She won't report them. She doesn't want anyone to know, apart from me.'

'That's a lot for you to take on. It's terrible what's happened to Hayley, but this goes back to what we spoke about before. You have to look after yourself. You can't save everyone. It will take its toll on you. It already is. Your body is telling you enough is enough.'

'I can't help Hayley. I know that now. I thought I could, but when I try, it just goes wrong.'

Roisin left one of her long silences for Catherine to fill.

'When I was younger, I would wish for someone to save me, I would imagine the door being pushed open and someone lifting me up and carrying me away to safety…but no one ever came. I don't want anyone else to feel like that. No one should have to. No one person should make another suffer. And if they do, they should be the one that suffers, that pays the price.'

'You're talking about revenge.'

'Revenge is just a word. What they've taken from Hayley can't be replaced.'

'That's for the police to decide. The justice system has a process.'

'And that process is flawed. You have no idea how many guilty people get away scot-free. Do you realise how hard it is to provide enough evidence to convict someone? It's completely set up in the criminal's favour. Look at all the women who don't report being raped, scared they won't be believed, ashamed and afraid of what others will think of them. What if I knew who raped Hayley? Do I leave it? Do I let them go back to their cosy little lives with their wives, their two kids, and their perfect homes? We aren't talking about masked men at night jumping out of the bushes. These are middle class, respectable, white, the type of white that juries find innocent. So, do I sit back and do nothing despite knowing they will rape more women? I can't…and I fucking won't.' Catherine was red faced and her fists were clenched.

'Catherine, I don't have all the answers. All I know is that you could get hurt or in trouble with the police if you do something silly. Hayley may change her mind. She may want to prosecute them when the time is right, when she's ready. It has to be Hayley's choice.'

Catherine raised her voice. 'She doesn't have a choice. She never did…but they did, and they chose to rape her. That was their choice…and now they don't have one in how this plays out. They will all answer for what they've done.'

"We play the broken string of our instruments one last time."

John Green

CHAPTER 22

'Alexis, I need your help. I'm happy to pay you for your time.'

'Catherine, I'm pleased you called. I hoped you would. Let me guess, our friend the policeman, David Worboys?'

'Policeman?'

'You didn't know?' Alexis chuckled. 'Please don't tell me you're surprised? Scumbags come in all forms, even the police. I don't trust anyone.'

'That changes things,' Catherine said.

'Why? Why does that change anything? He's just a man, two arms, two legs. He raped your friend, the same as the others did. He won't report you. How can he? If you can't do it, maybe I should—'

'No. I can do it,' Catherine interrupted. 'But he'll be harder than the first three, going by the photos I've seen. He's a lot bigger than the others, the risk is greater. I just want you to restrain him and leave him restrained for me to deal with. Could you do that for me?'

'Are you sure that's all you want? I can take care of him for good if you say the word. I'm no fan of a rapist or a policeman. It would be a pleasure.'

Catherine thought about it. She pictured Hayley laying in the hospital bed. The anger in her stomach was rising. She also pictured what her mum did to her. People should pay. The rage inside her wanted to let Alexis kill Rapist Number Four. But murder was another level. Taking a life would take its toll. The guilt and the repercussions were too much.

'That's very kind of you, Alexis, but no, I don't want him gone. I just want him to suffer. To suffer more than any of them, but I will need an advantage over him. That's why I need you.'

Catherine could hear Alexis breathing as she waited for him to answer.

'Very well, restraining it is. I don't know his address. I can find it, though.'

'I've got it here. Number two , Saltdean, Brighton. Tomorrow night, just after eight.'

'You are very resourceful, Catherine. I really wish you would consider working for me. You have all their addresses. Can I ask how?'

'Rapist Number One told me whatever I asked. He had no choice. The rest I got from their phones or social media. It wasn't hard.'

'Clever girl,' he said before he continued, 'And if anyone else is there, would you like them restrained?'

'If anyone else is there, it's off. No one else gets hurt. Especially family members. But from what I know about him, he doesn't have a wife or children.'

Alexis laughed. 'You're too nice, Catherine. If you want to live in the dark, you have to be prepared to do dark things.'

'This is my last time *in the dark* as you put it, after this I won't hurt anyone again.'

'If you say so, but there will be a reason, there always is. Bad people are born bad. That's just the way it is. Someone, someday, will upset you, and you will go there.'

'It ends tomorrow.'

'I understand. And, Catherine—'

'Yes.'

'Please don't offer me money ever again. You owe me nothing. I'm here when you need me. Mr Worboys will be there ready and waiting for you at eight o'clock. Good luck.'

Catherine arrived in Brighton by train. She didn't want her car being picked up by any cameras. The walk from the station to the address was long, but she used the time to go over in her head what she would say and do to Rapist Number Four.

In her all-black Nike tracksuit, she took a last look around before entering his road. Pulling her hood up, she made her way down the steep path. She walked past the house, allowing herself a quick glance. The light in the front room was on. Her phone pinged. She carried on walking as she looked at the message. *It's all clear, go straight in. Sorry about the mess, couldn't help myself. You can thank me later.*

'Oh shit, what's he done?' Catherine said quietly to herself. She knew Alexis was nearby watching her, but didn't know where. Bright car lights flashed in the distance. Another message. *Are you not even going to wave?*

Catherine replied with a waving emoji, and two words, *Thank you.*

The back door is open. Your gift is inside. Have fun, Alexis sent.

Catherine put her phone in her pocket and made her way to the back of the house. Catherine had every intention of going straight in, but her body tightened. She went rigid as she considered what was in there. Alexis said she could thank him later. Her gift was inside. What had he done to Worboys? Every movement she made to enter the house was met with anxiety tightening its grip. She bent forward, putting her hands on her knees and whispered to herself, 'Hayley, think of what he did. This is the last one.'

Pushing the door slowly, she crept in. She could hear a the whirring of a washing machine going. Looking around, she was in a utility room. Alongside the washing machine, a tumble dryer, and to its right was a giant chest freezer. Three pairs of shoes and one pair of wellington boots were perfectly sitting on yesterday's newspaper. She tentatively opened the next door and entered the kitchen. Plastic clear sheeting covered the floor. A trail of bright red blood led to a large man sitting taped to a chair. His hands were palms down on the top of his legs, industrial strength tape wrapped around his wrists and thighs. The blood was coming from so many different places, including every single finger. Catherine tilted her head as she looked closer at his injuries. She looked into Worboys' eyes. He didn't try to scream; he didn't try to move. But she could see from the whites of his eyes the pain he was in. She jumped as her phone rang. Startled and shaking, she ran back into the utility room. The gloves she was wearing made it difficult to get the phone from her pocket. The faster she tried the more she fumbled around in her pocket unable to retrieve it. Once she got a grip, she could see the number and answered, 'Yes.'

'I'm sure you have questions. I just wanted to let you know what I did. I know you didn't want me to kill him, and I didn't want to take all the fun away from you, so I did just enough. As you know, I like you, Catherine, and he's a big man. I wanted to give you an advantage.'

'Okay, I think. There's so much blood.'

'Do you know much about Greek mythology? Of how Achilles was killed?'

'Heard of Achilles,' she replied.

'Before they could kill him with an arrow, they disabled him by slicing his heel. I could have inflicted the same wound, but I don't want to be a copycat. But it got me thinking. I cut the tendons in each of his fingers. His fingers are now useless. He will be in terrible pain, and his fingers will feel and look like flaccid penises hanging in the wind. When you cut the tendon on a finger, it snaps like an elastic band. The bottom of said elastic band starts to slowly make its way down into the hand. He will never be able to straighten those fingers.'

Catherine remained silent.

'I used a Stanley blade, the Stanley Quick Slide Pocket Knife, a very handy tool.'

'You didn't need to—'

'Catherine, sorry to interrupt, but if he was uninjured and you went one on one with this guy, the odds would be in his favour. He's twice your size. Do not underestimate him. No amount of martial arts training will help you against this man. He's violent scum. I don't want you hurt. This is my parting gift to you.'

Catherine didn't know how to answer, so she gave another, 'Thank you.' It was all she could muster and before she could question him on how he knew she had trained in any type of martial arts, he spoke again.

'I will go now. You won't hear from me again tonight. But if you need me, I will be close by. I thought I'd treat myself while I'm down here at the coast. I'm staying at The Grand. The hotel where they tried to kill Thatcher – terrible business that was. Aside from the terrorist history, it's a beautiful hotel. I'm looking forward to it. I'll be there until Sunday evening. Goodbye, Catherine.'

Walking back into Worboys' kitchen, she couldn't take her eyes off his hands. They looked like a bear's claws. Each finger was unnaturally bent at the top, blood dripping from every deep cut. Worboys shook his head slowly from side to side. On the kitchen work surface was a block of knives. She removed one and checked it for sharpness and size. Walking towards him, she noticed he didn't flinch. Standing in front of this vulnerable man with a six-inch blade in her hand she knew what she could do, what she wanted to do. Physically, it would be so easy, but mentally, it would affect her the rest of her life. She gently poked the tip of the blade into the tape covering his mouth. Her chosen spot was where she guessed there would be a tiny gap between his lips. She cut a line big enough for him to breathe and then cut it more so that he could talk.

'Thank you,' he mumbled.

Catherine used her gloved fingers to tear it a little wider.

'Is that better?' she asked.

'Thank you, Catherine.'

Catherine nodded confirmation that he had her name correct.

'You knew I was coming?'

'I was expecting it.' He bowed his head towards a baseball bat that had been positioned behind the door. 'I have one at the front door as well. And a hammer by my bedside. I don't mind admitting it's been an anxious wait.'

'You know why I'm after you, don't you? If my friend had wanted to press charges, I would have left it to the police. You had to pay one way or another.'

'Can I have some water, please?' he asked.

She tried several cupboards before finding a glass and proceeded to fill it. She tipped it gently through the hole in the tape into his bloodied mouth. The whole time she kept the knife in her hand.

'Why? That's what I want to know. Why rape? You could find sex somehow, pay for it if you had to. Why rape?'

She put the glass on the kitchen side, blood sat on the rim.

'It's not rape. We've always liked to party. The girls we fuck are drunks. They're easy. They knew what they were doing at the time. By the time the morning came, they were too embarrassed to say anything, and they'd leave. We didn't need to rape. But as we got older it wasn't as easy, so we tried drugs to move things along a little easier.'

'She didn't want it, she didn't want you, did she?' Catherine's grip tightened on the knife as she pressed it against Worboys.

'She was different. I tried talking to her earlier in the night, but she acted like she was too good for me. She wouldn't give me the time of day.'

'Hurt your ego, did she? Because a girl doesn't fancy you, you decide to rape her instead?'

'I wouldn't put it like that. Girls come out wearing short skirts, dancing about like tarts, and then when you talk to them, they brush you off. Dick teasers. If you don't want sex, don't dress like that, don't take drinks from men.'

Catherine picked up the glass and threw it to the floor just in front of him. It smashed, sending shards into his face; she pointed her knife at him. 'Men like you need putting down. It doesn't matter what a woman wears. Even if she was naked, it wouldn't give you the right to touch her. You make me sick. And you're a policeman. You should be protecting girls like Hayley, not raping them.' She pressed the blade under his eye.

He was smiling at her. 'I'm finished with protecting anyone. I used to care. I really did. But it didn't matter what I did, the public hate the police, hated me. So, fuck them, and fuck your friend.'

Catherine narrowed her gaze at her victim. 'You really want me to stab you in the eye, don't you?'

Worboys was calm in response. 'You should. If you don't kill me, I'll keep coming for you. What you've done to me and my friends, I won't forget.'

Catherine could see Hayley's face as she pushed harder. The blade entered his sclera. Worboys let out an ear-piercing shriek.

'You fucking bitch, I'll kill you.' The chair was still strapped to his body as he threw himself forward at Catherine. The knife entered deeper into Worboys's eye as she landed on her back. She was unable to put her hands down, her back took the full impact, there was sickening thud. Worboys was on top of her up to her waist. His hands were still firmly strapped to his legs. He was shaking his head vigorously until the knife came out of his eye. Wild with rage, he started biting her upper thighs as she tried to push him off. She screamed out in pain.

She frantically looked for a weapon, but nothing was there. She pushed the top of his head with everything she had, once he was far enough down, she hiked her right leg up, bringing it over his shoulder, she crossed her ankles and bridged her hip upwards. Using her left hand, she grabbed her right ankle and pulled it towards her face. He was in a choke hold. She pulled her ankle until she couldn't physically do it anymore.

Eventually Worboys went limp.

As she let go, she let out a huge exhale of air and pushed his head from between her legs. Worboys's head crashed against the hard marble floor. The triangle choke Catherine had just performed was a move she had trained many times before, but she had never needed to use it outside of the gym. An opponent would tap out once they couldn't breathe. Seven to ten seconds can leave an opponent unconscious, more than thirty seconds can lead to brain damage, and anything more than sixty seconds can be fatal.

Catherine had no idea how long she had held Worboys in that hold for. He hadn't tapped out. He couldn't.

She shuffled herself back against a side unit, pulled her knees up to her chest, and watched Worboys's lifeless body lay in silence.

Murder was not part of the plan. She didn't want to kill anyone, just hurt them, to make them pay. Was she upset that Worboys might be dead? No. But it won't take much to link her to the murder. She slowly got to her feet and leaned on the work surface to steady herself. She must leave, but her mind was racing, thinking about how to cover up what she had done.

And then she heard his weakened plea, 'Just go.'

Catherine stepped back before shooting Worboys a look of disbelief.

'Go, you've done what you need to do. Look at me.'

'You're not dead?'

'It's over. We hurt your friend, you hurt us.'

She glared at the giant man in front of her, bloodied and broken. Picking up her knife, she leaned over him.

'You don't need to do this. If you murder me…'

She cut the tape from his hands and legs. 'She wouldn't want you dead. Stay down until I'm gone,' she insisted.

Worboys reached his hand up, blood pouring down his arm. 'I'm going nowhere.'

She backed up to the door and took one last look before making her way out of the house. The alleyway at the side of the house was in complete darkness. Every tiny sound was amplified, her senses betraying her.

Once at the front of the house, she could hear footsteps coming from behind. She shot a look over her shoulder and could see a shadowy figure closing in.

She sprinted towards the safety of the streetlights ahead. Running out between two parked cars she took another look behind before she saw the headlights and felt the impact.

"You often meet your fate on the road you take to avoid it."

French Proverb

CHAPTER 23

A single light bulb shone brightly in her eyes and each time she blinked, bright circles swirled in the darkness. Unable to move her left arm she used her right hand to rub her eyes. Crisp, clean linen sheets covered her body. Attempting to lift her head felt too much, the muscles in her neck tightened and the pain was overwhelming. She let out a faint cry.

'Please stay still,' he said.

This shadowy figure stood over her and gently touched her brow. 'If you move, it will hurt. You need to rest.'

'I need to get up,' she said as she attempted to lean on to her right arm before collapsing back down.

'You're in no state to get up. I can call an ambulance. I really want to, but you insisted I didn't. You didn't want to go to hospital. You kept saying no ambulance, and no police.'

'Who are you?' Catherine asked.

The man pulled a chair to the bedside. 'I hit you with my car. It was an accident. I wasn't going fast, but you ran out of nowhere, and the next thing you were, lying in the road.'

Catherine looked at him desperately, trying to make out if he could be trusted. He looked friendly enough, scared even.

'You were conscious at first. You made me promise not to ring anyone. Maybe I should. I can ring—'

'No, please don't,' she said as she reached out.

'Your upper body took most of the impact. Your arm is pretty bad, but not broken. It's badly swollen at the elbow.'

Catherine took in her surroundings. 'Where am I?'

'This is my apartment. You asked me to take you somewhere safe. I didn't know where you lived, you wouldn't say. Coming to my place was all I could think of. I haven't kidnapped you, I promise.' He let out a smile.

'Can you help me sit up? I feel dizzy lying flat.'

He helped Catherine move up the bed by adding another pillow. He held out his arm for her to use as support.

She grimaced before thanking him. 'I don't even know your name, and I'm in your bed.'

'I'm Christopher. And you're very welcome to share my bed.'

Catherine blushed.

'I'm sorry, I don't know why I said that. I just meant that I'm happy to help. Not that I wanted you in my bed with me. Shit, I'll stop talking.'

'You are making it worse.' She laughed just enough for it to hurt. 'Shit, that's painful.

'I'm Catherine, or Cat. Nice to meet you, Christopher.' She reached out her hand and placed it on his. She moved it back off once he smiled.

'I'll get us a cuppa. Is tea okay?'

'I'd like that. Sugar and milk, please.'

She watched him leave the room before she started looking around. On the bedside was her phone. She could see the screen was cracked. Her shoes were neatly put against the wall. .. Blinding sun rays shone in through the skylight. How long had she been out of it? And where was his apartment? Was she still in Brighton? Looking down at her bare legs, she could see the giant bite mark Worboys had left on her.

The door opened just enough, and Christopher spoke before coming into the room. 'Is it okay to come in?'

'It's your room,' Catherine replied.

'I know, but…but you might be changing or something.'

'Honestly, it's okay. I haven't moved. I'm lazy like that.'

He entered the room, two cups in his hands, steam rising from them both. A coaster with a Brighton and Hove Albion Football Club badge on it was where he placed her tea. He moved the coaster and cup so that she could reach it comfortably before he sat back down. 'You can stay here until you're ready to go. I mean, I don't mind if you need time. I have a sofa in the front room. I can sleep on that. It's just me here.'

'That's kind of you, but it wouldn't be right. You don't need me making the place untidy. Maybe a lift later, though, if that's not pushing my luck?'

'That's fine. Dorking in Surrey, right? You told me that much last night.'

She looked around the room. 'Where are we, by the way?' Catherine asked.

'Brighton, not far from where I found you. Or where you found me, I should say. Getting you in here wasn't easy. You were semi-conscious and in a lot of pain. I'm just glad none of the neighbours were about.'

'I'm so sorry. I'm sorry about all of this.'

She noticed Christopher's expression change before he spoke. 'I don't mean to get into your business, but what were you running from?'

'Don't. Can we leave it?'

'Don't worry, you don't have to say. I've sat here most of the night trying to work out what was going on. I thought maybe you were a burglar, but then I could tell you weren't. I'm no expert, but burglars are normally male, into drugs, and they don't look like you. Your outfit is more that of a jogger, quite a menacing one, I'll give you that. But jogging at night, alone, that's not right.'

Catherine sipped her tea. 'That's it. Just jogging. Got to get your ten thousand steps in.'

'You don't have to tell me if there's more to it. Probably best you don't as I'd be an accessory, or secondary party, if that's what they call it. I've seen enough police dramas to know the score.' He gave her a wink.

She had to lie. 'I haven't committed a crime. Let's leave it at that and stick with late-night jogger.'

'From Dorking? That's a hell of a jog.' He raised his eyebrows.

Catherine laughed as she was about to take another sip. 'What can I say? I'm a very good runner. Ultra-marathons are my thing.'

'It's fine. You can tell me when you're ready. If the police come knocking, I'll deny I knew you were here. I'll tell them that you broke in, and that it's been a long time since I've had a pretty girl in my flat, so I let you stay.' Another wink to let her know he was joking.

They lapsed into silence. His face glowing. She laid back staring at the ceiling, feeling herself flush with the on-set of redness appearing in her cheeks.

'Would you like to rest? I can leave you alone,' he said.

'No,' she said, her reply was instant before continuing, 'I mean, I'd just rather be with you, with someone.'

'That's fine. I can stay. Or if you feel up to it, we could go out for a walk. The beach isn't far from here. They do a lovely hot chocolate on the pier, and they sell those little ring doughnuts caked in sugar. It's not very warm out, but you could borrow one of my coats?'

'I'd like that.'

She lifted her hand to her forehead. 'Could I take a shower, please? We could go out after?'

'Of course, give me a minute,' he said as he left the room.

He came back in with a fresh towel and handed it to her. It felt warm and comforting, it smelt different, good different. She held it close against her chest.

'Thank you,' she said.

'I'll get out of your way. Would you like me to leave you out a clean T-shirt? It'll be a bit baggy on you, but I'm sure you can style it out. I've got some joggers, nothing fancy, but they are clean,' he said before grabbing them from his chest of drawers and putting them to his nose. 'Yep. Fresh and clean.'

'Perfect.' She gave him a nod.

As he went to leave the room, she called out, 'Christopher.'

He had his hand on the door handle as he turned round.

'I really appreciate this, all of this, thank you,' she said, not knowing if she was thanking him for helping her physically, or was she thanking him for not calling the police and being pushy with questions? 'But do you think I could go home? I need to sort a few things out. Another time, maybe, the beach. Give me your number. I promise I'll call, even if it's just to say thank you.'

'Of course, I understand. I'll run you home when you're ready.'

"Mother love is the fuel that enables a normal human being to do the impossible."

Marion C. Garretty

CHAPTER 24

She rubbed the hand sanitiser between her fingers and took in the strong smell of alcohol as she walked on to the ward. In front of her she could see five beds with patients in surrounded by loved ones, but the sixth bed, Hayley's bed, that was empty. Catherine's heart was racing as she looked around for answers. Helen walked towards her.

'What's happened? Where is she?' Catherine asked.

Helen touched her arm. 'It's okay, love. She's been taken down for more MRI scans, and God knows what else. Come with me to the canteen. You look awful. Are you okay? I'll get us a coffee.'

Catherine sat on one of the green plastic chairs and thanked Helen for her drink.

'I got two sugars. Is that enough?'

'That's fine,' Catherine replied.

They sat in silence for a minute before Helen reached across and placed her hand on Catherine's.

'Can I ask you something?'

Catherine nodded.

'Has Hayley asked you to do something for her?'

Catherine couldn't look her in the eye. 'Like what?'

'I think you know. She's been asking me to do the same thing.'

Catherine shook her head. 'I would never do that. She can ask as much as she wants. I'll never do it. I'll take Hayley in whatever condition she's in. I never want to be without her.'

'That's kind of the point though, isn't it?'

'What is?' Catherine asked.

'*We* want her around. *We* don't want to be without her. It's all about us. Can you imagine what she feels like, what she's thinking her life will be like? They're doing more scans today to give a final diagnosis. We both know it isn't good.'

Catherine leaned back in her chair and pushed Helen's hand away. 'No, don't even talk about it.'

'Catherine, I'm just trying to see it from her point of view. I was never a great mum to my girl when she was young. Her dad was a bastard, and I was too busy hating him and drinking to be there for her. I'm here for her now, though. I'll do anything for her. She would pass peacefully. I've researched a way. I can cause an air embolism by injecting air into a vein.'

'A fucking air embolism. Have you heard yourself? You're joking. You'd better be joking, Helen,' Catherine said through gritted teeth.

'This morning she looked at me with tears in her eyes and said, "Mum, you brought me into this world. Please help take me out." It was heartbreaking. When I said no, she stopped talking. Her trying to kill herself is my fault. I was a terrible mum.' Helen was sniffing and reached for a wrinkled-up, overused tissue from her pocket.

'It wasn't your fault. I know it wasn't.'

Helen's mouth opened, but nothing came out.

'What I mean is, there are many reasons someone suffers from depression. It could be something or nothing that caused it,' Catherine said.

'That isn't what you meant, and we both know it. You know something don't you? I'm her mum. I have a right to know. I need to know. Please, Catherine. The pain of hating myself is killing me. If something has caused this, tell me.'

Catherine closed her eyes briefly, searching for answers, but she couldn't lie, not about this. She knew Helen deserved to know.

'Please promise me you won't tell the police. Hayley doesn't want any of this becoming public knowledge.'

'I think it's too late to worry about what others think, don't you? Just tell me.'

Catherine spoke softly. ‘Hayley was raped.’

Helen’s hand went to her mouth. ‘No, not my little girl. By whom? Who is he?’

‘She was raped by several men…they drugged her. She didn’t stand a chance. She begged me not to tell anyone, and I haven’t…until now. And I’m only telling you because I want you to know that none of this was your fault.’

Helen slammed her fist down on the table. ‘Several? More than one? Those dirty bastards. Does she know them? Who did that to my girl?’

‘Hayley wouldn’t say, and please don’t ask her to tell you.’ Catherine moved her seat towards Helen, she put her arms around her. ‘I’m so sorry.’ She felt Helen nestle into her before bursting into tears.

‘This is no life for my girl. She doesn’t deserve this.’

PART TWO

Death in my hand

"If you want something you've never had, you must be willing to do something you've never done before."

Thomas Jefferson

CHAPTER 25

'Thank you for meeting me. I meant to call you sooner but—'

'That's okay don't worry. I'm just pleased you called,' Christopher said.

The parking bays on the beachfront were half full. This time of year was the quiet season, but Brighton still attracted its fair share of visitors. The paths were busy, cut in two by a busy cycle lane. Bells would be rung by cyclists as they did their best to move pedestrians from their share of the tarmac.

Christopher's car was immaculately clean, the dashboard was lit up like an airplane cockpit, a freebie car wash air freshener swung side to side hanging from the rear-view mirror.

Christopher chose a bay as near to the pier as he could get. 'You okay to walk from here?' he asked as he turned off the engine.

'Can we give it a minute?' Catherine said as she looked out at the waves crashing on to the pebbled beach. 'I've always found something so calming about the sea, and yet it's so dangerous.'

'I can go and grab us a drink and we could sit in here, in the warm and watch the sea.'

'Can you stay with me? We'll go together in a minute.' She looked across at him and felt he could read her as he looked intently into her eyes.

Catherine's hand was resting on her thigh, Christopher's was there on his own leg, inches apart from each other, but neither brave enough to make the move. She thought about it, how she would love him to reach across. She considered instigating the linking of hands, but what if he pulled away? Rejection at this point would be too painful. She hardly knew him and yet she felt comfortable within their silence. It felt safe, a homely feeling, not her home, but how a home should feel, safe and friendly.

A young couple walked in front of them. They exchanged glances as they shared what looked like a giant pretzel wrapped in paper. Catherine enjoyed seeing their happiness. She could feel herself glowing as she stole their moment and made it her own. The occasion was ruined by a seagull the size of a pterodactyl as it swooped down and snatched their food; the girl ducked as the boyfriend swung for the invading predator.

'Jesus Christ,' Christopher said as he started laughing and grabbed his phone to take a photo.

Catherine covered her mouth as she giggled. She hadn't laughed for a long time; it felt good.

Christopher patted her hand. 'Come on, you. Let's go and get that hot chocolate. You won't be disappointed. Big dollop of whipped cream on the top…it's so good.'

Hot chocolate in hand, they walked along the pier. The only noise was that of the waves crashing into the giant wooden pillars that had held up this pier for decades. Catherine took her napkin and held it out. 'Come here, you.' She wiped a small piece of the whipped cream off his nose.

'Well, that's embarrassing,' he said.

'I was going to keep quiet. It looked quite sweet.' She nudged his elbow.

Ahead, they could see flashing lights and hear the loud music, the entrance to the arcades.

'You any good on the grabber?'

'The grabber?' Christopher asked.

'You know, the claw thing? Comes down and grabs a Minion, or whatever other fabulous soft toy they're giving away.'

'Ahh, yes. I'm actually a professional at grabbing. Would you like me to win you something? You pick what you want, and I'll make it happen.'

'Oh really, a professional you say? I need to see this. Especially now you've promised to win me something. It's on.'

Christopher was reluctantly putting his fifteenth pound coin in the machine before Catherine questioned his grabbing skills. 'Are you sure you're a professional? We could just buy a teddy. To be honest, you could have bought two or three by now.'

A smile from Christopher was accompanied by a sarcastic but defiant nod. 'How dare you question my ability? This is the one I've got it.' The three metal rods closed in around the bright yellow Minion's head.

'Ooh that's tight, you've got it,' Catherine said.

The metal claw started to rise with its prize clamped firmly in its grasp. It moved left and headed towards the glass. The square hole was waiting for the prize to drop.

'See, professional. Get in there, you beauty,' Christopher shouted.

The claw released the toy from its clutches, and the Minion fell. Christopher's expression went from sheer happiness to despair as it landed on top of the plastic frame and hung over the edge.

'You bastard,' he shouted.

Catherine laughed so hard it hurt. 'Stop, my arm hurts when I laugh.'

Catherine watched a small hand tap Christopher's shoulder. 'Come on, mister. It's our go now,' the teenage lad said.

'Piss off, that's mine,' Christopher said as he kicked the machine. The Minion toy fell into the hole. Christopher reached down and grabbed it.

'See, professional. For you, madam.' He held out the toy for Catherine.

'That was impressive. You really are a professional. Apart from the telling the kid to piss off bit. That was harsh.'

'Was a bit much wasn't it?' He laughed and put his arm around her. 'Come on, let's go before someone complains.'

Time flew by, their date coming to an end.

'I'll drive you home.'

'I've got a return ticket for the train. I like the train. It gives me time to switch off mentally.'

'But if I take you home, I get another forty-five minutes with you,' Christopher said.

Her smile said it all. The journey back to Dorking was mostly silent but was filled with sideways glances and reassuring smiles. Stopping briefly to put some fuel in his car, Christopher came out of the garage with two coffees in hand. A simple gesture, but a gesture that took Catherine by surprise and gave her a warm feeling inside.

Once back to Dorking, Catherine directed Christopher to her house. She looked across at him and prepared to say goodbye, the desire to reach across and hold him was strong, to thank him for not probing her and asking too many questions, for taking her at face value, but most of all, for simply making her smile.

'You can come back with me if you want to?' Christopher asked.

'To Brighton?' Catherine replied in a higher tone than she meant to.

'Sorry, that was a bit forward of me. It's stupid. I shouldn't have said that.'

'Yes. I want to.' Her eyes lit up. 'I really want to.'

Catherine glanced over at her house as she continued, 'But I need to get some clothes and—'

'And what? What is it?'

'My mum…she's difficult.'

'I understand. Another time then?' Christopher said.

Catherine could see the disappointment on his face. 'I do want to, though. I could make things right here and come to you in a couple of days?'

'I work most days, but I'm always home by early evening. You can come down when it suits you, any time after six. Or I'll leave a key out,' Christopher said.

Catherine leaned across and put her arms around him. She felt his arms reach around her and squeeze her tight. It was a safe feeling that she wanted more of; she didn't want to let go. She waited for him to ease his hold on her first, but he didn't.

'Thank you,' she whispered.

Catherine looked at him as he leaned back. His hands ran up her body from her waist until he cupped her face gently and kissed her.

'No need to thank me. I've loved every minute of being with you. I'm so pleased you called,' he said.

Catherine kissed him back. 'In a couple of days, I promise,' she said.

'Or sooner,' he said with a cheeky grin.

Catherine opened the car door and stepped out. She was mindful he was probably watching her, which made this most normal of activities seem difficult. She closed the door and walked toward her house. Precipitously, she turned around and skipped back to the car. A huge smile greeted her as he opened the passenger window.

'I don't even know your surname, or, or what you do for a living. There's so much I don't know about you,' she said as she shrugged.

'That just gives us more to talk about when you come back, doesn't it?' he said as he reached across and touched her hand. 'Goodbye, Catherine Hart.'

'Goodbye, Christopher…whatever your name is,' Catherine said as she held her belongings close to her chest, she swayed slightly left to right, like she was hugging herself. He gave her one last smile before pulling away.

Catherine closed her front door and leaned against it. She looked at the ceiling and took in the feeling of someone who had won something by pure luck. Why her? She wasn't used to this feeling and wondered if other people felt this often. Reality returned, hitting hard from the front room.

'I don't really care where you've been, but who was that out there? The one in the fancy car. He looks trouble to me. Probably going to break your heart…men like that always do.'

Catherine stormed through the door to see her sitting in the same old chair, wearing the same unwashed nightgown. Her mum didn't break her gaze from the television.

'I take it you were watching from the window, being nosey as usual? You don't care about me, so why do you care who I go out with? He's just a friend. Keep out of it,' Catherine said.

'Cuddle and kiss all your friends do you?' her mum asked as she poured another drink.

'Just keep drinking, Mum, and if me being happy bothers you…good.' Catherine stuck her fingers up to the back of her mum's head.

'Oh, that's nice, isn't it? Who do you think you are? Proper little madam, aren't you? Well, don't mope around here crying like a wounded puppy when he shits on you.'

Looking away, Catherine exhaled while fighting off nasty thoughts of what she would like to do to her mum. Once composed, she had one more thing to say. 'I thought you'd like that. We could sit and drink together, feel sorry for ourselves until we both fall into a drunken coma. We could pour each other drinks and talk about what could have been and how cruel the world is. Talk about how unfair our luck is and go on about the Hart family curse. Your life is sad because you are. You're cruel and nasty, therefore your life is. You deserve to live in darkness…for what you did to me.'

Catherine hadn't mentioned anything to her mum about the abuse since she stood up to her as a teenager. Her hands were shaking, her chest tight. She had stuck her sword in the dragon and waited for its response.

She watched her mum walk towards the window and peer out of the curtains before returning to face Catherine.

'You are desperate to hurt me, aren't you?' her mum said as spit left her mouth landing on Catherine.

'Hurt you? You know what you did. You can't erase it by getting drunk every night.' Catherine put her hands on her head. 'Your own fucking daughter.'

'Oh, not this shit again. Stories made up in your head.'

'Do you know how disgusting that is? Do you know how many nights I've stood over you and contemplated smothering you or beating you to death?' Catherine had her finger against her mum's forehead.

'Your own daughter,' Catherine screamed.

Her mum's head dropped, her chin on her chest.

'Go on, say something, anything, just make me understand why?'

'I didn't touch my own daughter. You want to know why?' she said with a grin.

'Yes, fucking why?'

She prodded Catherine's chest. 'Because you're not my daughter.'

Catherine stiffened. She focused in on her mum's eyes, waiting for her to change expression. But she didn't. Catherine could see was enjoying herself, her grin was more of a satisfied smirk. She was in her element.

'You're lying. The one thing you know could hurt me the most is to say that I'm adopted. That you and dad aren't my real parents. I know how sick you are. That's your strength.'

Her mum's finger was touching her forehead when she replied. 'I never said your dad wasn't your dad, did I?' The smirk was still there.

Catherine took a step backwards, her body numb, the ground below her taken away.

Her mum continued with joy. 'You were his baggage. If I wanted him, I had to accept you. He even put it in his bloody will. The conditions of me getting what I got were that I bought you up as my own. I couldn't ever kick you out. I wanted to.'

Catherine sat down, head in her hands.

'He got some tart pregnant. She was young and couldn't handle the responsibility, so she gave full custody to your dad. He made sure he got you. Obsessed from day one. Once you showed up with your ugly little face, I was put in second place. When he got cancer, I told him I didn't want to bring you up, but he said if I didn't look after you, all his money would be signed over to you and you alone.'

Patricia moved back from Catherine and topped her drink up before sitting back in her usual grubby chair, the arms heavily stained. She sunk down low as one too many springs had given way over the years. Catherine looked across and watched in disbelief that this woman could give life changing news one second, then watch the television like nothing had happened. Patricia picked up the TV remote and turned it up to full volume. An episode of *The Sopranos*. Tony Soprano placed a rival gang member's jaw over a metal bar pole before stamping on his head. Teeth flew across the restaurant floor.

'Yes, Tony.' Patricia grinned.

'So why I am here?' Catherine asked.

Patricia ignored her.

'You heard me. I know you did.'

'You're here because your dad screwed a tart without protection.'

Catherine walked over and turned the television off. 'I mean, why am I still living with you? You only had to look out for me until I was an adult. I was eighteen over seven years ago. You could have kicked me out. I want to know why you didn't?'

'Put that back on. This is a good one. Coco deserved that for insulting Tony's daughter.' Patricia turned to face Catherine, 'His real daughter, not a fake one.'

'I'm not turning the TV back on, you mad cow. If I believe you, and I'm not sure I do, tell me why you kept me here?'

'You really want to know?'

'Yes.'

'I like seeing you unhappy. If I kicked you out…you could find happiness. That's the last thing you deserve. Now, turn my fucking television back on.'

Catherine dropped the remote control. Her breathing became shallow, chest tightening. She could see there was nothing in Patricia's eyes that said she was lying. There was nothing that said she cared what Catherine thought of her. Catherine's hand went to her chest as she left the front room, searching desperately for air. Patricia simply picked up the remote, grinned and turned it back on.

Three minutes had passed before Catherine returned with a hammer in her right hand. She walked towards Patricia and stood in front of her. Patricia's smile replaced by fear, she held her hands up in front of her face and curled into a ball.

Breathing heavily, Catherine's eyes widened as she raised the hammer.

'No, Catherine, don't, please.'

Catherine stopped, moved away from Patricia and walked towards Patricia's only source of happiness, her TV. She hit it repeatedly until sparks flew out of the screen, it fell to the floor. Catherine carried on hitting it over and over until she was exhausted. She stood up straight, wiped the hair from her face, and pointed the hammer at the frail, weak lady she used to call her mother.

'You are no longer the monster in my life. This ends today. You can't hurt me anymore. You will never see my face again.' Catherine dropped the hammer by her side and walked out of the room without looking back at the broken old lady she left behind.

****

Hayley's condition had worsened. Catherine and Helen had taken it in turns to sit by her side, but the conversations had reduced to visits where nothing was said.

As Catherine arrived for the latest visit, Helen had been called in for a chat with the specialist. She returned in tears just as the hospital porter wheeled Hayley's bed back in place and, in a friendly tone spoke to Hayley. 'There you go, Hayley. Thank you for travelling with Andy's Travels. I look forward to seeing you again soon.'

Hayley didn't flinch. Helen thanked the porter as he left, and Catherine moved next to Hayley so she could see her.

'Hey you, I've missed you. Can I get you anything?' Catherine asked.

Hayley didn't respond.

'Last time I was here, your mum and I were talking about what we can do for you and how we'll be there for you when you come home. The hospital will obviously help us and tell us what we need, but if there's anything else you can think of, just say.'

'I don't want anything. I don't want to go home. I don't want to go anywhere. Catherine, look at me, I can't even eat by myself, for fuck's sake, I can barely breathe without help.'

Catherine started stroking Hayley's hair. 'It will get easier, it's understandable you feel this way but, in time, you'll make a life that makes you happy. We'll all do it together,' Catherine said as tears fell on to Hayley's bed.

'Oh really, what, you think I'm going to have a great life, maybe aim for the Paralympics. What life will I have like this? They told me today just how shit my life will be. They said this is how I will probably be forever. Catherine, I won't ever get used to being like this. I wanted to die before this. Try to imagine how I feel now,' Hayley said as a tear left her eye, creeping slowly down towards her ear. She then moved her head back against her pillow and went into a distant stare. As Catherine moved her head away, she caught the look in Helen's eyes.

Catherine got to her feet, bent down, and kissed Hayley's forehead. 'I love you, Hayley. You're my best friend. You're my family. You always have been and always will be.'

Hayley closed her eyes. 'I love you too, Catherine.'

Catherine looked at Helen. Without using words, they said everything.

'I'll see you again, and when I do, we'll be happy. We will dance like we used to,' Catherine said.

Hayley opened her eyes and gave Catherine a smile. 'We will.'

Helen moved closer. She put one hand on Hayley's shoulder and her other on Catherine's. 'You girls will always have each other.'

Catherine let her tears fall as she looked back at Hayley one last time before running out of the ward.

That evening Catherine laid in bed sobbing uncontrollably. Her phone pinged and lit the room. She reached for it; the time was 22.22 and the name of the sender was Helen Flashman.

"We must be willing to let go of the life we planned, so as to have the life that is waiting for us."

Joseph Campbell

Chapter 26

Three Months Later

Catherine sat nervously in the waiting area, drinking her coffee and avoiding stares from the inpatients. She got her phone out and scrolled through social media to make it look like she was busy.

'Hi, Catherine, would you like to come through?'

Catherine felt comforted by the familiar voice. She put her phone away, smiled at Roisin.

'You can bring your coffee with you,' Roisin said.

Catherine followed Roisin down the corridor and into her office. She expected it to look different, but it was exactly the same, she smiled and sat down facing Roisin.

'How have you been?' Roisin asked.

Catherine noticed a thread of cotton on the hem of her skirt and started to pull at it. ‘I’m doing well. I wouldn’t say I’m happy, but I’m getting by. I’m using the tools you’ve taught me and I’m talking to those around me when I can.’

‘That sounds very positive. And I’m so pleased you decided to return to therapy. I hoped you would.’

‘After Hayley died, I didn’t want to see anyone but Christopher. He’s been amazing. He’s let me be me. He gives me space when I need it and he’s always there when I need him. Without him, I don’t know where I would be. But I think I now need a bit more. I need some outside help to keep me moving forward.’

‘Catherine, the fact you acknowledge that is a huge achievement. It’s so brave and you should be proud of yourself. In the past, you used anger as a way of coping, but you seem different. Christopher sounds like a good person to have around. Is he a friend, colleague?’

‘I suppose he’s my boyfriend. I don’t think we’ve ever put a label on us. You don’t, do you? But yeah, I’m living with him, so I guess he’s my boyfriend.’ Catherine smiled and shrugged.

‘I’m pleased for you, and I’m pleased you had Christopher to help you cope with the sudden loss of your friend. Would you like to talk about her?’

Catherine cleared her throat before replying. ‘The simple things have started to give me a glimpse of happiness. Chris greeting me at the door when I get home. The mundane things. A coffee when I didn't ask for one. Him stroking my head until I fall asleep. He's saved my life, but I miss her so much. She didn't deserve to die like that.'

'*Like that*, what do you mean?'

Catherine was biting her lip. 'I mean she was so young, to die in so much pain wasn't fair. Mentally, there was nothing anyone could do. I tried, but she was desperate to die. What makes it worse, it was because of others that she felt that way. They caused her death.'

'I'm sorry, Catherine, I really am. And how do you feel about those other people now? Are you able to walk away from them? You know your anger towards them will bring you down. I don't want that for you.'

'I don't have it in me any more to feel that way. The fight in me has gone. I just want to be left alone. I don't want any problems with anyone. I've not seen or spoken to Patricia in months, and I won't talk to her again. I can't do it.'

'Patricia, that's your Mum's name. You don't normally call her that.'

'Things have changed,' Catherine replied. She laughed briefly before taking a sip of her coffee that was now cold. Placing the cup back down, she looked at Roisin and felt the tears building. 'Turns out she isn't my mum. My dad was my dad, but my real mum is someone else. She could be out there somewhere right now.' Catherine waved her hand in the air.

'That's a lot to take in for you. Are you thinking of finding out who she is?'

'What if she's not about? She could be dead, in prison. Knowing my luck, she's probably Rose bloody West,' Catherine joked.

'From what you've told me your dad was a kind man. He wouldn't have been with someone unkind.'

'Then why did she leave? What mum does that?'

'From my years working in therapy there are many reasons people leave. It doesn't mean they're a bad person. She may have felt not good enough to bring you up, it happens. Mental health can affect anyone at any time, and it can make the kindest of people do things that others will never understand. I'm not making excuses for her, but it might be worth giving her a chance to explain what happened.'

Catherine gave a shake of the head before continuing. 'Christopher thinks I should let the past go, all of it. Forget what happened to Hayley, forget about Patricia and my past, just concentrate on the future with him. I think he's right. If I dig up more of the past, I could be asking for trouble, and I'm tired. I just want to be left alone.'

'It's your decision and if you feel that's what's right for you, then go with it.'

Catherine was flicking the heel of her shoe off and on again as they shared a moment of silence before Roisin spoke again.

'Are you working? Or volunteering still?'

'I'm just working back at the care home. It's a bit of a drive from Brighton and Christopher thinks I could get something closer, but I'd miss the people there. I like going there, it's not about the money. I don't need much to get by, so it gives me enough and I get to hang out with my elderly friends.'

'You didn't go back to Victim Support?'

'No, I didn't feel I was any help to anyone. I think the people there are wonderful and they do so much, but I had nothing to offer in the end. It was best all round. I'm content with life at the moment. Christopher and I walk along the beach most days. We talk a lot, and we're happy in each other's company. Even when we don't talk, if I'm just doing nothing at home with him, it's nice. He's kind, he doesn't drink too much, or do drugs, he's lovely to me,' Catherine said as her head lowered.

'You look upset when you say that. If he makes you happy, why the sadness in your voice?'

Catherine looked up. 'Coz I'm scared it will end. Happiness doesn't last.'

'But that isn't a reason to not enjoy it. It could last one year, it could last fifty years and there you are sitting with great grandchildren together one day. No one knows the future. You can't go into every relationship or friendship thinking about how and when it will end. You're in danger of causing it to end if you act that way. Take Christopher for who you think he is, a good man. He clearly knows what a lovely person you are. You deserve each other. Move forward together.'

Catherine moved her head to one side, hoping to hide her face.

'Is that a smile I see there? Catherine, you deserve this. Go with it, be happy.'

Catherine peered back at Roisin. She still had the smile, and her eyes glistened. 'I will, I promise.'

"There is no charm equal to tenderness of heart."

Jane Austin

CHAPTER 27

Desperate for sleep, Catherine had been awake in the darkness for over an hour now, she had shifted sides a dozen times, tossed her pillow looking for it to be cool to touch, nothing helped.

'Catherine, are you okay? Another bad night?' he asked.

She rolled to face Christopher. 'It'll be fine. You go back to sleep,' she said.

Christopher gently touched her face. 'If you can't sleep, then I won't either. I don't want you to be alone in the darkness.'

'Honestly, I'm fine. If I can't sleep soon, I'll stop fighting it and get up. You can sleep in peace then. Although stroking my face does feel nice.' She smiled at him.

He stroked her cheek softly before moving down her neck and onto her back. His touch gave her goosebumps.

'I love it when you touch me. You have some sort of magic spell over me. I go all weak. I think you're my kryptonite.'

'I love touching you, so I guess we're perfect for each other,' Christopher said.

After several minutes, the feeling was becoming less impactful, so she rolled on to her back so that Christopher could caress her elsewhere. He started on her stomach and then moved up to the side of her breasts. Her nipples were now hard, and she wished he would touch her there. He touched everywhere on her breast but there. She bit the inside of her lip and arched her back, letting out a soft moan. This had the desired effect as Christopher stroked her nipples. She reached across and could feel he was hard. He moved his hand down her body deliberately slow until he reached between her legs. Within seconds, she couldn't wait any longer. She grabbed her hair tie from her bedside table, put her hair up as she moved herself on top of him. Using her hand, she guided him inside of her. Any negative thoughts she had before were now gone. She pushed her full weight down as she moved her hips back and forth. Christopher had his hands on her breasts as she went faster. She wanted to cum; she moaned louder, knowing this would bring Christopher closer so they could finish together. She got louder as she felt herself reach orgasm in perfect sync with him. She let out a sigh as she collapsed on to his chest. He put his arms around her back and pulled her in tight.

'That was amazing. Quick, but bloody amazing,' he said.

Catherine chuckled. 'It was, we need to do that more often. Can we go again?'

'What, now? Give me a minute, or five,' he joked.

'I'll give you five minutes, no longer.'

She felt Christopher go to move. 'No, stay inside of me.'

He gave a gentle squeeze. 'I love you, Catherine Hart.'

That was the first time he had said those three words to her. Catherine kissed his cheek before putting her mouth by his ear. She whispered, 'I love you too.'

Catherine woke up as Christopher was putting a morning coffee by her side.

'Thank you,' she said as she gave him a huge smile.

He was in boxer shorts and had a towel over his shoulder. 'I'm jumping in the shower. After that, what shall we do today? We're both off work. Let's do something fun. We're in Brighton. There's plenty we can do. There's the Sea Life Centre near the pier?'

A huge grin appeared on Catherine's face. 'Ooh perfect. I haven't been there since I was a child. My dad took me. Give me ten minutes and I'll be ready.'

Within half an hour they had entered the Sea Life Centre, it had changed a lot since Catherine was young but the memories of walking in holding her dad's hand came flooding back.

'It's funny how certain places or songs can take you straight back to moments in your past, both good and bad. This is definitely a good memory. Thank you.'

He pulled her in for a cuddle. 'It's nothing. If you can think of other places you'd like to go, just say.'

After holding him tight, they made their way through the centre. Once inside the glass tunnel, Catherine stopped and took in what was above her. Small sharks and rays glided by.

'Beautiful. It looks so peaceful in there. The way they move is so graceful. Do you think they're happier than us?'

'They'd probably be happier in the sea, but I know what you mean. I don't think they're unhappy. There are so many predators in their world, safer here maybe.'

Catherine felt sadness come over her. 'There're plenty of predators in our world as well. Hayley found that out.'

Christopher put his hands on her shoulders. 'Catherine, we said we'd let that go. I know you said one day you'd tell me all of what happened, but whenever you bring it up, it upsets you. Let's enjoy today. We can't change the past, believe me, I wish we could. Let's get busy moving forward, you and me. Nothing about the future is guaranteed. I can't promise I'll be perfect for you, but I'll bloody try. It goes without saying there will be times we may fall out, piss each other off, everybody has that, but we can give it our best shot at being happy.'

They moved along a few feet before Catherine pulled him into her. She gently patted his chest as she looked up into his eyes. 'You're right, as usual. Let's go for it.' She smiled.

After leaving the Sea Life Centre, they walked across the busy road, past the pier, and down on to the beach. Catherine removed her shoes and felt the unforgiving pebbles under her feet. The tide was in; the waves crashing against the beach before the sea withdrew back into itself, leaving a white foam to dissolve into the beach. A group of boys were skimming stones across the surface of the water.

'Have you ever tried that?' Christopher said as he pointed at the lads.

Catherine looked at Christopher, bent down, picked up a stone the size of her hand and threw it in, causing a delightful plopping sound. Shrugging, she turned back to Christopher. 'No, I haven't,' she said and laughed out loud.

Christopher had a devilish grin. 'Truly awful. Best I show you how.' Christopher got on all fours and combed through the stones.

'That doesn't look mental at all. What are you doing?' she asked sarcastically.

'Well, it's all about the stone. It needs to be flat. Not like that boulder you just gracefully threw in.'

'Go on then, mister expert stone thrower inner.'

'It's called skimming, not throwing.' He winked. 'Ah, ya beauty, found one,' he said as he positioned himself. He bent his knees, leaned to one side, and threw it with the concentration of an Olympic athlete. It bounced across the water six times before being swallowed for good.

Catherine gave an exaggerated nod. 'Christopher Mason, I'm impressed.'

'Form is temporary, class is permanent.'

'Idiot,' she joked.

'Growing up in Brighton it's a required skill as a boy. Up until the age of about thirteen, it was our number one pastime.'

'And after thirteen?' Catherine asked.

'Girls, girls, and cheap cider under the pier.'

'You tart,' she said as she gently punched him on the arm.

'I wouldn't worry too much. I was short and shy. My mate Tommy Kenward was the local stud. I never got a look in.'

'I bet you did okay. And where's Tommy Kenward now?'

'Prison,' Christopher said before chuckling. 'Yep, he wasn't just good at pulling girls, turned out he was bloody good at pulling off bank robberies…until he was caught, that is. He's currently doing a twelve stretch in Parkhurst.'

'Think it's best we change the subject. Talking of when you were young, you still haven't taken me to see your mum. I'd like to meet her…if that's okay with you?'

'Right now?' Christopher asked.

'Not right now, but when it suits her.'

'Sod it, let's go today. She won't mind. It's not far away. She's in Eastbourne, where all the old people live. It's about forty-five minutes away. I'll ring her now and give her time to tidy up. Even though it will already be spotless, if she knows you're coming round, she'll still panic and get the polish out.'

Christopher's mum walked in with a tray of teas, cups on saucers, a china pot of milk, and a separate bowl of sugar.

'Here we go. Mum's got the best china out, she must like you,' Christopher said.'

'Oh, shut up you,' Mrs Mason replied.

Catherine felt herself going red. 'Thank you, Mrs Mason.'

'Please, call me Phyllis.'

'Thank you, Phyllis, and thank you for letting me come round at short notice.'

'It's no bother, love. I'm just happy to finally meet the girl that's making my son so happy.'

'All right, Mum, calm down. She's not supposed to know all that,' Christopher said.

Catherine blushed again and to hide it she picked up her cup. Only her forefinger could fit in the handle, which felt awkward at first.

'I can tell you're a nice girl, not like the other one. Right up herself, she was. Never said a word to me. Always looking at her phone waiting for the visit to be over so she could leave.'

'Mum, she wasn't that bad,' Christopher said.

'She must have been pretty bad. Your dad never warmed to her, and he liked everyone.'

'Dad was a good judge of character. That's a fair comment. I think she wasn't ready to settle down. A bit young at the time, maybe she's grown up since then.'

'If you say so,' Phyllis said, as she looked out of her window.

Catherine wanted to change the subject. 'This is lovely. I'd love a house where I could see the sea like you can here.'

Catherine felt Phyllis touch her hand. 'You can visit here as much as you like. And if you're still with this one, you can move in here with him when I'm gone.'

'Oh, don't say that. You have many good years left. But visiting you often would be a pleasure. You can show me around Eastbourne.'

'I'd love to,' Phyllis said.

'She'll have you at bingo next,' Christopher said.

They continued to talk about everything from Christopher as a young boy to when Christopher's dad passed away. Catherine felt a warm feeling. Being a small part of a family, she felt included.

'I didn't like some of his friends. I was glad when he stopped going around with them. His younger friends weren't so bad, even Tommy Kenward. He was always lovely to me, but his family had a history of crime and sadly, he followed them. It was at uni Christopher used to get up to no good. Too much drinking and partying. Some of his friends there weren't very nice. And you would have thought they would have been good 'uns as most of them came from money. We had to borrow to get him through university, took a long time to pay it back, but we always said we would. Once he knew what he wanted to be, we helped him the best we could,' Mrs Mason said.

'That's really good of you, and I know Christopher is grateful. He loves his job,' Catherine said.

Christopher looked at his watch. 'Mum, we're going to have to go soon. It's getting late. *Eastenders* is on in a mo, you can't miss it, I know my place.'

'I can tape it. Or whatever it's called these days.'

'We need to go, anyway. I've got an early start, and Catherine is back on nights tomorrow, so she'll want a good sleep tonight.'

'I think it's lovely you work with the elderly. It shows you have a caring side. It's a hard, underpaid job. The government should put more value on it. Get you carers paid more. The things you have to do are above and beyond.'

'Yes, Mum,' Christopher said as he smiled at Catherine.

They said their goodbyes and made their way to the car.

Before they got in, Catherine hugged him.

'What's that for?' he asked.

'For being you,' she replied.

Driving home, Catherine would randomly reach across and touch Christopher's hand. Each time she did, he would give a tight squeeze before looking across at her in a way she felt no one ever had before.

As they pulled out and exited the roundabout, a black BMW cut them up and sped past them. Christopher let go of Catherine's hand and flashed his lights.

'Dickhead,' he shouted.

Red brake lights shone brightly. Their car suddenly caught up with the BMW, which was now stationary.

'Go round them, don't stop,' Catherine said.

Christopher attempted to pass, but the BMW moved sharply, causing Christopher to stop. Catherine's attention was drawn to the driver. The anger in his face was real. She'd seen that look before. This was now fight-or-flight time. They'd tried to flee but couldn't. Catherine looked into her lap. Violence was in the past. She didn't want this anymore. In her world with Christopher, there was no need.

His door shot open, crashing against Christopher's front wing. Christopher tried to lock the doors, but it was too late. His door was pulled open, a gorilla-sized hand was grasping at his neck. Catherine watched as Christopher was pulled from the car. She removed her seatbelt and exited from her side. As she approached the fight, Christopher reached out. 'Go, Catherine, go.'

A woman got out of the BMW and ran towards Catherine. 'Keep out of it or I'll do the same to you.' The lady's hand was inches from Catherine's face.

Catherine sized her up before replying, 'Remove your hand and go back to your car.' The lady laughed before lunging forward to grab at Catherine's hair. Catherine took a step back, leaned slightly to her left before throwing a left hook to her ribs. The air was snatched from the woman's body as she collapsed to her knees. Catherine grabbed her hair and tilted her head back. 'You should have gone back to your car.' Catherine threw a punch down on to her nose.

'You fucking bitch,' the man shouted as he threw Christopher to one side.

Catherine switched stance, her left foot forward and right planted firmly to the ground. He was a big man, six-foot three plus and full of rage. Throwing her overhand right to a man this size would probably break her hand without hurting him. She had one option, an option taught to her back in the gym. It wasn't one to be used in the boxing ring or Octagon, it would be illegal. But Tony had taught her it early on. It was only to be used as a last resort.

He was heading towards her with chest puffed out, looking like he was carrying two invisible barrels under each arm. He was now within striking distance. Catherine bent her knees to help throw the shot upward into his windpipe.

He stood clutching at his throat. Eyes wide, the eyes of fear, fear of dying.

'Catherine, no,' Christopher shouted.

The man fell against his car before stumbling forward, one hand reaching out in desperation, his breath deserting him.

Catherine went behind him and kicked at the back of his legs, behind the knee, causing him to fall to the floor.

'Enough, Catherine.' Christopher was now behind her and had a hand on her shoulder.

She shot him a stare. One he'd not witnessed before. 'Don't touch me.'

She returned her attention to Mr BMW, kicking him repeatedly in the ribs.

'Think it's fair to attack people, do you?' She snarled before another kick landed.

'Going around bullying people smaller than yourself, a big man, are you?' Another kick, this one to his head.

Christopher got himself in front of her. 'No, Catherine. You're going to kill him. That's enough. This isn't you.'

Catherine was heavy breathing while looking Christopher in the eye. 'I can't—'

'Can't what?' Christopher moved forward.

Catherine lowered her fists and fell into Christopher's arms.

'It's okay, I've got you. Let's go.'

'I can't let him get away with it. He was hurting you. I'm not losing anyone else I love, I had—'

'I know. But it's over.' Christopher looked down at the man. 'He's breathing now, he'll be fine. But we need to go.'

Catherine stared at her hands as they shook uncontrollably.

Christopher walked Catherine round to the passenger seat, helped her sit, and put her seatbelt safely round her. He kissed her. 'Let's go home.'

"You are who you are when nobody's watching."

Stephen Fry

CHAPTER 28

It had been a week since the road rage incident. They didn't speak about it once they got home. Catherine wanted to move on, forget it, and make sure it didn't happen again. It was a glimpse of her past. She wanted a future.

Catherine had prepared the social room at the care home. The lights were low, some snacks were on the table, and three chairs were lined up in front of the television.

'Three? Why three chairs?' Betty asked.

'Because Bill is joining us. Turns out, he likes a bit of boxing too.'

'For God's sake, I don't want him here. He's a sandwich short of a picnic.'

'Less of that, Betty. Bill's a lovely man, and he's joining us, decision made,' Catherine said.

'If he talks during the fight, I'll throw something at him. I've got biscuits and I'm not afraid to use them.'

'I'm sure he won't, and you won't be throwing anything. Take a seat and pour some tea. It's ready in the pot. I'll go get Bill.'

'If he's already asleep, which he probably will be, leave him tucked up. You snooze you lose,' Betty said before continuing, 'Next thing we know, you'll be inviting Percy the ball grabber to join us.'

'Percy, I like Percy,' Catherine said.

'Do you now? I bet he likes you, too. Bit of a perv, that one. Have you noticed his hands are always in his pockets?' Betty said as she leaned in.

'I have noticed that. He said it was for comfort. That he'd done it since he was a lad.'

Once Betty stopped laughing, she replied, 'He cuts holes in the pockets.' Betty grinned.

'Cuts holes. What are you talking about, Betty?'

'You know, so he can grab his nuts and whatnot.' Betty chuckled. 'For comfort, you thought his hands were in there for comfort.' Betty laughed again, this time louder. 'For comfort, comforting his plums more like.'

'That's enough. I'm getting Bill. Not another word about Percy's balls,' Catherine said as she was about to leave the room.

'Percy's balls!' Bill said as he entered the room.

'Oh God, not you as well,' Catherine said.

'He cuts holes in the pockets, filthy man. Every pair of trousers he owns. He's an animal. You check 'em tomorrow. Every pair. He used to make me tea, and I'd drink it, not anymore.'

As Catherine sat back down, Betty tapped her shoulder. 'Told ya, Pervy Percy we call him.'

'Hello, Betty, thank you for letting me watch the fight,' Bill said as he took a seat.

'No problem at all. You're very welcome. I love it. More the merrier. More people, more noise, just bloody perfect,' Betty said with a sarcastic smile.

Catherine raised her eyes at Betty. 'This is nice, isn't it? So, who are we cheering for? I know Betty's a Tyson Fury fan, so no need to ask her. Bill, who are you going for?'

'I'll go for the other bloke, the tall black geezer,' Bill said, still smiling.

'Do what? You want an American to win, a Yank to beat our boy. What's wrong with you? No, no, no, get out, off you pop, I'd rather fat Pat came in here than you. At least she'd be quiet. I could throw a cake at her every five minutes. That would keep her piped down. Or bloody Percy. He can sit in the corner shuffling his sweaty nuts,' Betty said as she pointed at Bill.

'Betty, that's enough,' Catherine said.

Bill shrugged, 'Well, Tyson Fury won last time, and the first one was a draw, so it'll be nice if—'

'Bollocks to nice,' Betty interrupted. 'This is boxing, and if a Brit is fighting, we cheer for the Brit. I knew you shouldn't be here, you geriatric spastic.'

'Enough, or I'll turn the television off,' Catherine warned.

'I've said my piece, you'll hear no more from me.' Betty shot Bill a look that had him immediately look down at his feet. Betty carried on nodding in Bill's direction. Catherine could feel a rude comment incoming any second. Betty was on one. It had to happen.

'Bill, you're scruffy. Have a shave. And why don't you ever do your hair? You could try that Head & Shoulders stuff, stop your hair snowing all year round, ITS CHRISTMAS,' Betty shouted.

Catherine punched her fist down on the chair, she'd had enough and was about to send Betty to her room when she saw the look on Bill's face change.

'I was thinking the same about you, especially the shaving part. Women shouldn't have beards,' Bill said.

Catherine watched and waited for Betty's reaction. The sides of her mouth started to rise, and a smile formed, which turned into huge laughter.

'Oh, Bill, excellent. Good for you, Bill. That's made my day,' Betty said while giggling.

They sat watching the pundits do their usual guess work on the upcoming fight and the silence was only occasionally broke by Betty laughing at Bill's earlier insult as she replayed it in her mind. 'Especially the shaving part. I didn't know you had it in you, Bill.' They all giggled together.

Ten minutes later Catherine looked across and noticed Bill's head fall to his chest before mumbling, 'I'm awake, I'm awake.' And then his head would fall again like a dead weight.

'Another cuppa, Betty?' Catherine asked.

'Yes, please, love.'

Betty leant into Catherine and spoke quietly. 'How's your friend? The one that was hurt.'

Catherine moved back into her chair and stared at Betty. 'You remember me telling you?'

Betty reached for Catherine's hand. 'I told you before, I'm not as mad as you all think. It's okay love, I don't gossip. I'm not like Pat.'

'Let's leave it. Let's watch the fight.'

'I'm sorry, you don't have to say. I won't ask again,' Betty said.

'It's okay. I'd just rather not speak about it. One day we will.'

'Can I ask one question?' Betty said.

Catherine gave a single nod.

'Did you get the bastards who hurt her? Is it over?'

Catherine went back to watching the boxing before replying, 'I tried, Betty. They suffered, but is it over? No. I thought it was, but it's not. Not in here,' she pointed to her head.

Catherine had finished her night shift. She was driving away from the care home and her thoughts were on the nice evening she'd just had. She enjoyed their company, and it rarely felt like work. She was pleased Betty now had a new verbal sparring partner in Bill, and by the end of the big fight, they were all cheering Tyson Fury on as he celebrated keeping his heavyweight title.

Just as she was about to head up the A24 and head to Brighton, she switched directions and went into Dorking, towards her family home. She had no idea why she was going there, but as if on autopilot, she did, anyway. She slowed down as she looked in. Rain crashed against her windscreen. The grass on the front lawn was overgrown, and all the curtains were drawn. She parked and debated going in, but why? It wouldn't be to see Patricia. She told herself it was because of her dad and the memories; she missed him so much and the house held so many shared moments. But it also held so many nightmares and the person responsible. She put her foot on the clutch and pushed the gear stick into first; she wanted to see Christopher. She needed him.

Thirty minutes later she was nearing Brighton as she changed the radio station. The rain had grown stronger. The song playing triggered more memories, more pain hitting her in the chest. She turned it up. One line caught her attention. It was Rickie Lee Jones's, 'On Saturday Afternoons'. Thoughts of Hayley turned into memories of her dad. Thoughts of loss, loneliness. Dark memories. The hurt she had put upon her, the hurt she put on others. What kind of cruel world was this? Patricia abusing her had her hitting her steering wheel. The road was becoming blurry, her breathing shallow.

Her thoughts on Hayley returned. Should she have done more to convince Hayley's mum not to do it? What kind of person lets that happen? Catherine knew what she was walking away from that night at the hospital. The vision of Hayley suffering. The vision of her dying at her mum's hands, the guilt crippling. As she drove over Devil's Dyke, her poor vision and the rain couldn't go on. She screeched to a halt in the centre of the road and opened the door. She leaned out and vomited onto the wet tarmac. After wiping her mouth, she stepped out of the car and onto the grass; she looked to the sky for help, but all she could see was Hayley's face in amongst the heavy rain.

'*I'm sorry. I'm so fucking sorry*,' she screamed as she dropped to her knees.

Guilty, sorrowful tears streamed down her face, every ounce of heart-wrenching pain and regret leaving her body replaced by feelings of nothing. Her shouting replaced by muted mumbling, 'No more, I can't, not anymore. Let me go.'

PART THREE

Blood and Revenge are hammering in my head.

"We stopped checking for monsters under our beds when we realised they were inside us."

Charles Darwin

CHAPTER 29

EIGHTEEN MONTHS LATER

With Roisin's help, Catherine's recovery was steady and going well. That day on Devil's Dyke she was found by a passing motorist who called an ambulance after being unable to get any response from her. She remained in a dreamlike state for nearly two weeks before finally replying to Christopher from her hospital bed.

Over the last year, Catherine and Christopher enjoyed making a home together, they cherished their walks along the beach, spending time in the lanes of Brighton, their takeaway Friday nights in front of the television, afternoon trips to the cinema, but most of all, they just enjoyed being together.

'I'm in the kitchen washing up,' Christopher called out. He had his back to her as he was at the kitchen sink, washing up. 'My hands are wet. I'll finish this and then give you a cuddle.'

'No. Stay there,' Catherine said as she wrapped her arms around his waist and pushed her body against his back. 'I love you so much.'

'I love you, too. That's a big squeeze. Everything good? Nothing's happened, has it?'

'Nothing's happened. You don't need to worry. It won't happen again. I just love this, coming home to you. I'll never tire of this. I smile to myself every time I walk through that door.'

'I don't think it will happen again, but I'm allowed to worry about you. That's my job. Sod the washing up,' Christopher said as he turned around and held her tight. 'I smile too. When I hear your key in the door. I just you want you here with me. We are made for each other. If only I'd found you sooner…'

'We could have loved each other longer,' Catherine whispered.

Catherine didn't recognise the phone number when her phone rang later. She held it up to Christopher and shrugged.

'Answer it and find out,' he said before turning his attention back to the match on TV. Brighton v West Ham was now a big game in their house as bragging rights could go on for days depending on whose team were victorious.

'Hello, Catherine speaking.'

'Hello, my name is Mr Edward Fry. I'm a solicitor at Fry & Bray. I represent Mrs Patricia Hart.'

Catherine stood up just as Jared Bowen scored a penalty to put West Ham one nil up. Christopher pointed to the television and waved to get her attention. She ignored him and walked to the window.

'What does she want from me? Is she suing me? Has she run out of money?' Catherine asked.

'I'm terribly sorry. There is no nice way of saying this. Patricia has passed away.'

'She's dead?'

'She was found dead yesterday, but it would appear she had been dead for some time before anyone realised. I'm very sorry.'

'She's dead.'

'I'm sorry. She appeared to live her life alone, so no one was with her. No one has been with her for some time. Her body is currently at Leatherhead Crematorium. They had no one to contact initially.'

'Was it the drinking?'

'The official result of the autopsy is a massive heart attack, but there was also a considerable amount of alcohol in her system, enough to do serious damage.'

Catherine remained silent as she watched out of the window as children played across the road.

'I rang you as soon as I found your contact details. Miss Hart, the first question I have is, would you like to see her at the chapel before the cremation?'

Catherine turned to Christopher. By now he was standing behind her and mouthing, 'Who is it? What's going on?'

'Did you say your name was Mr Fry?' Catherine asked.

'Yes, Edward Fry.'

'Mr Fry, I didn't want to see her in life. I don't need to see her in death.'

'Okay, I er, I understand. Then my next question is, please could you come to my office to discuss your mother's last will and testament?'

'I'm not sure that's necessary. It's probably all going to a cat's home.'

'I'd rather discuss this in person as you're the sole beneficiary.'

Catherine sat down.

'Miss Hart, are you still there?'

'I'm here.'

'Would you like to visit me tomorrow? If you have a pen and paper, I'll give you my address.'

Catherine scribbled in the air with her hand, the universal language for get me a pen and paper.

'It's 211 High Street, Dorking—'

'I know roughly where that is,' Catherine interrupted.

'To the left of the pub on the high street, The Yeoman. Is 10 a.m. good for you?'

'Thank you, Mr Fry. I'll see you tomorrow.'

The next morning, they made their way to Dorking. The silence only broken when Christopher reminded Catherine that Brighton had won 2-1 in the end. His attempt to improve her mood worked briefly. And he hadn't stopped going on about needing breakfast after being rushed out of the door, Catherine hated being late. Christopher saw a sign for Surrey Hills Café on the A24.

'We are really early. Please can pull in? Pretty please, I'm starving,' Christopher begged.

'Yeah, go on then.'

They entered the village of Beare Green. Christopher wasn't in the door before he decided he was having the works, a full English breakfast. 'That smells bloody good.'

Catherine stuck to just a cup of coffee, her stomach in knots as she pondered the meeting they were about to have.

'It's going to be okay. Whatever happens, I'm here.'

'I know,' Catherine replied. 'What if she's having one final dig at me. Left me something that will hurt me, something about Dad.'

'She can't hurt you anymore, not if you don't let her. We go in, we listen to what Mr Fry says, and we leave.'

Catherine stirred her coffee for the third time and checked her watch.

Once at the meeting, they exchanged pleasantries before Mr Fry pushed his glasses slightly higher up his nose as he organised his paperwork.

'Right, here we go. There's a lot to go through here, but for now I'll just read out the main points. The house was originally left too Mrs Patricia Hart, but it was stipulated that the house would be then passed on to Miss Catherine Hart in the event of Patricia Hart's death. The current market value of this property, in its current state…an estimated one point two million pounds.'

Christopher was open-mouthed as he shifted his gaze towards Catherine. She didn't look back at him as he squeezed her hand. 'The house was paid off. It's all yours, Jesus,' Christopher said.

'She's leaving me the house?' Catherine said in disbelief.

'Yes. Well, technically, she had no choice. It was in your father's will. Next, there are several pensions that your dad took out, and a health insurance that paid out in the event of his untimely death. Again, these were left to Patricia, and in the event of her death, they move on to you.' He pointed his pen at Catherine.

'The amount left to you from the insurances, after fees and various deductions, is just over four hundred and twenty-five thousand pounds.'

'Bloody hell,' Christopher let out.

'Christopher, don't,' Catherine said.

Catherine could see Mr Fry was grinning, but he didn't look up from his papers as he continued. 'Oh, I get all kind of reactions in here. Bloody hell is wonderfully tame. This is the side of my job I enjoy. More often than not, I have bad news for people, but when it's like this, I'm happy. And Catherine' – he put down his pen, took off his glasses, and pointed at her with his glasses in hand – 'This is from your dad, you deserve this.'

Catherine felt tears forming when Christopher spoke. 'She does, she really does.' He leant over and kissed her cheek.

'We're not quite done yet,' Mr Fry said.

'What else can there be?' Catherine asked.

'Shit, there's more?' Christopher asked.

'Mrs Patricia Hart was left around nine hundred thousand pounds when your father died. I understand you were left the same for when you reached your eighteenth birthday?'

'That's correct,' Catherine replied.

'Your mum, she was a woman of simple means. Other than minimal living costs and the usual bills, she didn't need much else. Between what she spent, interest earned, and minus the taxman's take, there is seven hundred and two thousand pounds left. She's left that to you.' Again, he pointed at Catherine.

'But, why? She must have forgotten to change any will my dad set up.'

'To the contrary. Patricia contacted me a few months before she died and wanted to confirm it was all going to you. I sent her the papers, she signed and returned them within a day. It is my opinion that she knew she was dying when she contacted me. She was getting things in order, people do that.'

Catherine put her head in her hands. 'I don't understand. She hated me so much.'

Christopher rubbed her back.

'Why? Why hate me and then do this?' Catherine said before shaking her head as she wiped her eyes.

'I have been doing this job for thirty something years. I believe that before people die, they do one of two things, they either want to go out with hate and spite by giving their money to anyone but the expected recipient, or they leave us making amends. I believe this was Patricia's way of making amends. That's just my opinion,' Mr Fry said.

Catherine sat up straight, composed herself, and asked if she could use the tissues on the table. He handed them to her, and she wiped the tears from her face. 'Thank you.'

'The house will need clearing out. I have a key here. I can recommend a good cleaning company once you've emptied it, Domestic Divas. They clean our offices and my home, very professional.'

'That would be great.'

'Is there a total amount that all this comes to? I can't keep track of these numbers,' Christopher asked.

'Cash of around £1,127,000.00 is guaranteed, plus the family home is worth £1.2 million, so providing the house sells for what we estimate, around £2.3 million pounds is the total estate left too Catherine. Some taxes to come off that, the government always has their hand out, but still, it's considerable sum.'

'I'd have to do a lot of hours in the care home to earn that,' Catherine joked through her tears.

'You could buy your own bloody care home. Blimey, my girlfriend's a millionaire,' Christopher said.

'Stop it, you.'

'I can't believe how cool you are about this. You can do what you want now, retire if you wanted to. You're sitting there like this a few pence. This is life changing,' Christopher said.

'It's just money. I'd rather have my dad and Hayley for another ten minutes than all this money.'

'I know you would. Come here, beautiful,' Christopher said as he held her close.

She moved into Christopher, comforted by his words. Beautiful was how Catherine's dad referred to her.

'The funeral is next Friday. It's all arranged. Mrs Hart did that. Are you likely to attend? There's a piece going in the local newspaper for anyone that would like to attend. I will be going out of respect to your father more than anything, he was a good man.'

Catherine looked at Christopher. 'It wouldn't feel right. I don't think I can.' She turned to Mr Fry. 'Can I decide on the day?'

'Of course,' he replied.

'Thank you for everything Mr Fry. We better go now. I think I need a drink or two.'

'My pleasure. Before you go, I have a letter for you. It's from Mrs Hart. I have no idea what is in it. It's addressed to you only.'

Catherine reached across and took the letter. 'Do I read it now?'

'You don't have to. It's yours to decide,' Mr Fry said.

Catherine put it in her bag. 'I'll read it later. Let's not spoil the moment.'

'There's this as well. Your mum sent it on to me with the paperwork.' Mr Fry handed over a small memory stick. He couldn't look Catherine in the eye as he handed it to her.

'What is it? What's on it?'

'Catherine, it's your father. He recorded a series of messages for you before he died.'

Catherine felt Christopher put his arm around her. She felt weak. 'Now, why am I only receiving this now? He's been gone nearly fifteen years. Why now?'

Mr Fry looked into Catherine's eyes. 'Either she forgot or she held it back from you. Maybe your dad intended you to have it as soon as you were an adult. I'm so sorry. I wish I knew she had it. I would have passed it on if I could.'

Catherine bit down on her lip. 'She's done a lot wrong to me…but this is right up there.'

'C'mon, beautiful, let's go.' Christopher took her hand. Catherine stood and prepared herself.

As they went to leave the office, Catherine turned to face Mr Fry. 'I do have one more question.'

'Of course, Miss Hart,' Mr Fry replied.

'You knew my father. And I've heard things. Was he a good man?'

'Your dad turned to the quiet life some time ago, we lost touch in his later years, but I knew him well for a while, mainly from a business perspective. Your dad was brought up in a tough area of London. He had it hard. But he was a fighter. He wasn't handed anything by anyone, so he took it instead. To make his real money, he lent it to people. He would charge interest over the period of the loan, like a bank. But if people didn't pay as they'd promised, he would take it back in his own way…not like a bank.' Mr Fry shrugged.

'A loan shark,' Christopher said.

'I wouldn't call Eddie Hart a loan shark. And you certainly wouldn't have called him that to his face. He was a businessman, a good one, in my opinion. He was fair, but if they took his kindness for weakness, he wasn't fair anymore. That was their own fault.'

Silence filled the room, Catherine wanted to know more.

Mr Fry continued, 'He also bought other people's debts.'

'Other people's debts? How did that work?' Catherine asked.

'Simple, really. Say, Christopher owed me ten thousand pounds, and he didn't pay me what was owed, and I thought I wasn't going to get any of it back. I could go to your dad for help. Your dad would give me five thousand pounds there and then, which was a lot better than the nothing Christopher was going to give me. Then, the full ten thousand would be recovered by your dad and his friends, that ten thousand was all his, one hundred percent profit.'

'But what if I didn't pay him the ten thousand?' Christopher asked.

Mr Fry chuckled before staring intently at Christopher, 'You paid, everybody paid Eddie Hart. I used his services several times myself,' Mr Fry said.

Christopher's expression was that of a schoolboy who had just been told off.

'I remember sitting outside these different places as a kid, houses, offices, and pubs. That kind of thing. He'd give me sweets and a fizzy drink and ask me to stay where I was. He would then come back to the car several minutes later with an envelope in hand. He would take out one of the notes and give it to me, a five, a ten, and sometimes even a twenty-pound note. I never spent them. I didn't need anything when I had dad. I had all I needed.'

'He was a decent, fair man. Don't let anyone say any different,' Mr Fry said.

Catherine walked over to Mr Fry. 'Thank you. I know my dad would appreciate you being kind to me today.'

'Enjoy your life, Catherine. You're young and can choose what you do next. You have options. Be happy, that's what he would have wanted.'

Catherine hugged him before leaving with Christopher.

"We have two lives, the second begins when we realise we only have one."

Confucius

CHAPTER 30

Silence among so many people could only be possible when given out of respect, a minute silence at a football game, at church on a Sunday morning, and at a funeral. Patricia Hart's funeral was due to start at 10 a.m. Christopher kept his speed at 5 MPH as he drove into the crematorium grounds. Catherine could see around twenty people dressed in black standing near the entrance, smoke hovered above them as she watched them in conversation.

'They must be from the last funeral,' she said as Christopher found the right parking space. She touched her stomach and breathed deeply.

'You okay?' Christopher asked.

'I can't do this.' Catherine dabbed at her eyes. 'Why am I crying? I shouldn't be.'

Christopher started stroking her hair. ‘She was your mum in one way or another, she was a huge part of your life. There must have been good times.’

Catherine closed her eyes and pictured Patricia. They were at a beach. Her dad was messing about in the sea, and Patricia was smiling.

‘I don’t know, she was so horrible but maybe I choose to block any happiness when it comes to her.’

‘She was unwell when she did those things.’ Christopher said.

Exiting the car, Catherine pulled her skirt below her knee and brushed her top down before checking her reflection in the car window. She gave Christopher a nod when she was ready.

As they approached the entrance, the mourners were still there, checking her phone she saw it was 9.50 a.m., they’d have to move soon. She headed towards them and smiled politely.

‘You must be Catherine?’ The man asking was in his fifties, tanned and tall with the shoulders of a rugby player. His jet black her was gelled back and the scar on his cheek was enough to make you realise he wasn’t the kind of guy who worked a normal nine to five.

‘Yes, I’m Catherine. Did you know Patricia?’

‘I knew your dad, Eddie. I worked for him. Most of us here did at one time or another,’ he said as he pointed to the crowd he was with.

Catherine scanned the group. They were all of a similar build and appearance.

'I'm Lenny. Sorry for your loss, Catherine. Losing a mother is something we all have to face at some stage in our lives, but nothing prepares you,' he said.

Catherine smiled and said *thank you*, she didn't want to correct Lenny and tell him she was only here as she hoped to gain some closure from the hell Patricia put her through.

'Looks like we're going in soon. I'll maybe catch you after,' Lenny said as they watched the hearse pull up.

Catherine felt Christopher touch her hand and she gripped his tightly.

'Wouldn't want to mess with him, or any of this lot,' Christopher whispered.

The service went quick, no one made a speech other than the vicar who did a great job of paying respect to Patricia with the limited information he would have had on her. Patricia had chosen two songs, 'I Will Always Love You' by Dolly Parton and 'Alone' by Heart. Catherine clenched her fists when the vicar dedicated both songs to Patricia's Eddie. Once the curtain wrapped around the coffin and the exit doors were opened, Catherine turned to Christopher and said, 'Let's go, I've seen enough.'

Catherine walked out past the rows of headstones. She sped up as a light drizzle was falling and neither of them had bought their coats with them. Catherine heard her name being called and as she turned, she watched Lenny walk towards her.

'Look, I'm sorry I've not been in touch with you directly. I wanted to. I did try for some time when you were young, but ya mum, she wasn't a well lady by then. She wanted no piece of me, or anyone linked with ya dad. We couldn't get anywhere near you.'

Rain was getting heavier as Catherine replied, 'You didn't need to. It's fine. She wasn't a nice person. I'm sure you tried your best.'

'I did need to. I promised ya dad I would. But she made it impossible.'

'It's okay, honest. I understand,' Catherine replied.

'She wasn't always like that, ya know? She was fun and caring in the early days. That's why ya dad fell for her. And pretty, by God she was lovely. Everyone noticed her. But ya see, she liked a drink and dabbled in the other stuff, it messed her up. But Eddie still loved her. He wouldn't have it if someone spoke ill of her. And in the end, once he had enough money, he retired from our game and stayed at home with you and Patricia. He tried to get her help, but she wouldn't 'ave it.'

Catherine touched his arm and thanked him.

'Thanks for talking to us, Lenny,' Christopher said.

'If you ever need anything, anything, call me,' Lenny said as he handed Catherine a business card, *Steel Security Services*.

'That's my company. The mobile number on there is mine. I always hoped I could 'ave been some sort of uncle to you. When you were a toddler, I used to love seeing you and ya dad. He used to bring you out and show you off up until you were about four or five. But then she got ill, and it changed. When your dad, poor Eddie died, everything changed. In the early days after Eddie was gone, I would visit every week, even when she told me not to. I would check in on you. Make sure you had what you needed, but Patricia would never let me near you. Wouldn't take my money or gifts. She called the police on me for harassing her. All I wanted was to make sure you were okay. I had no choice but to walk away. I'm sorry, Catherine.' Lenny couldn't look her in the eye.

Catherine stepped forward and kissed Lenny on his stubbled cheek. 'Thank you.'

Lenny reached out to Christopher, and they shook hands. 'You both take care and you look after this one,' Lenny said. Christopher promised he would.

They left Lenny and rushed back to the car, jumped into their seats and Christopher started the engine. He turned the heating to full before kindly pointing the air vents in Catherine's direction. 'Should dry you out soon, beautiful.'

The rain running down Catherine's face hid her tears. She was looking out of the window hoping Christopher wouldn't notice her red eyes. 'Things could have been so different. Should I hate her the way I do, the way I always did? If she was unwell…'

Christopher's hand touched Catherine's leg. 'What she did to you was disgusting and evil. Yes, you should feel like that. Whether she was mentally well or not, people should be held accountable for their actions. She put you through hell. You're the victim, not her.'

Catherine turned to face Christopher. 'I'm not a victim. Not anymore,'

'You look lovely today, Catherine. Your eyes look full of life, and the way you are sitting, you look more confident and—'

'My fake mum died,' Catherine smiled.

'Patricia died? I'm sorry,' Roisin replied.

'Don't be. Why do you think I look better than usual? I feel lighter, like a heavy weight I've had on my shoulders has finally been lifted.'

Roisin remained silent.

'They said heart attack, but she killed herself with alcohol in the end.'

Roisin offered a compassionate nod.

'But she did leave me a load of money. That was a surprise for me.' Catherine raised her eyebrows and laughed. 'Nothing like a big bag of money to make me feel even worse than I did.'

'What do you mean?' Roisin asked.

'I hated her so much, and I wanted to hate her forever, but she leaves me everything which messes with my head. I now start to think that maybe she did love me in her own way. In death, she still gets to mess with my head.'

'I think she did love you, like you say, in her own way.'

'Then why do what she did to me?' Catherine's voice was raised.

'Only she knows why.'

'Still, me being messed up over her, it's what she would have wanted. But I'm determined to move on. I'm ready to. I can no longer think about her. My life is going in the right direction. She's gone, and she left me her money. I can do good with that. And besides, it was my dad's money, not hers. He gave it to me. The bit that hurts is…the letter she left.'

'What did it say?'

'I don't know,' Catherine said as she reached into her bag and held the letter up.

'Are you going to read it?' Roisin asked.

'I wasn't going to, it will probably just tell me I was responsible for my dad's cancer, or that I'm ugly and will never amount to anything.'

'Or it might say she was sorry for what she did,' Roisin said.

Catherine put the envelope on Roisin's desk. 'That would be worse. That's what I'm afraid of.'

Roisin put her hand on the letter. 'I'm not going to tell you what to do with this. It's not up to me, but if you want my opinion, I think you should open it. Whatever is in there will help with you moving forward. How can you move on if you're always wondering what it says?'

'Can you open it?' Catherine asked.

Roisin sat back. 'I'm not sure I should. This is your letter.'

'Please, I want you to. I feel safe here. Whatever it says I feel confident I'll be okay if I do this with you.'

Roisin reached for her letter opener.

'You use a knife to open letters?' Catherine asked.

'It's just a letter opener, blunt on the end, a bit old-fashioned, but I like it.' Roisin gently took the letter out.

Catherine reached for the envelope and smelt inside. 'Smells of her.'

Catherine watched anxiously as Roisin stared at the paper. 'Probably for the best you read it yourself first, then break it to me,' Catherine said.

She watched Roisin's face for any tells, nothing changed at first, just Roisin's emerald-green eyes shifting slowly side to side, and then her eyes looked past the letter direct into Catherine's.

'What, what is it? That bloody woman. What's she said.'

Roisin held the letter in her lap and exhaled. 'This is going to be a lot to take in, I'll break it down slowly.'

Catherine stood and rolled her head, first to the left, there was a click, then to right, another click, it didn't help ease the built-up tension in her neck. She did it this one more time finding the extra crack she was looking for. 'Now I'm ready.'

'She acknowledges what she put you through,' Roisin said.

'That's good of her.'

'She's sorry. She wishes she could have been the mother you deserved.'

Catherine stopped pacing the room and stood by the window. 'Can I open this please, it's so warm in here.'

'Of course you can, Catherine.'

Roisin continued, 'She wished your dad was still with us and says that if he was alive, life would have been good for you both. She calls him the glue. When he was around everything stayed together, without him your lives fell apart, especially hers. And that she regrets blaming you for that.'

Catherine poked her head out of the window thinking Roisin had finished reading. 'That's quite a bit to take in. I'm okay with that. It's better than I thought.'

'Catherine, there is more. You may want to sit down for the last paragraph.'

Catherine stood up straight, closed the window, and sat back down.

'Patricia has written in here who your real mum is' – Roisin lifted the letter – 'she's included where your mum lives.

Wide eyed, Catherine put her hands over her mouth. 'No.'

'I think you should read it.'

'I can't, please read it to me.' Catherine rocked back and forth in her chair.

Roisin read the final paragraph slowly and occasionally looking up for Catherine's reaction. 'Your mum's name is Lynda. She's married and her surname is Smail. She lives in Looe, Cornwall. I don't know her address but she won't be hard to find. Give her a chance to explain what happened when you were born. It wasn't her fault, it was your father's, and mine. She was young and had no choice but to do as your dad asked. No one on this planet would have got you from your dad. You were his everything from the minute he knew you were coming into the world. I'm sorry I wasn't able to love you. I'm sorry for everything. I was jealous that your dad loved you in a way he could never love me, and it hurt, it still does. But that wasn't your fault, I see that now. I wasn't always like the person you knew. There was a time when I was a good person. What I did to you was unforgiveable. I'll pay for my sins in the next life, I accept that. Find your mum. Find the love you are searching for. Patricia.

Catherine sat with her head in her hands, no screaming, no words at all. She felt Roisin's hand on her shoulder.

Catherine sat in a daze. The session earlier today with Roisin had taken it's toll. Patricia dying felt like the right time to move on, start a life with Christopher. Find her happiness. But now there was a curveball, she knew where her mum lived. She wanted a drink, hell, she needed one, but she dismissed the thought knowing it would lead to drunken misery. Instead, Catherine removed the business card from her bag and called the number.

'Is this Lenny? Lenny Steel. We met at my mum's, I mean Patricia's funeral. It's Catherine here.'

Lenny replied in his thick east end London accent, 'Hello luv, everything okay? You need sumink?'

'I'm fine, Lenny. I just wanted to talk about Patricia, and er…she's left me a note confirming she's not my real mum, that and some other stuff you might be able to help me with.'

Lenny was silent.

'She was a nasty woman at times, we all know that, so the words in this letter could be made up just to upset me. And you being a close friend of my dad, you might know what happened back then?

'Catherine, I'm sorry I didn't say more at the funeral. I didn't know whether to tell everything or not. I couldn't just come out with it all.'

'It's okay, I promise. I just want to know a bit more about my dad, and my mum, my real mum.'

'Ya dad was a good man, and all the time Patricia was normal it was all a bed of roses. But when she found out she couldn't have kids it drove a wedge between them. She turned bitter and nasty, turned to booze and drugs. Her mental health went downhill fast. She became a proper nutter, especially to ya dad. He went through hell trying to help her, doctors, therapists, you name it, he tried it. She told him that if he wanted a kid that badly, he'd have to find someone else. Well, by then he'd had enough, and once your dad went, he went. Her constant cries of find someone else came to bite her on the backside, coz that's exactly what he did. He'd had enough of her ways and his heart went elsewhere. Lynda worked in one of the bars, lovely girl, a bit younger than ya dad but she was old for her years. She was good for him. He was so happy when he was out with her. He'd bring her to the clubs and all of us got on with her. She was fun. Just what ya dad needed at the time. But despite loving Lynda, he wouldn't leave Patricia. He had a thing about his marriage, there was no way he would leave. His memory of the wife she was kept him from leaving.'

'So, my dad was in love with Lynda?' Catherine asked.

'Yeah, you were one hundred per cent conceived in love. But Lynda was only seventeen, and her parents weren't having any of it. They told her she was getting rid of the baby, and that was that. Ya dad would never let that happen. He went nuts. Then her parents turned up at your dad's house and told Patricia about Lynda and the baby, it all went off. Patricia went crazy. The whole thing was a nightmare. In the end, ya dad promised Patricia a fresh start. He wasn't allowed to see Lynda, her parents wouldn't allow it. So, he offered Lynda's parents a tidy sum of money to sign the rights away to the baby, you. Your dad wanted to bring you up in a family. No way on earth would he let Lynda's parents make her have an abortion. He convinced Patricia it would be good for them, that it would help her with her mental health, a child of their own. Poor Lynda didn't get a say, her family thought they were doing what was best for her, they knew what your dad did for a living. They were scared. They took the money and moved away. I know in the first few years, Lynda tried to see you, she tried everything. But Patricia made sure that didn't happen. And by then your dad was only interested in protecting you. He was fiercely protective. When it came to you, he would do anything, and he did. Lynda never stood a chance.

Catherine remained speechless.

'I'm sorry, Catherine. Truly I am. You want me to look into where Lynda is? It wouldn't be a problem. I'll get Baz on it. He'll have her address tomorrow.'

'No, Lenny, thank you though. I'll think about it, I think for now I'll leave it.'

'You know where I am. Anything, just call me,' Lenny said.

'Thanks again, Lenny, my dad would be happy knowing you're there for me.'

'Catherine, your dad would want you happy, start a life with your young man. Be happy. You deserve it.'

"The truth may be out there, but the lies are inside your head."

Terry Pratchett

CHAPTER 31

The memory stick was between her thumb and forefinger, she was about to insert it into her laptop, but stopped. How could something so small be the cause of such apprehension? Catherine knew she was about to see her dad but what would he look like? Would it be when he was starting to be unfairly stripped of his good looks and muscular physique, or worse still, when he was gaunt in the hospice barely eating and waiting for the day that was his last.

Catherine inserted the card and waited. Once the file was ready, she double clicked. A few seconds past and there he was, her handsome father. He wasn't in a hospice or hospital; he was as Catherine preferred to remember him, tanned, strong and hair perfectly gelled. The one thing missing was his smile, instead he was staring intently before taking in a huge breath before speaking.

Hello, beautiful, the fact you're watching this means you're eighteen and your mum has passed it on to you. I've decided to make a few of these videos. Hope you don't get too bored. And don't get upset. I hope by now you've found happiness and you've learnt to live without me. I don't want you ruining your life getting all upset and whatnot. Always remember, all my greatest memories were with and because of you. We never truly have to say goodbye, just close your eyes and see me. There I am. I'm there when you need me.

So, you're eighteen. That must mean you have signed professional papers for West Ham by now, maybe even had an England cap or two?

Catherine sighed, 'If only, Dad.'

I hope your mum is supporting your dreams. I've asked her to, and she's promising she will do her best. If it's not football, then I've asked her to help you in any career path you show an interest in, you will have a large amount of money coming now and you can use that for your education, or bribing someone to give you what you need, whatever works, beautiful. Eddie winked at his girl.

Catherine rubbed her eyes, could feel the tears forming, unstoppable despite her dad telling her to not get upset, 'Dad, I just wish you stayed, if you were here…'

Lymph nodes, I didn't even know what they were until yesterday…but according to Dr Eyebrows, that's where my cancer is. He doesn't shave or pluck that bit in the middle. It's one long eyebrow, like a giant slug, or an angry black caterpillar.

Catherine laughed through her tears.

Dr Happy said if I'd gone to them sooner, they may have been able to catch it before it went near the Lymph things, Nodes, whatever. But once it's in there, it works its cunning little way through all the wires in my body. When I think about the cancer eating away at me. I imagine the Death Eaters in Harry Potter, all black and wavy making scary noises whilst floating through my body. Nice, eh? And this is why I don't believe in God. You used to ask me about God, and for years I would lie. I'd go along with what your school told you. But you're clever, you have your own mind.

He can't be real. The stuff I've seen in my lifetime, the bad I've done, there just can't be a god. I guess what I'm trying to do here is tell you I'm not perfect, Catherine. For years I could be the bad guy, the black sheep of the family, but who do people turn to when they are in trouble, or scared? Me, and people like me. When someone dies, it's easy to put them on a pedestal. It's easy to only remember the good. I'm not all good, I never have been. But I wanted you to be. I tried, I tried to keep you blind to the bad side of life, blind to the bad in me and those around me. I probably shouldn't have. I regret that now. I need you to be tough. Your mum tries her best, but she has her own fight. Her mental health isn't great. It's not her fault. You will have to be patient with her. By now I would predict you're the one in charge, you're my girl, you're a Hart, Eddie Hart's daughter, you'll follow no one, you'll lead. I'm confident the eighteen-year-old you IS strong, independent, and brave. The world is yours.

Eddie grimaced, trying to hide the physical pain he was in as he leaned forward to turn off the recording.

'Dad, don't go,' she begged.

I'm going now, I'll report back soon. I know I've waffled on. I'll get better at these. I love you, Catherine Hart. You were my one good thing, my Catherine. And remember this, always try to see yourself through my eyes. To me you're perfect, you are perfect, don't let anybody tell you any different.

The recording ended. Catherine touched the screen.

'Dad, I miss…I just want one more hug.' She closed the laptop down, sat back in her chair, and pulled her knees in to her chest.

Lynda Smail. Catherine had now read the name and the letter over a hundred times. Christopher offered to start looking for her mum's address, but Catherine asked him not to. She was happy that she knew her mum's name, but was scared of making contact, scared of rejection. What if her mum had her own family and didn't want it disrupted? What if she was a drunk, or into drugs? She could be anything. Christopher reminded her that Lynda could also be a lovely person who would hold her arms out wide to her. She might become a big part of Catherine's future. It could be Catherine's chance to have a real family.

Christopher bought Catherine another cup of tea to the bedroom and removed the last one that was untouched. She lay there with the letter in her hand; the curtains drawn and the television playing to itself in the background. Christopher sat at the end of the bed.

'I know you might be angry with me…but I'm prepared to take the risk. I'm going to leave this at the end of the bed. When you're ready, you can read it.'

'What is it?' Catherine asked.

'Your mum's address.'

Christopher went to leave the bedroom. 'How did you find it?' Catherine asked.

'Facebook. There aren't that many Lynda Smails in Looe. There's a link to the business she owns with her husband. Their address is there and there's a phone number.'

'That could be anyone, Christopher. What if it's not her?'

Christopher walked around the bed and knelt in front of Catherine. He kissed her forehead. 'Catherine, there are pictures of her. She's beautiful, like her daughter. Trust me…she's your mum.'

The cleaners were due at Catherine's family home in two days; it didn't give her much time to get it emptied. Two giant skips had been placed out the front ready for Catherine and Christopher to fill. They started upstairs.

Catherine opened the windows to help clear the dust that circled in the light. The musky smell that lingered throughout slowly lessened. From the bedroom window, Catherine started throwing Patricia's clothes straight into the skip. Every item a memory, some good, but most were bad. Bedding, toiletries, used cups, and unused medication followed her clothing. Her dad's clothes had been gone for years. Patricia cruelly took them to a charity shop straight after Eddie died without a thought for Catherine.

Catherine finally found what she was looking for, a box full of old photos.

'I'll take these out to the car. Everything else can go,' Catherine said.

'I'll order a third skip. We're going to need it,' Christopher said.

Catherine came back into the house and stood where they'd found Patricia. The carpet was stained with a large red and yellow mark. Catherine imagined Patricia dying alone. Christopher came up behind her and kissed her neck. 'I know it's difficult,' he said.

'Christopher, I want to hate her, but I can't. For years, I wanted to kill her, but I couldn't. She wasn't right mentally. I hope Patricia didn't suffer at the end. I think she suffered enough in life. She doesn't need to anymore. Wherever she is now, I hope she's out of pain.'

By the end of the second day, Catherine had cleared everything out and organised a number of local tradesmen to help restore the house. Dorking Window Company were replacing every window. JS Plastering Services for any building work, and South-East Tree Surgeons for the grounds surrounding the house. She wanted it to be loved again, maybe not by her – she needed to move on – but by another family.

Catherine had her mum's contact details safely placed in her jean pocket. She still chose not to make contact, for now.

'Right, get your coat. We're going out. It's a surprise,' Christopher announced.

Catherine held her coffee mug in both hands, sadness in her eyes. 'Not today, Chris. Can we just *be*?'

'Normally, I would say yes, but I think I know what you need.'

Before Catherine could answer, he continued, 'I'm that confident it will help you. I've had this idea for some time, but I've been saving it for the right time. That time is now. And if when we get there you still feel the same, we'll come home. It's thirty minutes away. You don't even need to get dressed up, stay in your trackies.'

Begrudgingly Catherine did as she was asked, they headed down the M23 only stopping briefly at the services where Christopher picked up snacks and drinks. Catherine spent the journey looking out into the distance, but she was very much within her own thoughts as they approached Gatwick Airport.

Once parked in the multi-storey, she turned to Christopher. 'The airport. Are we picking someone up? You said not to get dressed up, I look a state.'

'Nope, trust me. C'mon, let's go.'

Christopher held her hand tight, giving several reassuring squeezes as they navigated through the swarms of holiday makers.

'There it is,' he said.

Confused, Catherine gave in to trusting her boyfriend.

'Right, we can stand here,' Christopher said.

Taxi drivers held up names in bold letters, families looked on desperately for the doors to re-open at arrivals.

'Chris, what are we doing here?'

'Wait for it, it's coming.'

'What is?'

The arrivals doors opened and a dozen people wheeling suitcases came through.

'Watch, watch their faces.'

Catherine looked at each individual until one face took her interest, a young lady looking tired, until it happened. The lady's face lit up. She left her suitcase where it was and ran forward.

Catherine turned her attention to where she was running. A man was standing there, arms wide open. They embraced and held each other tight not wanting to let go.

'Good choice,' Christopher said. 'I was watching the old couple, thought that was going to be lovely, but sadly no one's here to meet them. Yours was perfect.'

She pulled Christopher in close. 'Thank you.'

'You wait until you see a child alone greeting a parent. Crushes you inside. It's beautiful.' He opened out the bag of snacks. 'Right, what would you like? We're here for a while.'

It was Friday, Catherine didn't have to work until Sunday. Christopher had finished early and asked what would cheer her up if she could do anything tonight?

'Honestly, I'd like to get absolutely smashed, to the point where I forget, just for a few hours,' Catherine said as she gave Christopher a beaming smile.

'Your wish is my command.' He looked at his watch. 'It's four now. We could have a couple of glasses here while we get ready, and then around six we hit the town. Just you, me, and copious amounts of alcohol.' He started to do a little jig.

'You're a fool, Christopher Mason.' She got to her feet and gave him a kiss. 'I'll pour us a drink.'

'Yes, it's on.' He was now dancing behind her as she walked to the kitchen.

Catherine didn't turn around when she spoke. 'Enough of the dancing.'

Christopher stopped. 'Done. I'll be in the shower.'

As Catherine approached the bathroom, she could hear him singing, 'Happy Hour' by The Housemartins. She found him with his eyes closed, singing into a shampoo bottle. She wiped the glass shower door and put her head against it. Once Christopher opened his eyes, he jumped, causing Catherine to laugh hysterically. He opened the door and pulled her in fully clothed.

'Christopher, no! You dickhead,' she shouted as the water ran into her mouth. 'Not my hair. You know I hate that. I'll have to wash it again before we go out.'

'Too bad you're in now,' he said as he started kissing her. Catherine pulled back slightly, and they stared intently into each other's eyes.

'Isn't this supposed to happen at the end of the night?'

He kissed her again. 'There are no rules, we can do it now…and later, whenever we like, it costs nothing, we both enjoy it, we should do it as many times as possible until we're too old to perform such things.' She laughed as he started lifting off her top, Catherine undid her jeans and threw them on to the bathroom floor. He asked Catherine to turn her back to him, unclipping her bra. He lifted it past her arms and dropped it. Cupping her breasts, he kissed her neck as she tilted her head inviting him to keep going.

It was 7 p.m. before they made their way to the bar at the end of Brighton Pier. Horatio's Bar was Catherine's favourite, as they had karaoke. She wasn't one for getting up and singing, but she loved watching others do it.

'So much for leaving at six, dirty boy,' Catherine joked as they walked into the bar.

'Wasn't my fault you came to me in the shower, I was happy just singing.'

Catherine blushed and changed the subject as they approached the bar. 'What are we drinking?'

Christopher scanned the drinks behind the bar, then the drinks on tap before choosing his usual, a pint of Peroni. Catherine went for a double Jack Daniels and Coke with only one ice cube.

'A double, eh? Looks like I'll get lucky again later,' Christopher said.

They carried on drinking until gone midnight. Staggering along the pier arm in arm, Catherine suggested they sit on the beach, promised it would be romantic. Christopher replied, saying he was starving and asked if they could be romantic after a kebab.

The sea was calm, the moon full and beautiful. It lit up the sea's surface as the occasional small wave turned to nothing amongst the stones.

'I could sit here forever,' Catherine said as she reached for Christopher's hand.

'Me too. I do love you, Catherine. I love you so much. I know I've said this before and it's sounds naff and cheesy, but it's in these moments I wish I found you sooner. Hitting you with my car outside David's house was the single best thing I've ever done,' Christopher was slurring his words.

'I'm glad you hit me…' Catherine let go of his hand and glared at him. 'Who's David?' she asked.

Christopher's head wobbled. He blinked twice in an attempt to clear his vision. 'You know, David, that's where you were that night,' he said in an unclear, drunk tone.

Catherine's words were very clear and sober. 'David! I've never told you his name, or any of their names. I've told you some of the details, but I've never mentioned any of them by name, not Bryce, not Ian, a Tristan or a bloody David.'

'You must have. How else would I know? You talk in your sleep at times, it might have been that?' he said as he started to tickle her. 'C'mon, you. Why so serious?'

Catherine pushed him off. 'Stop it, Christopher.'

'I definitely remember a David being said. Come on. We're on a date night. A drunk date night. Don't spoil it.' Christopher laid back on to the pebbles and started singing 'The Whole of The Moon' by The Waterboys.

Catherine closed her eyes, searching her memories. When did she ever say their names? Maybe she did do it in her sleep or let them out when drunk one night. She could only remember discussing them with Hayley. She concluded the drinking had her paranoid. She looked across at Christopher. 'That's enough, you drunk fool. Your singing is terrible. Come on, let's get home.'

"Trust takes years to build, seconds to break, and forever to repair."

CHAPTER 32

'My God, who or what sat on my head last night? It's killing me, and my mouth is so dry.' Christopher poked out his tongue. 'I need water. I don't care where from.'

She usually laughed at Christopher's jokes, but not this time. She hadn't slept all night. Her mind had been racing at a hundred miles an hour.

'You okay?' Christopher asked.

'I'm fine,' Catherine lied.

'How do you look so good the morning after? I look and feel like crap. The last thing I remember is leaving the karaoke bar. I have no idea how we got home. I haven't drunk like that in years.'

'We walked.'

'Bloody hell, I must have been drunk. I never walk home,' Christopher said.

'We couldn't get a cab because they wouldn't take you. They predicted you'd puke up.'

'Cheeky bastards, I never throw up. I can drink for England and not throw up.'

'Christopher, you threw up three times on the walk home.'

'Must have been the hog roast thing on the pier.' He gave a wink.

'Yeah, that'll be it,' Catherine said.

Throwing the covers off, Catherine sat up and drank some water she'd grabbed from the kitchen through the night.

'Do you remember what we spoke about last night?' Catherine asked.

'The last thing I remember was singing, I mean murdering, Beyonce's 'Halo' on the karaoke. Quite the performance, if I say so myself.'

'You were on your knees at one point, pretending to cry while doing an air grab.'

'It's an emotional song. The crowd loved it,' Christopher said.

'You even did a bloody mic drop when you finished. DJ was furious…and you've definitely sung that before. You weren't even looking at the screen. Word for word you were spot on.'

'I might have a bit of Beyonce on my playlist from time to time.'

'I'll make us a coffee. You lay there and piece together what you remember about last night.'

Christopher shook his head. 'I'd rather not. I know I'm a bit of a prick once I've gone too far, and anyway, what happens when you're that drunk doesn't count? That's the rule.'

'If only,' Catherine said as she left the bedroom.

Returning to the bedroom with two cups of coffee, she called out, 'I'll put yours on your side,' as he was in the shower. He didn't reply, so she put it on there, anyway. His phone got her attention, she'd never had any desire to check its contents, trust had been established early on and going through his phone would break that trust. But he'd never used the name David before when talking about where they first met when he hit her with his car. Catherine had to know how and why he knew.

It took her two attempts to get in. First, she tried his birthday, which didn't work, then she tried her own and smiled to herself when it was successful. Scrolling through his contacts under the letter D there were no David or Worboys. There was no Ian Whiting, Tristan Bridger, or Bryce Bellfield.

Her hands were shaking as she checked over her shoulder. She could hear the water running in the shower. She knew she had time. His photos were next. She started scrolling through the hundreds that were on there, they were all of Catherine and Christopher, the odd one of his mum, some at Brighton football stadium, and one of a seagull attacking a child eating chips on the beach, that made her she smile, she remembered they both laughed out loud when that happened, she couldn't believe

Christopher took out his phone to get a picture. Content, she closed the phone and set it back down.

'Everything okay?' Christopher said.

Catherine reached for her chest. 'Bloody hell, you'll give me a heart attack. Your coffee's here,' she said as she pointed.

'Thanks, babe. What do you want to do today?'

'Not a lot, got work tonight so I'm happy to hang out here, crappy film, cheap food, and chill out,' Catherine replied.

'Sounds good. You pick what we're having, I'll go get it. Pizza or Maccys?'

'With this hangover, Maccys all the way,' she said as she walked over and hugged him.

With Christopher out of the house picking up the food, Catherine opened her laptop and clicked on the second message from her dad.

Me again, the one with the dodgy lymph nodes.

Looking at the screen, she could already notice a decline in her dad's appearance. How long had it been between messages?

I love you, Catherine. I already miss you and I haven't gone yet. In fact, you're in the house right now and I'm out in my car recording this for future you. I feel like I'm in Terminator. I'm John Connor, sending messages to the future. Was it John who sent the messages, or his mum? Or was it the Terminator? I don't bloody know, whatever it is, that's me. It's been a couple of weeks since the last message. Dr Monobrow has me starting treatment, which is why I look like this. They're basically going to poison me, near kill me, and that's what will hopefully make me better. Science, eh? Marvellous. I spoke to Lenny today. I've got him on to a few things for when I go. Just in case your mum isn't feeling great, he'll be checking in on you from time to time. You may not remember him, but he was the big lump who used to spend time with your dad. Not so much these days, but he's a good man. He'll protect you.

'You tried, Dad, I know you tried,' Catherine said.

Time used to pass by so slowly, I spent years wishing it away, and now I'm running out of it, and there's nothing I can do. I've got money, but it means nothing. No amount of money can buy me time. Don't ever waste time darling Catherine, enjoy every minute. As soon as I come off of this thing I'm going to go indoors and cuddle you, tell you I love you. You'll go red and tell me to get off, but I hope you remember our cuddles, remember I told you I loved you.

'I remember, every time, I remember,' she said.

Now, boys, I want to talk to you about boys. They are all arseholes after one thing, they think with their thingys, nothing else, and if I was still about, I'd slap any of them that came near you.

Catherine laughed. 'You would as well.'

I'm kind of joking. They're not all bad, just most of them. Seriously, be careful. If you get married, sign a pre-nup, keep your money for you. If you fall out of love, even the nicest of people try to take what isn't theirs. Pre-nup, make a note, go on, right now, I'm watching you.'

'Pre-nup, okay, Dad.' She sniggered.

You may think you have a good man right now. Things can turn, and if they do, be careful.

She raised her eyebrows.

I'm back to Dr Happy Brows tomorrow. Who knows, if he gets it right, you may never see these messages. But if he can't save me, you will. Sadly, I guess you are watching it right now. Anyway, I'm coming indoors to give you that hug. Hopefully, it can transcend into the future, and you can feel me squeezing you right now. Signing off beautiful, I love you, Catherine Hart.

'I love you too, Dad.'

On her way to work she was blinded momentarily by the oncoming headlights. Catherine snapped out of her daydream and wondered how she had driven as far as she had. She couldn't shake the suspicion. Her dad always told her to trust her gut feeling. She never understood that as a young girl, but growing up it had always proved right. When making a tricky decision, she would go with her gut, not her head. She couldn't leave it alone once she'd arrived at work. Parked in the usual bay, outside the care home, she opened her car boot and grabbed the bag before running in through the fine rain. She clocked in, shook herself off, and sat in the staff office. Peering into the bag, she could see the phones. They all had evidence of what they did. She charged Worboys first and left it there while she started her shift.

It had always upset her when people would make derogatory comments about care homes, saying that they smelt of death and urine and how they didn't want to end up in one when they were old. She would become defensive and say how nice the people were, that most of the residents have fun. She would explain that the smell was a chemical released by humans called nonenal. and that there was nothing anyone could do about it. It would happen to us all one day.

She'd been in with several of the residents and had a good chat about their day and then returned to the office where she unplugged Worboys phone and plugged in Bridger's. Worboys photos were just as she remembered. Her heart raced when she went into his contacts. There was a Christopher, a different to number than she had for her Christopher, but still. Catherine's heart thumped through her chest and before she could stop herself, she typed the number in to the office landline phone and rang it. It rang continuously and didn't go to a voicemail. Frustrated and hot in the high temperature of the office, she hung up, turned on the fan, and exhaled with frustration.

'Cup of tea?'

Catherine turned to see Betty standing there.

'Hi, Betty, a cup of tea would be perfect right now,' Catherine replied.

'C'mon then, Bill and I have a cracking game of poker going in his room.'

'Hope you're not playing for money like last time. You know the rules,' Catherine said.

Betty gave a mock surprise look. 'Of course not, we are playing for medication. If he wins, he gets my donepezil, and if I win, I get his Metformin.'

Catherine smiled. The warm feeling inside was a welcome relief from her troubled mind. 'Betty, you'll be the death of me. I'm glad you're only joking.'

'Ah, but am I? Quick, Bill is on one today, he's proper miserable, I need to get back and wind him up. He loves it. Silly old sod.'

After overseeing their poker game, and twice stopping Betty from cheating, Catherine headed back to the office where she discovered there was nothing on Bridger's phone, after a quick charge she was now going through Whiting's. The same number was in there for a Christopher, she made a note of it. The photos were all disgustingly similar. Catherine was going through them all again, zooming in from all angles. Nothing stood out.

'Come on, Catherine, just leave it alone,' she said to herself softly.

Catherine shifted side to side in bed. She always found it hard to sleep after a night shift, especially if she had something on her mind. She got up and pulled the blackout blinds down. The silence in the room was deafening. With Christopher at work, there was no one else there to make any noise. Catherine decided to put on an audiobook. One of her favourite ways of getting some sleep was listening to a good mystery thriller. After her third cry of *fuck it* in ten minutes, she sat upright, paused Mark Billingham's *Rabbit Hole*, and reached for her phone. In the contacts, she found the number again. Pressing *call*, she prayed a Christopher would answer, and that it wouldn't be her Christopher. She listened through the deafening silence.

It was ringing. Her heart felt like it would jump out of her chest. She heard a buzzing noise, hung up, and dropped her phone onto the bed before stepping away. Her mind playing tricks. Don't ring again, better not to know. Just leave it.

But then she remembered Hayley on that morning in Richmond with blood on her legs, Hayley attempting to hang herself. Her dad's face, him telling her that bullies shouldn't get away with it, they should pay.

She picked it up, this small device that held her future at the press of a button. She pressed redial, this time holding the phone away from her ear.

The vibrating was coming from Christopher's wardrobe.

"Sometimes losing everything is the only way to begin."

T.K. Kiser

Chapter 33

As Catherine dropped the phone, the noise stopped. She jumped back to her phone and rang the number again. As she tracked the buzzing noise, Catherine pulled out boxes, some empty, some full of shoes, and underneath the boxes was a small metal tin, the buzzing was inside. She pulled on the lid, but it was locked, so she picked it up and placed it on the bed. The buzzing had stopped. Catherine shook the tin gently. From the weight of it, there was more than just a phone in there. Thoughts raced through her mind. Where would she live? Who would she love? Who would love her? It wasn't too late to ignore the phone. But living a life as a lie was not a life worth living for.

She went to the kitchen; she needed tools. Grabbing a hammer and large flat head screwdriver, she returned to the bedroom. She pushed the screwdriver into the lock and twisted it. It wouldn't open. Using the hammer, she tapped the screwdriver, pushing it in further. She then twisted with force…the lock opened.

'Fuck.'

Once she'd composed herself, she opened the lid. Catherine could see the phone, and surrounding it was Christopher's passport, a few hundred pounds in notes, a few watches, and several wraps of what looked like cocaine. Catherine pressed the front screen. She was straight in; he hadn't locked it. She went into the photos. There were 855 photos. Catherine's heart was pounding, her hands clammy. Pushing her hair out of her eyes, she started scrolling through. She checked the dates; they were all before they met. This was a single man's phone. The pictures were all in bars, or on holidays surrounded by girls. Then she saw them, Bellfield, Whiting, Bridger, and Worboys. And there was Christopher with them. They looked like any other group of friends out enjoying themselves. Trembling, she took in a full breath of air as she carried on. Was he there on that night? She had to know. She scrolled and scrolled. No pictures of Hayley so far. Catherine could feel the tension in her jaw. She opened her mouth for relief. Coming to the end of the photos of the first scroll through, she was about to go again before having the urge to look in the videos section.

There were fifty-one videos. The first video started as she pressed play. Catherine covered her mouth.

'No, Christopher.' It was Christopher receiving oral sex from a girl, this was before they were together, technically he'd not done anything wrong, but for Catherine it was still disturbing to see. She stopped it. The next few were Christopher having sex with a random girl. He was so different, aggressive, and using words he never did with her. This wasn't her Christopher. Another video, another girl. Christopher filming himself fucking a girl from behind. A tear dropped on to the screen. This isn't the man she knew. To her he was caring, attentive. Their lovemaking was never rough or dirty. These videos were like watching a stranger. The next video, Christopher and two girls, both giving him oral sex as he encouraged them. Catherine pressed on the next video. Christopher's face smiling, he was sweating, red in the face. She turned up the audio. 'Go on, Chris. Fucking give it to her.' The video panned around the room. Bellfield was laughing, Whiting was naked standing behind him, Bridger was doing a line of coke off the girl's breasts.

The girl was quiet.

The girl looked unconscious.

The girl was Hayley.

Her face had a heavy hand over it, Worboys's hand.

'Shut it slut, there's still me to go,' he said before laughing. Hayley's eyes were now open wide and desperate like a scared child. Catherine dropped the phone and ran to the bathroom, she was reaching from the pit of her stomach, but nothing came up, she wanted to be sick, needed to, but it wouldn't come up. She ran the cold water and splashed her face. Looking in the mirror, she could see the redness in her eyes. Taking a step back, Catherine reached across and grabbed Christopher's aftershave, a large bottle of Oud Wood Tom Ford. Catherine threw it violently at her reflection in the mirror and screamed, 'You fucking bastard! How could you?' It shattered, sending pieces of glass around the bathroom.

Catherine's thirst for violence and revenge had all but gone from the moment she fell in love with Christopher. But not now. She was thirstier than ever. 'I'll kill you, you will pay.'

She didn't flinch even though her feet were bleeding from the broken glass. Red footprints lined the carpet as she went back into the bedroom. Catherine used her phone to take a copy of the video. She had around four hours before Christopher would be back from work. Going back into his phone, she searched again, this time into the deleted section. More videos, more girls. Her stomach was in knots. She fell to the floor, holding herself. The anger rising inside had to come out; she had to release it; she stood up and screamed until she was out of breath.

Catherine made the call to the only person she trusted. She answered after two rings, and Catherine spoke at speed. 'I know you said I could only call in an emergency on this phone. I'm sorry.'

'That's okay, Catherine. What's happened?' Roisin replied.

'I don't have anyone else, not anymore. Fuck, I've nothing left. Everybody leaves, I was right. I said it. Everybody leaves.' Her speech was rapid and manic.

'Catherine, please, take a moment. Remain calm, and tell me what's happened. Talk to Christopher. Maybe he can help.'

'Christopher, no, he's done. Christopher is going to be dead in a few hours. He won't be talking.'

'Catherine, why is he going to be dead? Where are you?'

'The video. It was him all along. He's one of them. There were five, not four, he's Rapist Number Five.'

'Number five, I don't understand,' Roisin said.

'Christopher raped Hayley, along with the others. He's one of them. I found a video of Christopher. He's on top of Hayley. He's one of those fuckers.'

'Catherine, I'm sorry. Are you sure? Could there be a mistake?'

'No. No mistake. He has to pay.'

'Come and see me. Come now. To my office. I can be there waiting for you. You can talk me through everything, we can go to the police together.'

'He has to pay, Roisin. How could he do it? And how could he start a life with me? All that bullshit he said about me letting everything go, about me letting go of the past. It was all to protect himself. He's going to die, has to.'

'No. I'll come to you. Where are you, Catherine? Are you at home in Brighton? It's an hour or so from me. I'll leave now.'

'Roisin, I wasn't ringing you to get you involved. I don't want you wrapped up in this, and I know you will have to tell the police what I've just told you. I understand. I'm ringing to say…goodbye. You've been good to me, the only person I could truly trust. I'm tired of it all, Roisin. I need it to stop.'

'I'm still here. I'll always be here. If you trust me, then please do as I say.'

Catherine's crying was uncontrollable as she spoke. 'I can't, it's over.'

'Catherine, just listen to me. You will wait until I get there. Promise me. Give me a chance to talk to you. I deserve that.'

Catherine stopped crying, but her breathing was shallow. 'I'll try, I don't—'

'Catherine, listen to me. Trust me and listen to me. Please do it my way, and if afterwards you feel the same, we'll work on that.'

'Okay, I'll wait.' Exhausted and wanting it all to be over, Catherine slumped to her side and listened to Roisin.

'Are you still there? Talk to me, Catherine,' Roisin shouted.

"Justice is like a train that is nearly always late."

Yevgeny Yevtushenko

CHAPTER 34

'Don't do it, Roisin,' her husband said.

'If I don't help her, she'll end up in prison herself, or hospital, or God forbid, worse.'

'You can't do this, you have to let the police handle it. You'll lose your career. Is she worth your career?'

Roisin held her head in her hands before replying, 'Yes, yes, she is. If that was my daughter, our daughter, I would do this.'

'That's it though. She isn't your bloody daughter.'

Turning away, Roisin covered her mouth.

'I'm sorry. I didn't mean it like that. Beautiful, please,' he begged.

Holding out both palms, she replied, 'No, she's not, and I'll never know again how that feels. But I am going to help Catherine. Fuck the consequences. This is real life, not some made up rule book. Life isn't straightforward, and neither am I.' Roisin left the room, slamming the door behind her.

Roisin had parked her car exactly where Catherine told her to. Catherine could see her walking towards her. Roisin wasn't in one of her perfectly fitted outfits, no high heels or long auburn hair. Roisin was in blue jeans, a T-shirt, trainers, and her hair was up in a bun. Catherine felt safe the second Roisin wrapped her arms around her and held her tight.

'It's going to be okay. Did you do what I said?' Roisin asked.

'Yes. I left his phone where it was, in the tin. I took the other phones from my car and put them in with Christopher's. I put Hayley's clothing with the tin. Everything they need, it's all there.'

'That's good. Are you ready to make the call?'

'I think so,' Catherine replied.

'What time will Christopher be home?' Roisin asked.

'Just after five.'

They stood together, far enough out of sight, but close enough to see the house.

Moments later, Christopher arrived as predicted.

'Look at him. He has no idea what's happened,' Catherine said through gritted teeth.

'Make the call, Catherine.'

'Emergency, which service?'

'Police, please.'

'Thank you. Go ahead caller you are through to the police. What is the address or location of your emergency?'

'Seventy-five Boleyn Road, Brighton.'

'Thank you. Can I take your name, please?'

'No.'

'Okay, what's the nature of your emergency?'

'Christopher Mason is a rapist. He lives at the address I've just given you, 75 Boleyn Road. Five men raped Hayley Flashman and all the evidence you need is in that property. Christopher Mason, Bryce Bellfield. Tristan Bridger, Ian Whiting, and David Worboys.'

'Is the incident happening right now?'

'No. It's already fucking happened. He's there right now. Please go and arrest him. Arrest Christopher and the other four will follow with the evidence in the property. David Worboys is one of your own, a policeman. All the evidence you need is in the kitchen cupboard under the sink. Please repeat that.'

'The evidence is under the kitchen sink at 75 Boleyn Road. I've got that. Is anyone in immediate danger?'

Catherine's face went red. 'Okay, if it will make the police arrive quicker, yes I am. He has a knife and he's threatening to stab me to death. so fucking hurry up.'

Catherine ended the call and looked at Roisin.

'Good girl. You ready for the next part?' Roisin asked.

'Not sure,' Catherine replied.

'This part is important. You'll need closure. This will help.'

Catherine could see Christopher was in the house. She pressed call and waited.

'Hi, babe. Thought you'd be here. You popped out?'

Catherine couldn't answer. She held the phone to her chest.

'Catherine, you need to do this,' Roisin said.

Catherine put the phone back to her ear. 'Christopher, was it ever real?'

'I don't understand. Was what real?'

'Us. Did you ever love me?' Catherine asked.

'I do love you. My world is built around you. My future is our future. What's going on, Catherine?'

'I thought I loved you, too. And I feel sick.'

'You're scaring me. Talk to me, please.'

'I know everything, Christopher.'

'Know what?' he asked.

'Hayley, and what you did, what you all did. There were five of you, not four.'

The silence lasted for around five seconds before Catherine spoke. 'Was there just five of you?'

'Catherine, let me explain.'

'You can't. I've seen it, I've seen you. You raped her just like the others.'

'It wasn't like that. It was just the lads being lads. Back then, we were different. We…we used to go out, get blackout drunk, wake up, and there would be girls, just as drunk as us. It wasn't rape.'

'No more lies, Christopher. When did you know? When did you know who I was? You hit me with your car on that night. Did you hit me knowing who I was?'

'No. I didn't mean to. Worboys called me in the day, said he wanted me to pop round later that evening. Said he'd taken care of everything, that he was paying some lunatic to stop you coming after us. I told him not to. I didn't want you seriously hurt.

'What a gentleman you are, you fucking liar!' Catherine screamed.

'I'm not like them. The night I hit you, I helped you up, got you in my car. I wanted to talk to you, tell you everything. Tell you how sorry I was. I assumed you knew who I was. But when you came round, I could tell you didn't know me. You were nice to me, caring, and funny. I thought if I was nice to you, and you got to know me—'

'And what, that we would live happily ever after? *You raped my best friend. You raped others.*'

'It wasn't like that,' Christopher replied.

'Christopher, I trusted you. Told you things I had never told anyone else, about my mum, about my dad. You and me, we were meant to be everything. You've ruined it all. You talked me into letting it go, to stop being angry and move on with my life. Oh God, how could I have been so fucking stupid?'

'Don't say that, Catherine,' Christopher pleaded.

'And now you're going to prison, and you're going for a long time. You have no idea how serious this is for you. No idea what you and your sick friends have done. I've watched the videos. I've seen the photos. It's not just Hayley. There were others. You drugged them so you could all have your fun.'

'That wasn't me. I never drugged anyone, not one girl. That was Bridger, that was his thing.'

'But you knew he was drugging them?' Catherine shouted.

'Not always. Most of the girls were just blind drunk, like we were. They were as much to blame. It happened all the time at uni.'

'They wanted it, did they?'

'It wasn't like that. I'm no rapist, you know me. I was so drunk the night Hayley came back. Once I sobered up, I left early, didn't want any more of it. I wanted it to stop.'

'You had your fun, then you left her there to be played with by those animals. You fucking arsehole. I know you now. I know the real you, and you are the very definition of a rapist. Look it up, Christopher, get a fucking dictionary and LOOK IT UP.'

Sirens could be heard. Catherine watched as two police cars screeched to a halt.

'What have you done, Catherine?'

'Time to pay, Christopher.'

'What's this number five you've written?' A huge number five was drawn in lipstick on the wall.

Catherine could hear him moving around. 'You're in the bedroom, I take it? Christopher, don't bother looking for it, it's not there.'

'Catherine, don't do this,' he pleaded.

'You won't find it. I've left your rape phone in it's lovely little tin for the police to find. And they will find it. They know where it is.'

'Please don't. I'm begging you. Tell them you lied, it's not too late. What about my mum? My mum won't get over this.'

'Don't you dare put that on me. You should have thought of your mum before raping all those girls.' Catherine's voice was now raised. 'Hayley is dead because of you. Think about that. You five killed her. People like you, rapists and abusers, think it's just about the rape, or just about the abuse, well it's fucking not. It's also about the life afterwards, the disgust you feel, the mental illness, the thoughts of suicide, hating yourself, harming yourself, thinking you're never good enough, not worthy of being loved. *It Never Fucking Ends*. You're not just rapists, you're murderers. Fuck you and fuck them.'

'Catherine,' Christopher cried.

Catherine could hear the police shouting, and doors being kicked in.

'Christopher, look out of your window. Past the large oak tree,' Catherine said calmly.

She saw him appear at the window.

Catherine could see Christopher's face. He looked pathetic and scared.

'Goodbye, Christopher.'

She watched as the police grabbed him. Catherine threw herself into the safety of Roisin's arms.

'I've got you. You're safe. We'll get through this together,' Roisin said.

"I suppose I should get used to being alone too. Not in the world, but in here. In my heart."

Victoria Aveyard

CHAPTER 35

FIVE MONTHS LATER

'I want to find a reason to live. I thought I had it. I had it with my dad, with Hayley, I had it with the Christopher I thought he was. Since the day Christopher was arrested, I've done nothing but think. I've come to the conclusion that we all have a shelf life.

'We're here for a reason, then that reason goes, and you can't see another one coming. We get to a point where we know that life can't and won't offer anything new, anything better than what we've had. I'm too tired to keep searching for the next thing. I know it's a depressing view, and I don't say this for attention. It's how I feel. I admire people who call time on their life. I don't see them as cowards for taking an easy way out. I mean, it's not easy, is it? Killing yourself isn't easy. It's painful whichever way you choose to do it. But the way I see it now, these are the ones who are lucky enough to choose when they go. I want to be one of those people.'

'You say something, love?' Betty said with her eyes half open.

Catherine sighed. 'It's okay, Betty. I'm rambling, you go back to sleep.'

'These bastard pills they give me. One minute I'm wide awake eating my dinner, the next I'm asleep with a face in my food. The other day I had a brussels sprout stuck to my face, right above my eyebrow. And no bastard in here told me either. I walked around until bedtime like that. I should have known something was up. Bill was laughing at me all evening, but he wouldn't say why. Silly old twit. You wait, I'll have him for that. I'm going to swap his sugar for salt.'

'Everybody is on something, Betty, even me. You have to take your pills.'

Betty touched Catherine's arm. ''Ere, I'd love to mix everyone's pills up in this place, and then sit back and watch the carnage. Can you imagine? We'd have Fat Pat not getting her water retention tablets. Just imagine if that happened? She'd wobble about like a—'

'Betty, what have I said about Pat? She's a nice lady. Don't be mean.'

'I'm not being mean, I'm just saying. I look at her legs and think about getting a pin and poking it in to watch them go—'

‘Betty, come on.’ Catherine was trying not to smile.

‘Bang, explode everywhere they would.’

‘Betty, stop.’

‘Probably take a knitting needle to pierce her skin, or a sword, tree trunks. Like a big old grey elephant.’

‘No more,’ Catherine said.

‘Okay, all right, no more Fat Pat talk. What about Flakey Albert? You seen him recently?’ Betty gave her very best acting performance and started to heave like an old dog about to be sick.

‘Betty, enough.’

‘I can’t eat when he’s about. Scruffy retarded scaly git. Skin and stuff falling off him, he leaves a trail wherever he goes. Like Hansel and Gretel. Leaving a trail so he can get back to his room. There can’t be much skin left on him. I think he’s part reptile. Bet he even sleeps under a hot light. What was that programme years ago, *The Singing Detective*. That’s him.’

‘Betty, I hope you don’t say these things to him or any of the others.’

‘Of course not. And anyway, it’s not just me, Bill joins in now. He’s good at it too. Every time Reggie, you know Reggie, the new one who can’t stop shaking. Well, Bill calls him Shaking Stevens and sings ‘Green Door’ every time Reggie goes past. Gets me every time. Laughing, I can’t stop. I peed myself one time. Not much, just a dribble. Good job I double up on my knickers.’

Catherine afforded herself a chuckle.

'Reggie supports Tottenham, so it's his own fault. Anyone who supports that lot deserves the piss taken out of them. Half of the nutters in here don't even know where they are, they don't care if I rib 'em a bit. All I have left is my sense of humour. If I lose that…' Betty drew a line across her neck with her finger.

'Look. Watch this.' Betty picked a boiled sweet out from her handbag and threw it at Mavis. It landed in Mavis's grey curly wig. 'What a shot! Bullseye.'

'Betty, no,' Catherine snapped.

Mavis looked up and dabbed at her wig. 'Is it raining? Get my brolly, it's raining.'

Catherine looked into the distance, avoiding any eye contact for fear of laughing.

'C'mon, Cat, that's funny. Let yourself go. You need a laugh. I know I do. Look at her, barking mad, that's my point. I'm not hurting anyone, they don't even know. And when I finally lose all my marbles, I hope they do it to me. I don't care.'

Mavis went back to staring at nothing. 'I'm sure it's raining,'

'You okay, Mavis?' Catherine called out.

Mavis raised her head slowly, squinted her eyes and replied, 'Tuesday.'

Betty laughed aloud. 'There you go, nutters.'

Bill arrived with a packet of biscuits in hand. 'I've been on the rob. Got these for us.' He held them out. 'You want one, Cat?'

'Nice, Custard Creams. My favourites,' Betty said as she took a few.

As they spoke, Reggie walked past in the corridor. Catherine looked at Betty, Betty looked at Bill.

Bill sang 'Merry Christmas Everyone,' as he raised one of his feet on to it's toes.

Catherine stood up and covered her mouth with her hand. 'I'm going. I can't be part of this.' She pointed at Bill. 'Don't let her corrupt you any more than she already has.'

Bill pointed back at her and spoke in his best Shaking Stevens / Elvis accent. 'Okay, baby.'

'I'm done, goodbye you two.'

Catherine could still hear Betty and Bill laughing from the end of the corridor.

The rain crashed against the window. It was two o'clock in the afternoon, but the darkness outside gave the appearance of much later in the day. Roisin turned the table lamp on as Catherine entered the room.

'It's good to see you, Catherine. Please take a seat.'

Catherine thanked Roisin and sat down as she ran her hands through her wet hair. 'I should have brought a brolly with me. It wasn't raining when I left.'

'How have you been? Have you had time to make any sense of it all?'

'No. I've done a lot of feeling sorry for myself. Why me and all that. I thought my bad luck would be having Patricia as a mum for all those years. I didn't think I'd have anything else bad come my way again.'

'Catherine, you're entitled to feel sorry for yourself. You loved Christopher. He was your future. It's a life-changing event. It will take time to digest before you can feel ready to move on.'

'I think I'm done with moving on. I'm tired. I'm tired all the time. I wake up in the morning, have a coffee, and then go back to sleep. I only stay awake to go to work. And even then, I nick a few hours when everyone is asleep. Sleeping saves me from thinking.'

'Is there anything or anyone that makes you happy? Do you have people to talk to?'

'I have you, and Betty. She's one of the ladies at the care home. Everyone else has gone. Everyone leaves, don't they?'

'I'm worried about you. Could we go to two appointments a week? Or—'

'Or what?' Catherine asked.

'I've been unprofessional by meeting up with you outside of here, but I don't regret it. I've only ever broken away from being professional once before. And that was for another person I cared about. I wanted to help you. I still do, so if it would help you, we could meet more often. Maybe out of the office? For a coffee now and then.'

'Like friends?' Catherine said.

Roisin gave a nod. 'Yes, like friends.'

'I'd like that.'

'Catherine, your mum. Have you thought any more about contacting her?'

'Every day, but I'm too scared.'

'Of rejection?' Roisin asked.

'Of loving again.'

'Catherine, never be afraid to love.'

'I don't know if I could find her. Christopher tried to give me her address once, but I wasn't ready. He said she's in Cornwall but—'

'She is in Cornwall. I have her details here,' interrupted Roisin.

'You know where she is?'

'I do. I have her address and phone number. I wanted you to have the option. I'm not making you call her. That's up to you. But, when you feel you're ready, you have what you need.' Roisin passed the piece of paper to Catherine.

Roisin leaned forward and held Catherine in her arms. 'Catherine, all good people deserve to be loved. All good people deserve a family. Find your family and be what you deserve to be…happy.'

'Dad, I need you. I don't know what to do,' Catherine said as she pressed the icon on her laptop.

Look at my slap head. I thought I'd look like Jason Statham, Bruce Willis, someone cool. Your mum says Little Britain, the fat bloke on there. She wasn't even being funny. She meant it. I think she's getting worse. I'm worried, Catherine, worried she won't look after you properly. I've changed my will slightly. She has to do right by you until you're an adult. I'm sure she will, but just in case I want it in writing. Lenny can make sure it happens. I'll see to that.

I'm getting weaker now, beautiful. I don't know how long I have left. Dr Eyebrows has done all he can. He's a good man. I know I make fun of him, but if he can't help me, no one can.

'You're never scared, Dad.'

I'm scared. Not scared of dying, not scared of pain. I'm scared of never seeing you again. You're my girl, my Catherine. When I go, I'm gone, but you have the pain and that hurts me.

'Oh, Dad, don't,' Catherine said as she lowered her head.

Never seeing you again is a pain so bad, the hardest pill to swallow. I've never known pain like it until today. Today I realised it's over, I'm not going make it. Eyebrows has done his thing. We had a go…but we lost. Today I'm saying goodbye, I'm not recording anymore of these, I can't. Soon I'll be in the hospice, I'll lose more weight and I'll probably talk nonsense. I don't want your last memory of me being like that. So, this is goodbye, Catherine.

'No, Dad, don't, don't go,' Catherine cried as she touched the screen softly.

I'm sorry for the tears, but your dad is a big softy when it comes to you. I love you. I love you like I've never loved before. My chest aches at the thought of leaving you. I want to take it out on someone, but I can't. Who can I blame? Who can I hurt? It's at this point I wish God was real, because if he was real, we have a chance of seeing each other again. I've never wished for anything before, but I now hope he is. I pray he is.

'I hope he is too, Dad. Don't go, don't leave me. Not again.'

Catherine, I love you. Please never forget me, but move on without me. Use my memory as a strength. Look to the sky at night, if a star is flashing…

'It's you looking over me,' Catherine said as she cried uncontrollably.

I love you. I'll miss you. You are the only reason I fought this disease. I just wanted extra time with you. You kept me fighting. Now it's your turn. Fight to have a good life. Find a family if you don't make your own. Family comes first. You will love no one like you love family, like I love you.

The screen faded to black, and Catherine threw the laptop across the room.

"Failure is not fatal, but failure to change might be."

John Wooden

CHAPTER 36

Catherine had requested a visit at Wormwood Scrubs, wanting to see him one more time. Christopher Mason and the prison governor had approved it. The rules would be strict. Catherine had to dress appropriately. She could be turned away if she wore a low-cut top, only a vest, high shorts, or a dress. No ripped jeans or flip-flops. No hats, scarves, or sunglasses. She could bring up to £25 to buy food and drink, and she would need a pound for her locker.

Christopher sat down opposite Catherine, not close enough to touch, but close enough for her liking. Catherine pushed back into her chair, causing it to screech on the linoleum floor.

'Thank you for visiting, Catherine,' Christopher said. He was looking gaunt; blackness surrounded his eyes and his hair was greying on the sides.

'I wanted to see you one more time. This won't happen again. After today, we both move on. I now know my future, and you know yours,' Catherine said before looking around the visiting room.

'I'd like you to visit again. This doesn't have to be the last time.'

Catherine transfixed her eyes on Christopher before putting her elbows on the table. She grew in confidence and stature as she leaned forward. 'I have something to show you.'

Christopher shrugged his shoulders.

Catherine went into her jeans pocket and removed a piece of paper, half the size of a piece of A4. She slowly unfolded it and placed it on the table with her palm on top. Christopher inched forward. Catherine pushed it slowly towards him. A prison guard approached. 'That's close enough,' he barked.

Catherine removed her hand, revealing a baby sonogram.

Christopher tilted his head before looking at Catherine with glazed eyes. 'You're pregnant?'

Catherine moved closer still. 'I was.'

'*Was*, what does that mean?' His tone of voice changed.

'It means I wouldn't have a baby of yours for all the money in the world. You're disgusting. That there was your son. You don't deserve a child. What if he ended up like you, a rapist?

Christopher's eyes narrowed, he was about to unload but Catherine beat him to it. 'Think about this Christopher Mason, you're in your late thirties, and looking at receiving a long sentence. Hopefully you'll never get to have children.'

'Bitch,' Christopher snarled as he inched forward.

Catherine rose to her feet, pushing her chair back sharply.

The guard approached.

'It's okay, I'm going,' Catherine said.

Christopher sat there, broken, unable to speak, unable to show any emotion.

Catherine turned back one last time and took in just how broken he was. Her conscious clear as she thought of Hayley, satisfied she did the right thing.

As she left the prison, she threw the scan picture into a bin. She'd purchased it for £9.99 plus postage, on a website called babymaybe.com, which sold all things to do with fake pregnancy.

Catherine had listened to everything Roisin had said about moving on, about doing things the right way. She intended to…but does anyone really change? Revenge was in her blood. Christopher being arrested and sentenced had not felt enough. Crushing him for what he did to Hayley was the outcome she wanted, and after visiting that pathetic excuse for a man, it was the outcome she had got.

"The bond between a mother and her child is the only real and purest bond in the world, the only true love we can ever find in our lifetime."

Ama H. Vanniarachchy

CHAPTER 37

The drive to the West Country was straight forward, M25, M3, and then on to the A303 where Catherine would pass Stonehenge at a stagger due to the holiday traffic all slowing down to look across at the ancient stones. She only stopped once to re-fuel and buy a cheap meal deal at the garage. A family sat parked opposite, the windows of the car were open, she could hear the arguing from the children in the back, followed by the mum threatening to turn around and head back home. Catherine smiled to herself knowing this was the emptiest of threats, no parent has ever turned around and missed their holiday that they've saved all year for. Catherine re-entered the M5 and was close now. The narrow roads of Cornwall were waiting for her.

Catherine drove across the seven-arched bridge in Looe, went up a steep hill, and then down an even steeper one that had her being overly cautious on the brakes. Once she had paid to park her car, she headed into the town. She removed her small cardigan and wrapped it around her waist; the sun was unforgiving, and a vest top would do. With no sun protection, she headed for shade in a small gift shop. Fridge magnets, crabbing nets, sticks of rock, toy guns, fudge with a picture of Looe on the front, mugs with Her Majesty the Queen on, ice cream made locally was in all flavours, even bubble gum. Catherine watched a dad as he was explaining to his son that they were on holiday, and that he wasn't buying him a Harry Potter Lego set for fifty quid, he told him to pick a bucket and spade, and hurry up. Catherine found the sun cream. That's all she needed for now.

The information Catherine had was a phone number, an address, and an address of her mum's business. She'd still resisted the urge to look at her mum on social media. She wanted the first time she saw her to be as real as possible. She wanted to judge everything on that initial reaction; she was confident she could tell if there was anything there by her mum's first look, first touch, and first words. Catherine found the café, simply named *Lynda's*. It was summer, so it was full of tourists. Catherine could see the staff were busy, rushing in and out with their next order. She waited patiently until she could see a woman around her mum's age, could it be her? The woman had the friendliest smile. She was dressed casually but looked unintentionally perfect; she wore no make-up but looked beautiful. Catherine watched her go from table to table, noticing the customers' faces light up as she greeted to them. Catherine knew who she was, Catherine knew her name, her name was Lynda, and Lynda was her mum. Her mum looked so happy, so content, maybe too happy to have her world turned upside down by her broken first born. With tears in her eyes, Catherine turned and walked away.

'Are you okay?'

Catherine stopped and looked at the girl in front of her. She had a friendly, confident demeanour, and was in her late teens.

'Can I help you? You look upset?' the girl said.

'I'm fine, just having a tough day. It'll pass,' Catherine said.

'Are you alone?'

Catherine paused and looked back at her mum's café. 'I think I am, but I'm used to it.'

'My mum owns the café. Would you like to come in for a drink? My treat,' the girl said as she pointed in the direction of Lynda's.

Catherine couldn't stop her tears as she stared at the girl in front of her with the same eyes as her own. Different colour hair, but everything else could only be that of a sister.

'I'm…I'm not sure where I'm going. I may come in soon. It's my first day in Looe. I need to check in to my hotel and get cleaned up.'

The girl touched Catherine's shoulder. 'If you're sure? When I'm upset, I hate being alone. Please come back and find me once you're settled. No one should be alone on their holiday.'

Catherine smiled and watched her walk away. The girl turned and faced Catherine. 'I'm Hanna, by the way. And I mean it. Come back, we do a great cheesecake. I know, I make it. I'll cut you a slice ready.'

'Can't wait,' Catherine said before walking away into a sea of people. Surrounded by so many people she had never felt so lost and alone. She felt the tap on her shoulder.

'I'm not leaving you on your own. Come on, my mum's let me have a longer break. I'll get us an ice cream,' Hanna said.

'You honestly don't have to do that. I'm just being pathetic.'

'What's your name?'

'Catherine.'

'I'm not sure what it is, Catherine. There's something about you. I can't explain it. You ever had that thing where you meet someone and feel like you know them?'

'I think so,' Catherine replied.

'I'm not on the pull or anything weird like that. I'm into boys, maybe not at the moment, as they're all bastards, but I am when I'm looking.' Hanna laughed.

'Ice cream sounds good,' Catherine said. Hanna pointed over to a tiny shop and led Catherine to the front of the queue.

'Two butterscotch two scoops please, Janet.' The lady gave Hanna the ice creams and said she could pay her later.

The girls sat together perched on a wall overlooking the clear blue sea below.

'I often come here to think. It's better late at night, so peaceful. This time of day you have to watch the bloody seagulls don't have your food away. Some of them are huge.'

'Nice ice cream. I love butterscotch,' Catherine said as she raised her ice cream.

'Me too. It's my favourite. And my sister's.'

'You have a sister?' Catherine said as she felt another knot in her stomach.

'I have three,' Hanna said. 'Don't think Mum and Dad had a tele back then.'

Catherine laughed. 'Four girls in one family. Any boys?'

'No boys, there is my dad I suppose. He's in Scotland until next week, a family issue. That's where his side of the family are from. Our surname is Smail. He says it's a true strong Scottish name, and that's where we get our strength and bravery from. He also says we get our sense of entitlement and sense of humour from Mum's English side,' Hanna laughed.

'My dad never got a blue one. He tried his best. That's why there's four of us. Nicola, Sarah, Claudia, and me, Hanna, I'm the oldest.'

Catherine stayed silent as she looked down into the clear blue water.

'You?' Hanna asked.

Catherine was desperate to say her truth. 'It's kind of complicated. It's just me. Over the years, I've got used to being alone, even liked it…but not anymore. I don't want to be alone.'

Hanna nudged Catherine gently with her shoulder. 'Come and meet them if you like?'

'Who?' Catherine asked.

'The Smail clan, my mum and my sisters are all in the café. We all work there in the summer, just to help out during the crazy season. In the winter, we do our own thing. All the tourists are gone then. It's lovely and quiet at that time of year.'

'It looked busy. But fun,' Catherine said.

'Even Claudia is helping today. She's only ten. She's proper cool. She'd love you.'

'What do you mean?' Catherine asked.

'Well, look at you, you're beautiful. Like a famous person or something.'

Catherine blushed.

'C'mon, come and meet them,' Hanna said as she nudged Catherine with her shoulder.

'Do you mind if we do it another time? I would love to meet them, but maybe later?'

'We close at seven,' Hanna said as she looked at her watch. 'Shit, I better get back or Mum will send out the search party.'

'I'll come back later. I promise.'

Catherine had checked in to her hotel. Thoughts of driving home were strong. It would be the easier choice, the safest choice. The potential rejection would be crippling, but she also had Roisin's words resounding in her head, that she deserved happiness and to take the risk in her pursuit of it.

Catherine's phone lit up and vibrated extra loud as she had left it on the flimsy tea tray in her hotel room. She watched as it danced about, bumping into the tiny plastic pots of long-life milk. The screen read, *Alexis*, a reminder of the problems of her recent past, a past she wanted to move on from. But he was there for her when she needed him and offered more help, which she declined.

'Hello, Alexis,' Catherine said.

'I wasn't sure if you would answer. I'm glad you did,' Alexis replied.

'How are you?'

'How am I? How are you more importantly? Your boyfriend, young Christopher, turned out to be quite the bastard, didn't he? I checked up on you several times. I was assured you were happy, so I kept my distance. You were living in Brighton, and you had settled down with a nice fella. I was happy for you. And then when I checked up on you yesterday, well, put it this way, Christopher has made me quite cross.'

'Men, you can't live with them—'

'And you can't kill 'em. Well, you can, you just needed to call me.'

Catherine smiled, but she was unsure if he was serious or not. 'He's no threat where he is now. He's out of reach. Prison will look after him.'

'Cat, I can assure you he is not out of reach. If anything, it is easier to reach someone in there. Christopher isn't exactly going anywhere. I'm owed a lot of favours by men in that prison. Accidents happen every day in there. The stairs in those places are made of rock, one little slip and it's bye bye Christopher.'

'No, leave him alone,' Catherine snapped.

A moment of silence before Alexis replied, 'Ah, okay. Do you still have feelings for him? Let that go if you do.'

'It's not that…I just want away from that world. I want to move on. I'm going to move on.'

She could hear Alexis sigh before replying, 'Moving on is something I've thought about many times, to just up and go, to Spain or Thailand, somewhere sunny and stress free, but I'd get bored, the only thing worse than being bored is being boring.'

'I'll take boring, I want boring.'

'Okay, Catherine Hart, I'll leave you in peace. But promise me something?'

'I will try, but I don't know what you are going to say.'

'The next time you have a problem like Christopher, I'm sure you won't, but if you do, you will call me. I was upset you didn't come to me. Helping you makes me feel better about myself. I don't know many good people…and you are good people. Your dad was good people. Let me be there for you.'

'I can do that…I promise, Alexis.'

'Thank you. Goodbye, Catherine Hart. Oh, I forgot to mention, Worboys is gone.'

'Where?'

The silence was interrupted by a siren going off in the background, Alexis's end.

'He's gone, for good. After that night, he refused to tell his colleagues who had inflicted those gruesome injuries. But the police being the police let him take early retirement. Nothing made the press. They're careful like that when one of their own is bent.'

'How is he gone?'

'Done himself in. Guilt can be a terrible thing. Drive a man head on into his demons.'

'Was it suicide? Really?' she asked.

'He's gone. Take care, Catherine. You know where I am.'

Catherine left her hotel just after five and made her way to Lynda's. When she arrived, it was half full. Unlike earlier, there were plenty of available tables.

She sat out front and chose a table away from anyone else, sitting with her back to the café staff. She could feel her heart pumping. She could see her chest rise and fall when she looked down.

She reached for a serviette and used it to dab at the sweat on her brow. She paused when she could hear the footsteps of someone approaching; they stopped at the table behind her. A chair was pulled out and the person sat down.

A shiver went through Catherine's body as she felt eyes staring into her. Muted crying started behind her, but Catherine was frozen in her seat, unable to turn around.

'No, no, it's really you,' the voice said.

Catherine gave the gentlest of nods.

'Cat…Catherine, I knew you'd find me one day. God, please say it's you. I know it is. As soon as Hanna told me she'd met someone today, she described you and I knew. I knew before she said your name. I just knew.'

Catherine took in a huge breath of air before standing and turning to face her mum.

'My Catherine, I knew it was you. I've dreamt of this. Look at you, you're beautiful. I knew you would be.' Lynda covered her face with her hands before reaching out for her daughter. 'I'm so sorry, Catherine, I'm sorry.'

Catherine closed her eyes as she felt the warmth of her mother's love touch her, the kind of warmth she last felt at twelve years old from her dad.

'Don't say sorry, never say sorry. You don't need to. I know what happened,' Catherine whispered.

Catherine pulled back slightly, wiped the tear from Lynda's cheek and looked into her eyes, eyes of different colours, one sky blue, one hazelnut brown, the same as her own.

'Mum, it's you.'

EPILOGUE

The sisters had spent the last two months filling Catherine in on their life growing up in Cornwall, and Catherine shared parts of her childhood, just the good parts of which there were few, she made up the rest. The summer evenings were a gift, and the sisters loved nothing more than getting to the end of the working day and spending precious time together.

Catherine and three of her sisters sat in the garden late into the evening as they watched the summer sun disappear. Hanna poured Catherine another drink just as their attention was drawn elsewhere when they heard the front door slam, followed by raised voices. Hanna, Nicola, and Claudia looked at each other nervously, a look that said they'd heard this before.

'Everything okay in there? Should I leave?' Catherine asked.

'Best ask Mum. She doesn't want us involved.'

Catherine made her way into the kitchen. Lynda stood there with a glass of wine in hand, staring out of the window.

'You okay?' Catherine asked.

'It's Sarah, a boyfriend issue. He's a cocky piece of shit, and no matter what I do or say I can't stop her seeing him. But this time it's gone too far. I'm stepping in.'

'Do you mind if I talk to her? I've had my share of cocky pieces of shit.'

Lynda turned to face her. 'Cat, I don't want this for you. Your life has been hard enough. I want to make things right, make it up to you, and that doesn't start with you clearing up any mess in this house. I want us all to be happy. The last couple of months have been so special. I don't want it ruined for you, for any of my girls. I'd hoped she'd finished with him.'

'Mum, I don't mind. These things happen. I want to help. This is a family problem and I see you all as my family. You are my family.' Catherine stroked her mum's arm as she walked past her and went to Sarah's room.

Her mum called out, 'Cat.'

Catherine turned round. 'Yeah.'

'Thank you for calling me Mum. I don't deserve it yet but thank you.'

'You deserve it. You are my mum.' Catherine smiled and headed to Sarah's bedroom door.

She knocked gently. 'Sarah, it's me, Cat. Can I come in?' She pushed the door gently and peered through. Sarah was lying on her bed facing the wall.

'I tried to finish it. I told him we aren't good for each other, that I just want to be friends,' Sarah said.

Catherine sat on her bed and put her hand on Sarah's back. 'That's fair, beautiful. You did the right thing. It will hurt for a while, but you'll get over him, and maybe…'

Sarah turned onto her front, and that's when Catherine saw it. Sarah's eye…red, half closed. Catherine tilted her head as she moved the hair out of Sarah's face and studied her injury. Catherine's jaw clamped shut as she looked to the ceiling for answers.

With the vision of her father in her mind, Cat received the answer she always received when a loved one was hurt.

'Give me his address.'

ACKNOWLEDGEMENTS

To my wife Claire and my four sons, Henry, Freddie, Cassius and Jackson who make me proud every day. I would like to say thank you for allowing me to follow my dream.

For her mentorship through my writing journey, I would like to thank Lynne Hackles. To Amanda Horan at letsgetbooked.com for a great book cover design.

To my early readers, Claire Cox, Vicky Roberts, Mark Dunmall and Chris Joy, thank you for all your vital feedback.

Thank you to anyone else that has taken the time to read my book, reading a novel from start to finish is a big commitment and I'm humbled you have chosen mine.

About the Author

Cassius Cox lives with his wife, four sons and Dobby the house dog in Dorking, Surrey, England. This is his second novel and is part of *Vengeance Is in Their Heart* series. The first book in the series *Living Is Losing* was an Amazon best seller.

FROM THE AUTHOR

Suffering with depression often means my thoughts are drawn towards the dark side of humanity.

The subjects I write about are issues that upset and anger me. That may not sound healthy, mentally, but it does mean I write with passion.

I would also like to say that I don't take these subjects lightly and my heart goes out to anyone who has suffered any form of abuse and I hope you are receiving the love and support you deserve.

REVIEWS:

Please can I ask you to kindly leave an honest review on Amazon. Reviews are vitally important to authors.

I love to hear from readers, so make sure to connect with me on the following social media platforms:

CassiusCox.Com

Instagram

Facebook

Threads

You can sign up to my mailing list on my website cassiuscox.com or you can email me directly on: cassiuscoxauthor@gmail.com

Thank you so much.

Cassius.

CASSIUS COX
LIVING
IS
LOSING
GRIEF IS THE PRICE HE PAID FOR LOVE

Help and support:

If you, or someone you know, have been affected by crime, including sexual harassment or any sort of sexual harm, help and support is available.

Victim Support is an independent charity for victims and witnesses of crime. They offer free, confidential help to anyone who has been affected by sexual harassment.

Call 0808168911 or go to Victim Support's website:

www.victimsupport.org.uk

Drinkaware Home | Drinkaware

The following websites offer help and guidance for survivors of rape:

Support Line

Victim Support

The Survivor's Trust

NHS

Rape Crisis charity helplines for support and advice:

England and Wales: 0808 802 9999 (12–2.30pm and 7-9.30pm every day)

Scotland: 0808 801 0302 or text 07537 410 027 (6pm - midnight every day)

Northern Ireland: 08000 246 991 (Monday and Thursday, 6 – 8pm)

Printed in Great Britain
by Amazon

30833506R00215